# DRESSED TO KILL

# DRESSED TO KILL

## Patricia Hall

CRÈME de la CRIME

This first world edition published 2013
in Great Britain and the USA by
SEVERN HOUSE PUBLISHERS LTD of
19 Cedar Road, Sutton, Surrey, England, SM2 5DA

Trade paperback edition first published 2018
In Great Britain and the USA by
SEVERN HOUSE PUBLISHERS LTD
Eardley House, 4 Uxbridge Street, London W8 7SY

British Library Cataloguing in Publication Data
A CIP catalogue record for this title is available from the British Library.

ISBN-13: 978-1-78029-046-1 (cased)
ISBN-13: 978-1-84751-903-0 (trade paper)
ISBN-13: 978-1-78010-431-7 (e-book)

# ONE

K ate O'Donnell stood open-mouthed in a corner of Andrei Lubin's studio, where work had been brought to a standstill by the arrival of a small woman sporting a very short skirt, very long boots and a very unpredictable temper. She had marched into the room ten minutes earlier, red hair flying, and speaking loudly in a language that Kate assumed was Russian. She had barely paused for breath since and the three young models who had been gyrating in short skirts of their own in front of a virulent puce backdrop had been left standing listlessly like marionettes unable to move unless someone pulled the strings.

Kate glanced at Ricky Smart who, as usual, was standing rather closer to her than she appreciated, and raised an eyebrow. Although she was determined to give him no encouragement, she could not resist a question.

'Who's this? Andrei's wife?' she whispered.

Smart sneered slightly, his sharp foxy face full of the contempt with which he generally seemed to face the world. 'Andrei doesn't go in for wives,' he said. 'Tatiana's his cousin who seems to think she's gone from refugee to aristo in three generations by marrying some dozy lord with a crumbling pile in the home counties somewhere. But she's not satisfied with that and is trying to set herself up as a dress designer. Claims she has all these contacts in Paris but still thinks Andrei should help her out by providing her glossy fashion pictures on the cheap.'

'And I take it he won't?'

'I've never known Andrei do anything for nothing, darling,' Smart said. 'I expect your boss has paid a heavy price to have you here looking on. Or maybe Andrei has something else in mind.' This time he gave her an open leer and ran a clammy hand thoughtfully down her arm. She pulled away sharply just as Andrei Lubin turned his back on his cousin, causing her to curse in English in an accent that Kate thought came straight from the East End, although as a born-and-bred Scouser it was difficult for her to be sure.

'Get lost, will you, la,' she said to Smart in her strongest Liverpool brogue, wiping a hand down her arm where Smart had touched her and moving away from him. Evidently their manoeuvring caught the attention of the redhead across the room who marched in their direction as soon as she took on board the camera Kate was carrying. She cast an unappreciative eye over Kate's outfit, a blue cotton shirt and medium-length grey wool skirt worn with sheepskin-lined boots. Kate flushed slightly. She had lost most of her wardrobe in a fire and was gradually trying to piece it together again. She knew only too well that she couldn't compete with this tiny woman in the latest styles whose every inch, from her short glossy hair curling round her sharp cheekbones to the tips of her patent boots, seemed groomed to perfection.

'Who are you?' Tatiana demanded as she crossed the littered space between them, a minefield of cast-aside clothing, coat hangers, sandwich wrappers and empty beer bottles.

'I could ask you the same,' Kate came back sharply. Andrei and Ricky were enough of pains to deal with without someone from outside the studio she was temporarily attached to exhibiting the same peremptory tendencies. The intense young woman's eyes flashed for a moment before she offered a placatory smile. Kate had not been happy when Ken Fellows suggested this assignment as a preliminary to launching his agency in general, and Kate in particular, into some fashion photography, and she was getting less enthusiastic by the day. She knew little of fashion and cared less. Another temperamental Russian on the scene might be too much, she thought.

'Tatiana Broughton-Clarke,' the redhead said. 'Princess by rights, but no one wants to know about Russian princesses any more, so Lady will do. My husband's only a Lord but it's better than plain Mr, I suppose. So who are you? Do you take pictures with that machine?' She gestured at Kate's precious Voigtlander camera, which had survived the fire by being hung around her neck as she escaped, and was one of the items that had persuaded a sceptical Ken Fellows to take on his first female photographer; something, Kate thought, he sometimes still regretted.

'I have been known to take pictures,' Kate admitted cautiously, having learned by now, during her few exciting months in London, that pictures taken out of turn were sometimes more likely to threaten than reward. 'Ricky says you're Andrei's cousin. I'm supposed to be here to learn how to take fashion shots but I'm more confused than enlightened so far.'

'You've only been here five minutes,' Smart responded snappily. 'And you should know better than to smoke in here,' he threw at Tatiana who had pulled out a packet of Balkan Sobranie and made to offer one to Kate. 'If there's one thing Andrei is strict about it's that. If we singe the client's merchandise, we're sunk.' Kate vividly recalled the acrid smoke after an arson attack on the Ken Fellows Agency where she was officially employed, and shuddered, while memories of the night she and her flatmates had narrowly escaped a conflagration from their top-floor home in Notting Hill she seldom dared recall. It was as close as she had ever come to death and the possibility of repeating the experience in one of the fire traps lurking in Soho's old buildings horrified her.

'Come outside, darlink,' Tatiana said, closing the packet of cigarettes and putting an arm round Kate in a totally unexpected embrace. 'Let's have a little chat. I'll buy you a coffee if you like.' Kate glanced at Andrei who had turned his attention back to his models and was urging them into ever more athletic poses as he pirouetted around them with his camera. Kate shrugged. Lubin had offered her nothing that could be called serious tuition since she had arrived early at his studio – at his insistence – three days ago, only to wait two hours until he turned up to announce that there would be no shooting that day as his main model was ill.

'I'd love a coffee,' Kate said. 'The stuff Ricky brews up here is horrible. And what the secretary makes is not much better.' She was conscious of Ricky Smart watching their departure with a crooked grin and wondered what he was thinking.

Tatiana led the way down the flight of dusty stairs leading

from the rooftop rooms – which had been converted into studio space – and darkrooms and out of a red painted door into a narrow alleyway running between high brick walls and then into Berwick Street, where the market stalls were attracting a Soho clientele bearing little relationship to the pleasure-seekers who poured into the narrow streets of the area later in the day. These were serious shoppers seeking out fruit and veg and groceries from all over Europe that were not readily available in the suburbs.

'Coffee we can get here,' Tatiana said, leading the way into a narrow Italian cafe where a large woman in a white overall presided over the hissing coffee machine. She sat down at a very small table pushed against the side wall of the narrow room, and pulled out her cigarettes again. She offered Kate one of the unusual dark-coloured cigarettes, and, when she declined, lit one herself, blowing an aromatic smoke ring in Kate's direction.

'I don't smoke,' she said.

'So a coffee then?' Tatiana asked. 'This is much better than the rubbish they call coffee in the coffee bars. This is the real thing. Try an espresso. As a Russian – well, part Russian if I'm being honest but a bit of exotic goes down well with the clients – I suppose I should be looking for tea in a samovar, but I have to say I've been converted to coffee since I came to London. I was brought up in Paris, you know.' She ordered and the Italian woman in charge eventually brought them two tiny cups of a dark brew that Kate stared at in astonishment.

'Is that it?' Kate asked.

'It's very strong but very good,' Tatiana said, her accent switching now to standard English instead of either East End or Russian, though whether either was genuine Kate doubted. Even she knew that the Russian connection for an alleged princess must be way back in time. 'You may need to put some sugar in it,' Tatiana advised. Kate took a suspicious sip, stirred a large spoonful of sugar into the cup, tried again and nodded.

'I see what you mean,' she said. 'So I've learned about something at last through Andrei's studio.'

'You're supposed to be learning something from my cousin?' Tatiana asked, not hiding her scepticism. 'In bed maybe?' Kate flushed slightly. 'Nothing like that,' she said. 'I work for a picture agency and they want to take on some fashion work. My boss arranged for me to shadow Andrei for a couple of weeks. To be honest I don't know much about fashion except that skirts are getting shorter and boots longer.' She glanced at Tatiana's crossed legs, which revealed what seemed like acres of thigh between boot top and skirt hem and grinned. 'Maybe it's you I should be taking lessons from. Andrei's offered me some time tomorrow evening, after work. I'm not too sure about that.'

'I might be more reliable than Andrei,' Tatiana said. 'And with less of an ulterior motive. He only sees women in two ways: modelling clothes or in bed without any on at all. Don't say you weren't warned.'

'What about as a photographer? Is he any good?' Kate asked.

'If you want the honest truth, he's still stuck in the 1950s. He's much happier snapping debs in white dresses and society mamas in pastel suits and long gloves than he is learning about the cutting edge of the rag trade. That's how he's earned a crust for years. But now he's realized that David Bailey is flying high with all those skinny girls posing against scruffy street scenes, so he's trying to catch up. But Andrei doesn't really know how to get it right. And he won't listen to me. It's Ricky who holds that place together.'

'Should Andrei listen to you?' Kate asked, puzzled.

'I've started to do some designing myself. My husband has set me up in a bijou studio down the road behind Peter Robinson. The rag trade is big down there. It's only on a small scale so far, just a couple of girls to help me, but I've got friends in Paris who keep me up to date with the latest ideas. No one here is coming close yet. Courrege is way out in front. It's all changing almost overnight.'

'I thought there was some shop called Bazaar here in London . . .'

'Oh, she's quite clever but she won't last,' Tatiana said dismissively. 'So, what do you think? If Andrei won't give me any help promoting my designs, how would you like to take some shots for me?' Kate hesitated.

'Do you mean me personally or my agency? I'm not sure what my boss would think about me doing a freelance commission. I've a nasty feeling he'd want his share of the fee.'

'Oh, I'm sure we can keep this a little secret between ourselves,' Tatiana said airily. 'Let's not make any firm agreements until I've seen what you can do. I'll have some designs ready to show in a week or so. If you want to see what you can do with them, you can come to my studio one evening and we'll take a few shots.'

Kate looked dubious. A designer's studio was hardly likely to have the lights and other equipment a photographer would need to produce high-quality fashion shots. That much at least a couple of days in Lubin's studio had taught her. 'It might make more sense to do some shots out of doors. More like the stuff David Bailey is doing for *Vogue*,' she said.

Tatiana looked interested at that. '*Vogue* I like. Give me your phone number,' she said. 'When I've got something fit to show I'll give you a ring. And keep a close eye on my cousin while you're working with him. We're not really Russian, either of us. It's all a couple of generations back. But he plays at it and thinks it gives him free license to sleep around with pretty well anything that moves. And keep an eye on Ricky Smart too. He's mainly into the skinny little models, but he might make eyes at you just for a change. And darlink . . .' She hesitated for a moment with a wicked grin. 'Do buy yourself some new clothes,' she said. 'You look as if you're straight off the boat from Dublin.'

'The train from Liverpool, actually,' Kate admitted.

'Isn't that the same thing?' Tatiana asked.

Detective Sergeant Harry Barnard sat at a front table in the dim and cavernous Jazz Cellar, nursing a Scotch and half listening to the two musicians rehearsing on the tiny stage. He was not a great follower of jazz but he knew this place was something of a legend and the black man playing the sax a greater legend still. Muddy Abraham was an American who had somehow managed to remain in England at the end of the war instead of returning to the States with the rest of the GIs and claimed to have acquired British citizenship along the way. He would have to check up on that, Barnard thought. Over the last year or two Abraham had become an almost permanent fixture at the Cellar and was now top of the list of staff and musicians at the club that DCI Keith Jackson wanted interviewed, though not, Barnard knew, with any great urgency. For Jackson there was a hierarchy of crime, even when it came to murder, and this case came pretty far down it.

Two days ago Jackson and the full murder team had descended on the club when one of the cleaners had called 999 when she discovered the naked body of a young girl partly concealed by the rubbish bins in the back yard of the club. That the girl was very young – no more than fifteen, the pathologist thought – was obvious from the start; that she was on the game and pregnant, became apparent quickly enough at the post-mortem, which Barnard had attended. Little more came out of the routine examination apart from the pathologist's conviction that the girl had not been killed where she was found. The blood flow after death showed she had been moved at least once. In any case, he had said, she had been dead, he reckoned, at least twenty-four hours and the body would not have gone unnoticed for long in broad daylight. She must, he thought, have been brought there and dumped in the back yard after dark. Her body was badly bruised, black and blue and yellow, as if she had been beaten over a period of time, but the actual cause of death was a single stab wound to the heart.

That DCI Jackson would soon lose interest in the investigation Barnard had not needed to be told. He had seen it too often before. What he had done to deserve being landed with the cursory interviews, which was all the DCI was now interested in, he did not know. But he resented it enough to feel a growing determination to give the unnamed girl, bruised and battered and finally stabbed and tossed aside in death, while still looking like a child, at least a shot at justice.

The blues being explored on the stage finally wailed to a plaintive close and the two musicians jumped down to Barnard's level, and glanced desultorily at the warrant card he waved in their direction. They looked neither impressed by his rank nor particularly helpful.

'I know you all spoke to my boss, or maybe someone else, the other day,' the sergeant said. 'But there are a few follow-up questions you might be able to help with,' he said. 'Perhaps I can start with you, Mr Abraham, and then catch up with you in ten or fifteen minutes, Mr . . .?'

'Chris Swift,' the second man, tall and rangy with a sparse beard, National Health glasses and an open-necked check shirt, offered without enthusiasm.

'Clarinet, obviously,' Barnard said.

'Obviously,' Swift said. 'I'll be at the bar if you want me.'

Muddy Abraham sat down at the table opposite Barnard, putting his saxophone carefully into a case which he pushed under the table. 'So how can I help you, Sergeant,' he said, the southern American drawl in no way diminished by almost twenty years in Britain, although Barnard guessed that he looked significantly different from the young GI who must have crossed the Channel from the south coast to Normandy in 1944. His eyes were bloodshot, his jowls loose and his skin an unhealthy colour like chocolate kept too long. 'It's a terrible thing to have something like that so close. Poor kid.'

'Did you know her?' Barnard asked, but the musician just shrugged.

'How do I know?' he asked. 'I don't know what she looked like. There's always a lot of young girls hanging out aroun' outside here at night. Stan Weston doesn't like them coming into the club but now and again they come in with some guy and he doesn't notice. Jail bait most of them. There seems to be something about musicians that brings them in.' He gave a lopsided smile. 'It's not just the Beatles, you know, who pull the girls. Though the ones who hang about here are usually a bit more savvy than that. Generally a bit older, too. Jazz goes back further, much further that this new stuff, even this side of the pond. The club don't let them inside, the kids. But it's difficult sometimes to know how old a girl is, ain't it? Or what she's up to.'

Barnard reached into his inside jacket pocket and pulled out a photograph which he passed across the table.

Abraham took it and stared, almost transfixed, by the black-and-white image of a young girl's face, eyes closed, half-turned away from the camera. 'She dead?' he asked quietly.

'Her face wasn't too bruised,' Barnard said. 'It was possible to take a picture at the post-mortem.'

The musician nodded. 'Yeah, yeah,' he said slowly. 'I seen her. I guess a lot of people round here have. She's been hanging around for a while. Seemed like a nice kid.'

'She was on the game. A tart,' Barnard said.

'That's a shame, man,' Abraham said. 'That sure is a crying shame, a young kid like that.'

'It happens,' Barnard said flatly. 'You haven't used her services?'

Abraham did not look shocked but shrugged massively. 'I have a lady, man. I don't need to be sleeping with no bits of girls who should be in school.'

'OK,' Barnard said. 'But if not you, who? She wouldn't have been hanging around unless some people weren't taking an interest in her. Stands to reason.' Abraham nodded but looked uncertain.

'I don't know that, man,' he said. 'You'll have to ask around.'

Barnard did not believe him, but did not want to push him too hard right now. He did not really think that the musician was a likely murderer and he did not look the type to quit a good job and run. 'Do you know her name?' he asked instead of pushing harder.

Abraham shrugged again. 'I never spoke to the girl, man, but I think I heard her called Jenny.'

'Probably not her real name anyway,' Barnard conceded. 'But at least it gives us something to use if we ask the other girls on the street.'

'How was she killed, man?' Abraham asked.

'We're keeping that to ourselves for a while,' the sergeant said. He glanced round the dimly lit club, only the lights over the tiny stage and the much bigger bar area casting a glow over the tables. Within hours the place would be packed and smoky and throbbing to the music a self-selected clientele often came miles to hear. And round the edges would hover the Soho locals, the tarts and con men, dealers in dope and fake booze, looking for a mark and, occasionally, surfacing from the sludge, dealers in death who had been crossed in business or even in love and arrived looking for revenge. Barnard had long ago ceased to be surprised by what emerged on his patch, but something about DCI Jackson's lack of interest in this case offended him. This kid deserved better, he thought.

'We don't think she was killed here,' he said. 'Were you doing anything unusual the day before, or the night before?'

'I lead a borin' life, man, with my woman,' Abraham said. 'I come to work, I go home an' go to bed, I wake up, eat an' come to work again. My music an' my woman keep me content.'

Barnard nodded and leaned back in his faded and worn plush seat. This place needed someone with a bit of money to put into it, he thought. He wondered vaguely whether Ray Robertson might take an interest, but he suspected that Ray was only interested in clubs if they paid a social as well as a financial return. This place was being blown out of the water by the sudden changes in taste that had hurtled the Beatles to the Palladium this year. The musicians were middle aged at best and the majority of their fans probably even older.

He glanced across to the bar where Chris Swift was leaning, staring in their direction, a glass raised to his lips.

'Could you ask your clarinet man to come and have a word?'

Abraham shrugged and got to his feet.

'You're not thinking of taking a trip any time soon?' Barnard added quickly. 'Not a trip to New Orleans?'

Abraham laughed but it was a sour sound. 'If I'd wanted to go back stateside I'd have gone a long time ago,' he said. 'Bein' black ain't all roses here but it's a damn sight better than there. I'll get Chris for you.'

Swift took Abraham's place with even less enthusiasm than Abraham had showed. His expression, Barnard thought, was quite simply hostile, his mouth a pursed line behind the whispy beard, his eyes blank, and he wondered why.

'What's all this about then?' he asked. Barnard showed him

the photograph of Jenny Maitland and he looked at it impassively. 'Who's she?' he asked.

'The kid who was found dead in the club's back yard last week,' Barnard said. 'Have you ever seen her in the club, or anywhere else for that matter?'

Swift shook his head. 'Never,' he said. 'I thought the rumour was that she was a tart. Old man Weston keeps the whores out of here. Quite right, too. They're a distraction from the music. If people want sex they can find it easily enough on the streets here around here, can't they? You lot don't seem to do much to keep it under control. Grease your palms too well do they, the pimps?'

'All that bothers you, does it, Mr Swift?' Barnard asked, slightly surprised by the aggressive tack the clarinettist was taking. He hadn't expected such a puritanical reaction here.

'Yes it does,' he flashed back. 'I'm a serious musician, Sergeant, and most of the people who come to the club are serious about jazz. In many ways it's a pity the club is in this neighbourhood, amongst the poofs and pimps and good-time girls.'

'Can't be much different from New Orleans in the old days,' Barnard observed mildly.

'That was then, and in another country,' Swift said flatly. 'In America jazz is shaking off that sleazy reputation. Jazz is filling the concert halls. Can you imagine us being offered the Albert Hall?'

Barnard tired of this argument quickly. 'So do I take it you've never seen this girl? Or any others like her in the club?' he asked.

'Never,' Chris Swift said. 'Can we get on with our rehearsal now?'

Barnard nodded, wondering why Swift was so sure that the club was clean while Muddy Abraham had recognized Jenny immediately as someone who had definitely been around. He watched Swift hurry back to the bar and suddenly recognized a lever, if a dirty one, to persuade DCI Jackson to launch a serious investigation into the girl's death. Whatever Swift said, Abraham had offered the possibility that soliciting was going on inside the Jazz Cellar and the DCI would not like that one little bit. In fact he would be determined to put a stop to it. And that, Barnard thought, might be just the sort of aggravation, carefully embellished, that would help him find Jenny's killer.

# TWO

'Come,' Andrei Lubin said imperiously. 'We go on location. If that is what the magazines want, that is what we'll give them. We'll do a little recce with the girls we shot indoors yesterday. Offer so-picky Miss Greenaway two sets of prints. See if she seriously likes her clothes being pawed over by hoi polloi, blown about in the rain, all that nonsense.'

Kate O'Donnell and Ricky Smart were crammed into the tiny room Andrei called his office, although it was in just as much a state of disarray as the rest of the studio, with clothes hanging apparently randomly on the backs of chairs and the door, and piled high on a low red-velvet chaise longue that was parked against a wall. She wondered what the purpose of that was at the same time as she felt Ricky Smart's hand fumbling where it had no right to be. But she had very little wriggle room to escape his attentions and guessed that if she complained to Andrei she wouldn't get much sympathy.

'Stop that,' she hissed at Smart, who stepped back slightly. 'Where will we go?' she asked Lubin, interested in his latest idea almost in spite of herself.

'David Bailey went to New York,' Lubin said. 'But there's no money for that sort of caper so I think for a start we'll go to Highgate Cemetery. Lots of nice monuments. Even Karl Marx, that old bastard. A couple of tasty girls round his tomb will make him look like the old fraud he really was.'

Kate grinned in spite of herself. The combination of years of tub-thumping sermons from militantly anti-communist priests and the stark fear, which lingered, of the night the nation went to bed not knowing how Kennedy's and Khrushchev's brinkmanship would end, gave her little sympathy for the Russians, who had apparently chased Andrei and Tatiana's ancestors out of their homeland with little more than the clothes they stood up in. The idea of fashion shooting, if not actually dancing, around Marx's tomb quite appealed to her.

Little more than half an hour later, Kate found herself shivering in the back of Andrei Lubin's sleek open-topped car with the wind blowing her hair wildly, sitting behind the driver and Ricky Smart. She could feel the power of the Mercedes and held on to the grab handle for dear life as Andrei weaved in and out of the traffic in Camden and Kentish towns and then accelerated with a roar up a steep hill with dense trees on one side until he screeched to a halt outside a massive entrance on the left side of the road and a similar entrance on the right. A funeral cortège was passing slowly ahead of them down the avenue between the trees to the right as they parked the car. Their vantage point high above the city gave glimpses down from Highgate across the river Thames to the hills of Surrey and Kent beyond.

'They still use it then?' she asked as she got her breath back and tried to restore her unruly dark curly hair to some sort of normality.

'Not the Victorian side. That's more or less full up,' Lubin said. 'The east side is still in use. That's where old Karl's monument is. Come on. I'll show you.' He put the hood up and led the three of them across Swains Lane and into the eastern part of the cemetery, slightly downhill to a fork in the pathway where he swung left and there, looming over them and attended by a handful of visitors was the massive bust of Marx amongst the encircling trees, with a couple of fading bouquets of flowers on the floor at the foot of the plinth.

'He looks a bit like Father Christmas – or God,' Kate said, earning herself a filthy look from a serious-looking couple reading the inscription on the plinth closely.

'A bit of a fraud either way,' Ricky Smart muttered, glaring at Marx's disciples and giving Kate a slight shiver at hearing aloud what she might have thought but had never dared voice in the community she had grown up in.

'Come on, let's have a recce,' Lubin said. 'What do you think, Kate? Cast your artistic eye over it, why don't you?' Kate glanced around critically, taking him seriously although she was never sure how serious he was with her. Like most photographers he did not regard his trade as a suitable one for a woman and she guessed that Ken Fellows had paid more than he really wanted to for her temporary apprenticeship in Lubin's studio.

'I'm surprised it's so close to the road,' she said. 'You won't want those buildings in, will you?' She waved in the direction of Swains Lane where some unattractive modern property could be seen. 'But maybe this way, in amongst the trees, you could drape a few girls in there p'raps.'

Lubin took out his camera and began to shoot quickly around the monument and a little way into the trees. 'He's not under there, you know,' he said, waving at Marx. 'He's actually buried over there somewhere.' He waved vaguely towards the ranks of tombstones spreading down the wooded hill. '*Workers of all lands unite*,' he quoted from the inscription. 'That didn't go so well, did it? There's as many workers fighting against them as there are for them.'

It was on the tip of Kate's tongue to dispute that but she decided against it. She was in London now, not Liverpool, she told herself. Best to ignore the politics of the generations of dockers and seamen she sprang from, so far from home.

'What about all those Victorian monuments over the other side, where we came in?' she asked instead. 'Some of those look pretty amazing. They might make an even better backdrop.'

'Go and take some shots over there then, and we'll look at all of them when we get back. I think this whole place has real possibilities. Go with her, Ricky. It's a bit overgrown and gothic over there. You never know who might be lurking in the shrubbery like that old villain in the Dickens story.'

'I'll be fine by myself,' Kate said, but Ricky Smart just gave her a leer and followed her back across the road anyway. Overwhelmed by the sheer volume of tombs and the amazing wealth of imagination that had been put into their creation, some of it leaning now at crazy angles, a few showing signs of deliberate damage to the statuary, Kate tried to concentrate on seeking out the backgrounds that Andrei might find attractive for his outdoor shots. But Smart was always there and almost always too close for comfort. Finally, when he had brushed against her suggestively once too often, she snapped and slapped his face.

'For goodness' sake, can't you take a hint, la?' she demanded. 'Leave me to get on with my work. I'm supposed to be learning something useful here. You're just a bloody distraction.' Smart stepped away and, leaning back against a massive plinth with a one-armed angel on top raising its eyes to heaven in prayer or supplication, laughed loudly.

'Too good for an East End boy like me, are you, you little Scouse slapper? I don't think so. I reckon if it was Andrei making a pass you'd be up against the wall in his office like a shot.'

'Don't kid yourself,' Kate snapped, setting off back towards the Marx monument at a brisk pace, just short of a run.

Later, when Andrei had ferried them all back to Soho, and begun to draw up an extensive list of possible outdoor locations which to Kate, who was still learning her way round the West End, seemed like a veritable safari, she decided to call in on her actual boss on the way home. She found the agency almost deserted and Ken Fellows himself in his office studying contact prints in his shirtsleeves with fierce attention. He looked up when she came in without much apparent enthusiasm.

'How's it going?' he asked.

Kate dropped her bag on the floor and shrugged as she dropped into her chair. 'I'm not sure,' she said. 'I'm not sure Andrei knows which way fashion photography is going, to be perfectly honest. I met his cousin, who's trying to break into the rag trade and she says he's much happier doing society photography, daughters of the county set in long white gloves and pearls on their way to hunt balls, that sort of stuff.'

'I shouldn't think that's got much of a future in swinging London,' Fellows said.

'Oh, I don't know,' Kate said. 'It's not just the poor who are always with us. Who do you think buys those posh frocks in *Vogue*? And what about the *Tatler*, for God's sake? Or *The Lady?*' She had done a brisk survey of the upmarket women's magazines when Ken had suggested a venture into fashion and reckoned she sounded authoritative, even if her knowledge was little more than skin-deep.

'But someone will be into the short skirts and long boots, won't they?' Fellows said. 'They're out on the street right in front of our eyes, aren't they? The lads' eyes are out on bloody stalks every time they go down Oxford Street. Some girls are wearing combined knickers and stockings as well. Tights, for God's sake, like bloody Laurence Olivier. That'll cause a lot of disappointment to the "get a flash of that" fellers, believe me.'

'Well, that's one reason why I wondered if I should take Lubin's cousin more seriously than him. Tatiana may be what we're really looking for. She's into designing cutting-edge clothes for the teens and she's looking for someone to take some pictures for her. Lubin won't help her, but I could. And I thought if it went well and her collection goes well, we could get a new client . . .' She stopped, taking in the sceptical look in Ken's eyes. 'If you let me use the darkroom?' she said.

'In your own time,' he said. 'I suppose it's more practice. But I want the rights. If they're worth selling, I'll sell them on.'

'OK,' Kate said. 'I'll give it a whirl, la. See what they both come up with. At least with Tatiana I won't have Andrei and his sidekick trying to get into my knickers by the minute.'

Ken Fellows threw back his head and laughed. 'You'll have to take that in your stride if you're going to last in this game,' he said. 'You're not in your Liverpool convent school now, sweetheart. You're on your own. And in a job where girls are a rarity.'

Harry Barnard began to think he might win his point when his boss leaned back in his chair and nodded thoughtfully to himself. He had spent some time poring over the post-mortem report on the dead girl, which catalogued thirty-five separate injuries she had suffered, mainly from a blunt instrument, before she had been stabbed in the chest with what the pathologist judged to be a kitchen knife.

'A pretty frenzied attack then?' DCI Jackson asked, placing the report meticulously at the centre of his ultra-tidy desk and steepling his hands thoughtfully, his eyes gleaming. Barnard often amused himself wondering what his Scottish upbringing had been like and whether the DCI had ever worn a kilt. He could see him now casting a disapproving eye over this morning's new Liberty's tie and his slim-fitting Italian suit and knew the suspicions both would usually arouse. In self-defence, Barnard never failed to hide his strictly hetero conquests around the nick.

'Looks like it,' Barnard agreed quickly.

'Not a very big girl?'

'Tall but skinny,' Barnard said. 'Quite a looker but very young. About fifteen the pathologist reckons.'

'But sexually experienced?'

'Very,' Barnard said. 'And about three months pregnant.'

'Not someone we're likely to get anguished parents chasing up as a runaway just this last weekend?' Jackson asked. 'I don't want complaints on the front page of the *Standard* or the *News* about us failing to even try to trace this girl when she went missing.'

'If she's a runaway it looks like it's a good while ago and we haven't had any approaches from other divisions to try to trace anyone who looks like her. I'll check the missing-person files. Double check to see if there's a photo that matches. Get a firm ID that way, maybe.'

'And you say she's been hanging around this jazz club for a while? Weeks? Months? How long?'

'One of the musicians I talked to said that, yes. He knew her by sight though he claimed he hadn't slept with her,' Barnard said carefully. 'She'd been around the neighbourhood for weeks, they thought. The other didn't think he'd ever seen her, but I'm not sure I believed him.'

'Musicians?' Jackson said explosively. 'I wouldn't dignify them with the name. Jungle music, more like, straight out of Africa. I don't understand why white men get involved with it. And you say this Abraham is black? I missed him when I was there the other day.'

'He came here during the war as a GI, he said. Should have gone back to the USA but somehow didn't. Says he prefers his treatment here to there.'

'Check out his status,' Jackson said. 'Find out exactly why he didn't go back. Talk to the US army authorities. Get his military record if you can. Bells begin to ring when you get American black men in a jazz club. It's hard for foreign musicians to get permission to play over here. Chances are he shouldn't be here at all, or if he should, he's up to no good. I'll ask uniform to organize a raid on the club to see who's got drugs, who's running the girls in the neighbourhood and in the club. May turn up something interesting on this little tart. With a bit of luck we might be able to close the place down.'

'So we treat this seriously, guv?'

'Of course, we treat it seriously,' Jackson snapped, as though the idea that some deaths were worth more attention than others would never cross his mind. 'It's a murder, isn't it? Why would we not treat it seriously? She's somebody's daughter.' Jackson straightened the papers on his desk into an even more meticulously tidy pile than before and gave Barnard a dismissive nod, as if the very idea of not taking the girl's death seriously had never crossed his mind. The sergeant knew better. The bait he had dangled in Jackson's mind's eye had been snapped up enthusiastically but it was not the prospect of convicting the killer of young Jenny that had tempted him to maybe commit some of his budget to the events at the Jazz Cellar. It was the potent mix of, in his mind, decadent music, drugs and a possible American deserter that had tempted him. And if his trawl netted a few homosexuals – who, to his mind, infested every alleyway and entertainment joint in Soho – so much the better.

'It's on your patch. Deal with it,' the DCI said.

Back at his desk in the CID office Barnard gazed thoughtfully at his phone for a moment, then shook his head irritably, picked up his trench coat from the coat-hooks by the door, crammed his hat on his head at a rakish angle, and left the nick. Heading across Regent Street and into the warren of narrow streets that make up the heart of Soho, he barely noticed the numerous people who either crossed to the other side of the road when they saw him or acknowledged his presence with

a more or less shifty nod. This time he had no interest in the
tiddlers who inhabited the upper reaches of this murky pond;
this time he was after one of the sharks. And he could see as
soon as he approached the Delilah Club, where a Jag was
parked outside the main doors with two wheels on the pavement and a bulky man in a dark suit lounging in the driver's
seat, that the shark was at home.

Barnard flashed his warrant card at the doorman and crossed
the dance floor inside, weaved between tables, where cleaning
was still in progress, to a door to one side of the bar marked
Office. He tapped on it, and put his head round.

'Can I have a word, Ray?' he asked the man who looked
up with a flash of extreme annoyance on his face at the inter-
ruption. Ray Robertson was sitting at a massive desk with a
pile of what looked like correspondence strewn in front of
him, envelopes screwed up on the floor, For a moment Barnard
thought he would refuse to speak to him but after a brief
hesitation Robertson's heavy face relaxed slightly and he
nodded the sergeant in.

'Morning, Flash,' he said. 'Long time no see. How's it
going?'

'Not bad,' Barnard said. 'Just wanted to pick your brains
about the club scene, if I can, you being the king of the circuit,
as it were.'

'Might have been once,' Robertson said gloomily. 'Doesn't
look like it any more, judging by this little lot.'

Barnard raised an eyebrow. He knew better than to question
Robertson in this mood but guessed he would tell him anyway
in his own good time.

'It must be down to Georgie,' Robertson snarled. 'His
shenanigans are frightening the best people away. I sent out
invitations to a boxing gala and I've had more rejections than
acceptances so far. What the hell is all that about, Flash?
People who've been coming for years have turned me down
this time. Have I got a black mark against my name because
I'm his brother?'

'I expect it'll all calm down once the trial is over,' Barnard
said soothingly. 'Once he's safely inside people will forget.
Why don't you leave your next gala until the spring? He's due

at the Bailey in March, isn't he? Keep a low profile until the verdict's in.'

'Pity they won't hang him. That would fix him once and for all. Though my mam would go bananas, poor old biddy. He was never anything but trouble, that boy. *You* remember.'

'I certainly do,' Barnard said, his mind flashing back to the younger Robertson brother's delinquent habits when the three East End boys had been evacuated together to a farm during the war. He wondered whether, this time, Georgie Robertson might not end up in Broadmoor rather than jail. But that was not a thought he chose to share with Ray just now.

'So what's to know about the club scene?' Robertson asked.

'The Delilah's doing OK, that's all I'm interested in.'

'What about the Jazz Cellar?' Barnard asked. 'What's the word on the street about that place? We're making inquiries about a little tart they found dead in the back alley behind the place. Is it being used as a knocking shop?'

'Not to my knowledge,' Robertson said. 'He's on my books for protection. The Maltese shouldn't go near him. But the owner's a law unto himself. Does as he pleases, which isn't the way it's supposed to happen. Could have gone in for a bit of private enterprise I suppose. D'you want me to check it out?'

'Discreetly,' Barnard agreed cautiously. 'Don't wreck the joint when it's at the centre of a murder investigation or my guv'nor will go crazy. I'll talk to the owner myself. Stan Weston, isn't it? Trumpet player.'

'That's right. I've never had any trouble with him. But everything seems to be going down pear-shaped just now. I seem to be someone no one wants to know, either side of the law. Notting Hill turned out to be a no-no. They ganged up on me, those beggars. No place for a born-and-bred Londoner down there, apparently. Wrong bloody colour, ain't I? Looks like I need a spectacular like Biggs and his mates last summer. What do you think?'

'Not if you get nicked as fast as they did,' Barnard said, not entirely sure that Robertson was kidding. 'They'll go down for as long as Georgie will, if not longer.'

'Yeah, you're probably right,' Robertson said. 'Well, thanks

for your thoughts, Flash. You'll come to the gala, won't you?
And bring that pretty little photographer with you if you're
still seeing her.'

'I'll be there, Ray,' Barnard said. "But I'm not sure about
the delicious little Kate. Bit problematical, she is, most of the
time. We'll have to see.'

# THREE

When Kate arrived at Andrei Lubin's studio the next morning she found the place strangely deserted, although the door was unlocked. She knew she was late because she had been delayed by not one but two phone calls which she had taken on her and Tess's proudest new possession, a smart cream telephone installed only a couple of weeks' earlier in their shared flat and barely used yet because hardly anyone had their number. The first call had come from Tatiana Broughton-Clarke.

'Did you talk to your boss?' she had demanded peremptorily. 'Will he let you do it?'

'He will, but he wants the rights to the pictures,' Kate said.

'What does that mean exactly?' Tatiana asked.

'It means they belong to him and he has the right to sell them on to newspapers or magazines. I would have thought you'd be happy with that. He's got a lot of contacts in Fleet Street and on some of the magazines.'

'Do I get to have some for my own publicity?' Tatiana asked suspiciously.

'You probably need to discuss all this with Ken himself,' Kate said. 'I'm just the hack who clicks the shutter. I don't know much about the contract arrangements the agency makes. But let's get some pics together first. Then you should talk to Ken Fellows.'

'All right,' Tatiana agreed reluctantly.

'I need to go now. I have to get to work,' Kate had said, anxious about being late for her unpredictable Russian boss.

'Can we meet when you finish at Andrei's?' Tatiana persisted. 'Just for a coffee, maybe. To make some plans?'

'Call me about five at the studio,' Kate had said and hung up slightly irritably. She wondered if linking up with this bossy cow with far too high an opinion of herself was really going to turn out well. Two Russians, or pseudo-Russians, in her life might be at least one too many.

She had been just about to leave the flat when, to her surprise, the gleaming new phone rang again. She had run quickly through the list of people she had passed the number to since the phone had been connected only to find that the call had been disconnected before she picked up. If it was anyone from work they would have been more persistent, she thought. It certainly could not be either Andrei Lubin or Ken Fellows, her ill-matched duo of bosses. Either of them would be far more determined to persuade her to answer.

By the time she got to Lubin's studio she had almost forgotten about the aborted phone call, but when she found the place deserted she wondered if perhaps he had wanted to redirect her to some other location. The man was more impulsive than anyone she had ever met. She stood in the doorway indecisively for a moment before taking off her coat with a shrug and putting the kettle on in the tiny kitchen and making herself a cup of coffee. With the mug in her hand, she wandered around the small space looking at equipment and the many folders of glossy pictures that Lubin stored in carelessly stacked piles on almost every flat surface. Tatiana was right, she decided. The photographer seemed more at home with society beauties and debutantes that he did with the cutting edge of the new fashions that were beginning to dominate the women's magazines. In his world skirts were still decorously below the knee, necklines concealing rather than revealing and silk stockings no doubt held up with suspender belts. He might imagine that he could launch himself on to the streets with his young skinny models with skirts up to their knickers but Kate had her doubts. He was, she thought, too old and too set in his ways.

A slight noise behind her made her jump and she spun round to find herself being watched by one of those models, a girl she knew only as Sylvia, who was standing on the threshold clutching an over-large coat around her.

'Hello,' Kate said. 'Do you know where they've all gone? I was a bit late and there was no one here when I arrived.'

Sylvia came right into the room, but shook her head. 'I had to go to the doctor,' she said. 'No one said anything to me last night about going anywhere this morning.'

'Nor me,' Kate said. 'Do you want a coffee?' The girl nodded, took off her coat and perched herself on a tall stool with a sigh. She looked pale, Kate thought, and barely fit for work. 'Are you not well, la?' she asked, and was surprised when the girl burst into tears.

'You could call it that,' she muttered through her sobs. 'I'm only up the duff, aren't I? Having a bloody baby. And how am I going to work when I'm pregnant, I'd like to know? Andrei will be furious. And I've been trying so hard with him. This was my chance, wasn't it? My chance to get somewhere. Now he'll just bloody sack me.'

Kate knew how hard some of the girls worked to produce the look and the moves Lubin wanted and how quickly they were likely to be ditched if they failed. Pregnant, which would soon become obvious in revealing clothes, Sylvia would not stand a chance. Even the fact that she had come in late this morning would be a black mark against her. The girl blew her nose viciously and dried her eyes, glancing in one of the mirrors to push her bottle-blonde hair back into place and mopping up the mascara that had run down her cheeks.

'Look at the state of me,' she said. 'I told the doctor I didn't want it but he just went all high and mighty on me. "Don't even think of that, my dear. I can put you in touch with people who will give you all the help you need if you can't go home to your mother." Fat chance of that, I said. There's no way that's going to happen. My mam didn't want me to come up west in the first place and she won't want me back now.'

'What about the baby's father?' Kate asked. 'Can't you get married?' She knew that might not be a long-term solution but at least it would make the child respectable and she knew how important that was in many people's eyes

'I don't even know who the father is for sure,' Sylvia said, her eyes full of desperation and her cerise lips trembling. 'I wasn't surprised when Andrei took me to bed. I half expected that. You know what they say about these artistic people. The other girls had said it was more or less part of the deal. But then Ricky too . . .'

'Ricky as well? And neither of them's the marrying kind,' Kate said angrily.

'I can't get married, can I? I'm only fifteen. I'm not bloody old enough.' Kate felt an emptiness in the pit of her stomach and she put an arm around the girl, feeling the bones of her shoulders sharp under her sweater. There was nothing of her, she thought, she was all skin and bone, and she found it hard to imagine how she could carry a baby to full term in even the best of circumstances.

'You'll have to tell Andrei,' she said. 'He's going to notice and he's responsible for this anyway, one way or another. It's down to him.'

'That's the theory,' Sylvia said dully. 'Anyway, don't say anything to anyone just now. I need time to think.'

'Talk to Andrei,' Kate insisted. 'You must do that. Promise?'

Sylvia nodded glumly and as they both became aware of people approaching from the street the girl scuttled away into the rudimentary bathroom at the back of the studio and Kate rinsed their coffee cups at the corner sink. Andrei Lubin came in first, black coat draped around his shoulders like a cloak, closely followed by Ricky Smart, in a blue three-piece suit, and three of the young models.

'Ah, there you are,' he flung at Kate. 'You missed us. We've been down by the river, by Blackfriars, where the trains go over the top, fantastic gritty backdrop for the girls. I think the next time we have some really up-to-the minute dresses we'll go down there, snap a train going over the bridge, a couple of tramps – some of them sleep down there – put them in the background, fantastic stuff.'

Kate nodded without enthusiasm just as Sylvia emerged from the bathroom looking pale but relatively normal.

'Sorry I was late,' she said to Lubin. 'I overslept.'

'Silly cow,' Lubin said. 'You could have phoned.'

'I did,' Sylvia said. 'I went out to the phone box with my coat over my nightie. There was no answer.'

Lubin shrugged and handed Ricky his camera. 'Get them developed, Rick,' he said. 'Then we can see what we've got. We'll give Bailey a run for his money yet, you'll see. Now girls, let's have you all in that new consignment of dresses I see's arrived at last. This shoot's needed like yesterday so don't be surprised if you're still here at midnight. Kate, can

you help me unpack? See what we've got? You can do some
shots today. Take them back to show your boss. Show him
he's getting value for his money, so they'd better be good.'

Harry Barnard had parked his red Ford Capri coupe half on,
half off the pavement and sat staring thoughtfully at the
entrance to the Jazz Cellar in the narrow alley leading off Frith
Street, watching a straggle of early arrivals make their way
inside. It was nine o'clock and the street lighting did not
penetrate far into the alley, making it difficult to see just who
was going in. Earlier, when he arrived to put in what he
regarded as some necessary overtime, he had ventured round
the back of the building to the area where dustbins were stored
and a separate door served staff of all kinds, from the musicians to the cooks and bar staff, and seemed to be left unlocked
long before the paying public were admitted at the front. It
was here that the body of the girl they knew only as Jenny
had been found by a cleaner arriving almost before it was
light. The police guard had gone now that the area had been
thoroughly surveyed for clues and there was nothing there
except some bags of rubbish spilling out of the dustbins and
beginning to rot.

His main objective now was to talk to the club's owner and
star trumpeter Stan Weston, a legend, he was told, amongst
traditional jazz musicians who had so far been mysteriously
absent from the club since the girl's body had been found. No
one, it seemed, amongst the original investigating officers, had
seen fit to attempt to track him down. But he was advertised
as top of the bill with Muddy Abraham tonight and Barnard
was determined to talk to him before the show began. He did
not see Weston arrive but when the tall, dark, easily recognizable figure of Muddy Abraham turned into the alley and then
in the direction of the back entrance Barnard reckoned it was
time to move.

Inside the dimly lit club early arrivals had already taken the
tables nearest the small stage, drinks set up, and recorded
music was playing over the speakers. Barnard made his way
to the door at the side of the stage and pushed it open. He
could see no one in the cluttered space beyond but he could

hear raised voices and when he pushed open the next door he found Abraham and a tall white man in a tweed three-piece suit, bow tie and a luxuriant beard and head of hair in a heated discussion. Both stopped dead when they saw him.

'Who the hell are you?' the bearded man demanded.

'DS Harry Barnard,' Barnard said, flashing his warrant card in his direction. 'Looking for Stan Weston. Been looking for him for several days as it goes.'

'He's the cop I been telling you about,' Abraham said, pushing his fedora to the back of his head. 'He's looking for anyone who knew that poor kid they found out back.'

'She was nothing to do with my club,' Weston said angrily. 'This is a music joint and I'm particular about who – or what – I let in.' He flashed a glance at Abraham as he spoke and Barnard guessed that he was not always successful in enforcing his rules with the American.

'But you know there are tarts around here. Can you be sure no one here was making use of her services?' Barnard said bluntly.

'Not on these premises, Sergeant,' Weston said. 'In the back yard, who knows? You know as well as I do that some people aren't particular what they do where. When we close I've seen girls outside, propositioning my clients. It's not something your people seem to bother about much. It's a thriving trade. You'd be better making inquiries amongst some of the other girls on the street.'

'Don't worry. I've got that in mind,' Barnard said, nettled by Weston's tone. He could not slot him easily into the usual run of Soho club owners. His style of dress looked more suitable for a country squire than a jazz musician and his accent did not belong to London. And he was well aware that the reason he had never come across him before was that the Jazz Cellar was, as far as he knew, clean.

'You don't get any approaches from the Maltese?' he asked.

Weston scowled. 'You know how these things work, Sergeant, I'm sure,' he said. 'I pay for security. Who doesn't round here? You probably know exactly who I pay. And so far I've found the service very satisfactory. And now, if you've no more questions, I have a show to put on. If you don't mind.'

'I do have one more question for Mr Abraham, as it goes.'
The American gave him a lopsided smile. 'Only one?'
'Are you still an American citizen, Mr Abraham? Or have
you taken out naturalization papers?'
'Sure,' Muddy Abraham said easily, though Barnard was
not sure he believed him. 'I'm in the process. I can't imagine,
when you see those southern rednecks blowing up li'l black
girls in Sunday school, why I never got round to it before.
Typical lazy nigger, I guess.' He gave Barnard a faint smile
and a shrug. 'Make what you can of that,' he said wearily and
walked determinedly out of the room.
'This isn't New Orleans, Sergeant,' Weston said angrily.
'That is a good man. And a bloody fine musician.'
'He may well be, Mr Weston,' Barnard said. 'But it's not
necessarily going to be easy for him to prove he's an innocent
man. We may not be in Alabama but there's plenty of people
here who don't like blacks.'

Tatiana Broughton-Clarke swept into the Blue Lagoon, where
Kate had arranged to meet her when she called the studio, and
turned every head in the room, which Kate accepted wryly
was precisely the intention. She was wearing a minute skirt
under a cape of some soft black leather, and above knee-high
red patent boots, all topped off with a Russian-style hat in
black fur.
'Darlink,' she greeted Kate with an unexpected kiss on each
cheek. 'I'm so glad you could make it. And so glad your boss
is amenable. Andrei is such a pig when it comes to helping
me. He doesn't think I'm being serious, you know. He thinks
– what was it he called me? – a play girl. He's jealous of
course. Jealous of me and of Roddy.'
'Roddy?' Kate asked, bemused.
'Roddy. My husband,' Tatiana said airily. 'He's paying the
rent for my little studio. I can't work at home. We're right out
in the country, in the Chilterns. You know the Chilterns? Lots
of hills and trees and narrow roads. Lots of big houses, old
and not so old.' Kate shook her head and Tatiana shrugged
and slipped out of her cape, revealing a cerise silk shift-like
shirt, sleeveless and cut low and attracting some startled

glances from nearby tables. 'I can do some of the initial planning and cutting out there in the sticks, but for most of it I just have to be in the West End – suppliers, clients, models, everyone and everything, you know. Andrei understands that too, of course. He just likes to be as difficult as possible.'

'Why do you live out there if it's so inconvenient?' Kate asked.

Tatiana raised her perfectly plucked eyebrows. 'It's his ancestral home, darlink. You don't sell your ancestral home unless you're totally bankrupt and we're not that quite yet. Six hundred years his family has been there, he says. I sympathize. My family was the same once, before the Bolsheviks. In fact the whole object of my little enterprise is to mend the hole in the roof. The place was taken over by the army in the war and rumour has it that the young officers played hockey in the salon and ran races down the grand staircase on tin trays. Anyway, one way or another, the place suffered. So now we're looking for any way we can to make a bit of money. Roddy thought we could open the house up to the public, offer tours and cream teas, roundabouts for the kiddies, but his mama stamped on that idea pretty firmly. So far we've only hosted private parties and made a loss. So I've decided I'd better do my bit. So far the people who've seen my work think it's cutting edge. So now we have to prove it.'

Kate glanced at Tatiana's outfit and smiled. 'It's certainly unusual,' she said. 'I've not seen Andrei snapping anything quite so way-out.'

'Good,' Tatiana said. 'When can you come round to my studio to plan a shoot?'

# FOUR

Harry Barnard knew better than to interrupt the street girls when they were working. He would make himself very unpopular with the women themselves and with the shadowy men of the Maltese mafia who mainly controlled them. Tracking down the friends and acquaintances of the murdered girl would have to wait until tomorrow. He drove home to his Highgate flat thoughtfully and unusually early, hung his leather coat up carefully in the hall cupboard and poured himself a large malt whisky from a carefully chosen selection in the teak cocktail cabinet in his living room. He put a brand new 78 on his radiogram, a new band recommended by one of his CID colleagues, unusual in being still unattached and with money to spend. Steve reckoned that the Rolling Stones were likely to be next year's big thing, better than the Beatles maybe, certainly different. Barnard was not that impressed by the number, *I wanna be your man,* which was in any case penned by Lennon and McCartney. Steve, he reckoned, was way off beam with this lot. They wouldn't survive long.

He sat in his favourite Heals' spinning bucket chair, sipping his drink and contemplating his own love life. His flat, as a project, was pretty well complete and occasionally he fantasized about having someone to share it with. But surprisingly for a man who prided himself on the ease with which he attracted women, his list of available candidates was not that long. Working in Soho as he did, sex was readily available. For a frisson of danger there was Shirley Bettany, snug in her luxurious Hampstead home and never likely to contemplate abandoning all that, even if he were fool enough to try to tempt her and risk the wrath of her husband Fred and his boss Ray Robertson. Then, as Ray himself had reminded him, there was Kate. Kate O'Donnell, beautiful certainly, passionate quite possibly with the right encouragement, but with an accent as thick as the waters of the River Mersey and an unaccountable habit of landing herself in predicaments that were dangerous and unpredictable and had involved him in situations twice already that had threatened to put his own career on the line.

Impulsively he pushed his chair to the telephone on a side table and dialled the number of Kate's new phone, which she had written down for him when he had last bumped into her briefly in Greek Street on her way to Andrei Lubin's studio. Kate answered herself and sounded slightly surprised to hear his voice.

'How's it going, la?' she asked. 'Have you found your murderer yet?'

'It's not as easy as that,' he muttered, disconcerted. 'We don't even know who she is yet.'

'Seems to me there's a lot of lost girls in Soho. Some of them seem to be working as models – all expecting to be the next Jean Shrimpton I expect – but I bet a lot of them get chewed up and thrown away. I met one today who's only fifteen and pregnant. Is that legal?'

'Working is legal. She doesn't have to be in school. But having sex isn't.'

'And do you bizzies do anything about that?' Kate came back quickly.

'Jesus, Kate, controlling the sex trade's a tall order, let alone girls who may be sleeping with their boyfriends.'

'Pity,' she said.

'I called to ask if you fancied a meal tomorrow night,' Barnard said, wondering already if the invitation was not a mistake. But he need not have worried. Kate turned him down flat.

'Can't do that,' she said. 'We're having a little Scouse night out tomorrow, me and Tess and some old mates from home.'

'Anywhere nice?' Barnard asked, trying to inject some friendly enthusiasm into his voice.

'We thought we might go to this Jazz Cellar place. Something new. My ex-boyfriend thinks jazz might be the next big thing, so he's organized us a table.'

Barnard groaned silently. 'I doubt it,' Barnard said. 'It's

been going to be the next big thing since about 1920. Anyway, I wouldn't recommend it right now.'

'Why? Are you lot going to close it down?'

'Not immediately,' Barnard said grimly. 'But it may not be long, since they found this girl's body suspiciously close to their back door, and anyway my DCI is sure it's a sink of iniquity, cannabis on tap.'

'We'd better go while we can, then,' Kate said lightly. 'It is supposed to be famous.'

'Famous, or notorious, take your pick,' Barnard said. 'Anyway I can't stop you, can I. Just take care. And don't accept drugs if they're offered, right? I'll see you around.' He hung up angrily. He was wasting his time there, he thought, and poured himself another Scotch. She was far too young for him anyway, and he couldn't live with that Scouse accent, which did not seem to be softening at all under the influence of southerners. The few days she had stayed with him when she was burned out of her flat in Notting Hill was a one off and that looked like the end of it.

The next day Harry Barnard was on Evie Smith's threshold as early as he dared – which was not much before noon. There had been a time when Evie's charms lured him into pressing this particular doorbell – one of six all with women's names alongside on the door with peeling red paint – more often than was probably wise, even though such relationships were regarded as one of the perks of the job in the police canteen. But Evie's looks were fading and with them the attraction. He had not seen her for a couple of months and did not know how welcome he would be.

She came to the door in silky housecoat with no make-up and a half-smoked cigarette in her hand. She waved him in without saying anything and as she let him into her room, which was better lit than the hallway, Barnard realized that she was looking far worse than he had seen her before. Her face was distinctly lined around the eyes and mouth, her hair was lank and dark at the roots, and as she sat in the sagging armchair crammed into the small space beside the double bed she began to cough.

'You look rough,' he said. 'How bad is that cough?'

'It comes and goes,' she said, stubbing out her cigarette in an overflowing ashtray on the bedside table and picked up a cup of something standing beside it.

'Have you seen a doc?'

'It'll get better when we get some warmer weather,' she said. 'I'm as tough as old boots really. Always have been. You don't survive long in this game if you're not. Anyway, what can I do for you? You haven't favoured me with a visit for a long time.'

'Been busy,' Barnard said.

'New girlfriend more like,' Evie said. 'It's about time you settled down, Flash.' She gave him a smile that reminded him of why he had once found her so attractive but he merely shook his head at her suggestion.

'I really came round to pick your brains, Evie. You know a young girl was found dead at the back of the Jazz Cellar the other day. General impression is that she was on the game but no one seems to know her name or where she came from. She's only a kid.'

'I heard,' Evie said before dissolving in a fit of coughing again.

Barnard waited until the fit had subsided. 'See a doc,' he said, as he reached into his jacket and pulled out the photograph of Jenny and handed it to Evie. 'This is her.'

Evie gazed at the picture for a long time before she spoke and Barnard was surprised to see tears in her eyes.

'Yes,' she said. 'I wondered if it was her. She's been around for a couple of months at most. 'I came across her one night up in Soho Square, sheltering with a couple of winos. She said she'd been with a couple of blokes and they'd ended up hitting her and refusing to pay. They drove off in a car. I was on my way home and I brought her back, put her to bed, I slept in the chair. But she was ready for off as soon as it was light. She didn't tell me much. Said she was called Jenny, she came from the East End, had come up west to work as a model, but that didn't work out and she ended up on the streets.'

'No second name?'

'No. She seemed very worried about saying too much.'

'No hint as to whereabouts in the East End? There's a lot of it,' Barnard said. 'No idea why she didn't simply go home when the modelling failed?'

'Clapton, I think she said. She talked a bit about her school, though she didn't say what it was called. She hated it, she said. Played hookey a lot of the time. Spent more and more time in the West End when she could find the money for the bus fares, looking for jobs in the fashion business. She said she knew other girls who had come up here and found work as models.'

'Well, that gives me a lead at least. I'll call the local nick and see if she's been reported missing for a start. If not I could try the photograph at the local schools. Was it a grammar school? A girls' school? Any idea?'

'She only talked about girls,' Evie said before collapsing into another paroxysm of coughing.

Barnard sighed. 'You really should have that cough seen to,' he said. 'Thanks, Evie. And look after yourself, for God's sake. If you go on like that how are you going to be able to work?'

Evie nodded bleakly and lit another cigarette before walking slowly with him to the front door. 'Find the bastard who killed her,' she said hoarsely. 'None of us are safe, are we, if you don't.'

Barnard put his head round the door of the Jazz Cellar as he strolled back to the nick, but there was no one inside except a couple of cleaners wiping tables and a stale smell including an undertone of marijuana which he knew would be enough to spark DCI Jackson into a raid. He shrugged. There was nothing much he could do to prevent that. He just hoped that Kate O'Donnell was not there when the uniformed plods stormed in.

Back at the nick he put in a call to the nick in Hackney to inquire about missing persons. But according to the WPC who looked at the records for him without much enthusiasm there was nothing there: plenty of teenagers leaving home but no Jenny or Jennifer who fitted his description.

'They bugger off all the time,' she said. 'The bright lights seem attractive, God knows why. Sometimes their parents report them missing, sometimes they don't. The children's homes generally let us know if they abscond. But if they're sixteen or thereabouts, working age, age of consent, all that, and no indication of foul play, we haven't got the resources to follow up. Some come back, some don't, some are never seen again. You could try the Sally Army. They try to trace a few.'

'I need this girl's name,' Barnard said with an edge to his voice. 'This is a murder case. She probably went to a girls' school near you. Clapton is the best guess. What have you got?'

'A girls' grammar and a girls' secondary in Clapton,' the WPC said. 'I'll get the addresses for you.'

It took Barnard a good half hour to grind out east to an area way beyond where he had been raised in the tightly packed streets of Whitechapel until the land began to drop away into a landscape of marshes and reservoirs and derelict sites left to fester since the war. Hackney, which contained Clapton, was the last of the boroughs he found recognizable as real East End and was where he found the secondary school that he thought Jenny might have attended. An elderly building, much extended over the years, was crammed into a mainly residential road with, as far as he could see, shockingly little outdoor space for the crowds of neatly uniformed girls who were pouring out of the doors at the end of the school afternoon. Asking directions three or four times he found reception and asked to see the head teacher.

The woman on the desk looked dubious. 'I'm not sure she's in,' she said. 'Are you a parent?' She looked anxious and he flashed his warrant card impatiently. The woman looked slightly shocked but picked up her telephone without comment and within a minute Barnard was being ushered into the office of a smartly suited middle-aged woman, her gray hair in a neat bun, who glanced up from a cluttered desk with a look of slight exasperation.

'Mrs Bradley,' the receptionist muttered at Barnard, and scuttled off, looking as if she feared being chastised for bringing in a visitor, even though he carried a police warrant card.

'What can I do for you, Officer?' the head asked. She glanced at her watch. 'I have a governors meeting beginning in fifteen minutes.'

Barnard pulled Jenny's photograph from his inside pocket and handed it to the headmistress. 'I'm trying to trace a girl,' he said. 'She can't be more than fifteen or sixteen and we believe she went to a school around here and wondered if she was one of yours.'

The head took the photograph and Barnard knew immediately from the way her lips thinned in head-teacherly disapproval that he had struck gold.

'She was one of our failures,' she said tartly. 'Jenny Maitland, always a difficult child from the start, by the time she had reached the fourth form she was playing truant regularly and her parents seemed only marginally interested in what she was doing. We try very hard for these girls, you know. This is not an easy area to grow up in. And on the whole we do well by them. Some of them go on to take O levels and A Levels elsewhere. Most of them find reasonable jobs. But some of them we lose. Jenny was one who wasn't interested. Said she wanted to be a model. One or two others the previous year took themselves off for the same reason. And we all know where that can lead. Why do you have her photograph, Sergeant?'

'I'm afraid Jenny Maitland is dead,' Barnard said. 'Her body was found in Soho, brutally murdered. I need to contact her parents urgently.'

Olive Bradley gave him her full attention then, looking appalled. 'How dreadful,' she said very quietly. 'That is truly dreadful.'

'Presumably you still have Jenny's records, her home address, all that?'

'Of course. I'll get my secretary to retrieve them for you. Presumably you won't want this to go any further until you have seen her mother and father.'

'I'll ask the local police to contact you when it's appropriate to tell her teachers and friends,' Barnard said. 'When we have formally identified her we will want to tell the Press that we've done that. So far all we have is an unidentified body in the mortuary. When I've got an address I'll go round straight away to try to contact her parents.'

Olive Bradley stood up and held out her hand to shake Barnard's. 'In a big school you don't get to know many girls as individuals,' she said. 'Mainly it's the very bright ones – the ones who should have gone to grammar school – or the very naughty ones. Jenny Maitland was both, as it happens, but she couldn't – or wouldn't – make use of her brains. A great shame. I will write to her parents in a day or two. It is a tragedy to lose a child, however difficult.'

'Thank you,' Barnard said.

The street Barnard located with some difficulty was in the throes of demolition. On the left, as he turned the car in and slowed down, the terraces of small houses had been reduced to rubble, with demolition balls and bulldozers still working in clouds of dust at the far end. On the right, the even numbers were, to his relief still standing, but some were already boarded up. This was local government finishing off what Hitler had begun, he thought. He knew only too well from personal experience how unsatisfactory a lot of these East End houses were, with their outside toilets and no bathrooms at all. But he also knew that many of the communities were strong, three or even four generations living in close proximity, and were unlikely to recover as families were split apart and decanted into more modern housing scattered across the edges of London. He sighed and got out of the car and began to count down to number thirty-four where the Maitlands had lived until recently and he hoped still did.

To his relief he found the house was still standing and the windows were not boarded yet, though the front door looked dilapidated and he knocked on the almost bare wood with some trepidation. To his surprise it was opened quickly by a careworn woman with graying hair who looked surprised to see him.

'Oh, I was expecting Mr Deedes from the council,' she said. 'Who are you?'

He showed her his warrant card. 'Can I come in, Mrs Maitland?' he asked quietly.

The woman looked up and down the street quickly and then pulled open the door to allow him in.

'It must be difficult living with all this going on,' he said as she closed the door with some force against the obviously warped jamb. The door led directly into an untidy living room and she waved him vaguely into a seat which he noticed was faintly covered with dusty deposits which he guessed must have drifted in from outside.

'Mr Deedes from the council,' she said, appearing to be on the verge of tears. 'He was bringing me the offer of a house in Billericay. We need to get out of here but they keep saying they need to know how many people are in the family and my husband's done a bunk. I don't know where he is. He buggered off soon after Jenny left . . .'

'Ah,' Barnard said. 'It was Jenny I came about.' He pulled out his photograph of the murdered girl again and showed it to her. 'Is this your daughter, Mrs Maitland? Is this Jenny?'

She took the photo from him, her hands shaking. 'Yes,' she whispered. 'That's Jenny. Have you found her?'

'I'm very sorry, I'm afraid we have found Jenny dead,' he said and watched helplessly as her face crumpled into despair. 'Is there anyone else in the house?' he asked. 'Or a neighbour who could come to be with you?'

'The boys are at school,' she said. 'They go out to the Marshes to do sport after they finish lessons. The neighbours have all gone. We're almost the last to be moved. There's almost no one here now . . .' She broke into heartbroken sobs.

Barnard got up and went into the kitchen at the back of the house, rummaged through the cupboards until he found what he wanted and made her a cup of hot, sweet tea. He put it on the table in front of her and handed her a handkerchief.

'I don't want to harass you at a time like this but I do need you to tell me a little about Jenny and how she came to leave home. And later, or maybe tomorrow, we'll ask you to come into the West End and identify her body. So far we've been looking for the killer of an unknown girl. What you can tell us about her will make it much easier to track her movements since she left home and find her murderer. Do you understand that, Mrs Maitland?'

She drew a deep breath and dried her eyes, although she was still wracked with shuddering sobs. 'I understand,' she said. 'What do you want to know?'

'Tell me about your family, for a start,' he said. 'What's your husband's name?'

'Walter,' she said. 'He was working at Fords in Dagenham when we got married and had Jenny. She was our first and he adored her. But when she was about eight or nine he got laid off and it turned out he'd started drinking, hadn't he. It was never the same after that. We had the two boys by then and all the kids were affected. Jenny was naughty at school. Her teachers said she should have gone to grammar school but she didn't pass. I don't think she tried. Her dad was angry about that. He started hitting the kids – and me – when he was drunk. And then they started talking about all the houses coming down. That made it worse.'

'I spoke to Jenny's headmistress. She said she'd started playing truant.'

'She did. We didn't know at first but the school told us she wasn't turning up. She's got in with some girls who'd all decided they were going to be models. As if that was likely. But she wouldn't listen. And a year ago she packed her stuff and said she was going. Her father went berserk but she went anyway. We've not seen or heard from her since.'

'Did you report it to the police?'

Mrs Maitland shook her head glumly. 'My husband wouldn't let me. He said that if that was all she thought about her family she wasn't worth looking for. He said she was old enough to look for a job so she could look after herself now, save him some money. And then he went too . . .' She broke down in tears again.

Barnard sighed. His imperative was to get on to the next stage of his investigation and he couldn't sensibly transport this distraught woman to the mortuary to make an identification of her daughter right now. It would have to wait.

'Do you have a phone?' he asked but she shook her head. 'Then I'll ask the local police station to send a woman officer down to see you,' he said. 'I'll ask her to help you get a relative or friend to come round to be with you, at least until your sons come home. And she can arrange for a car to collect you tomorrow to bring you to identify your daughter at the hospital. And I'll ask the local nick to try to track down your husband. He needs to know about Jenny too, and we will need to talk to him.'

'He's at the root of all this,' Mrs Maitland said bitterly through her tears. 'He drove her away.'

'But he didn't kill her, I'm sure,' Barnard said. 'And what I'm sure you want me to do is catch her killer. So I'll ring the local station and make the arrangements, then I'll see you tomorrow. Right?'

'Right,' Jenny Maitland's mother said, though it was obvious that for her nothing would ever be right again.

# FIVE

D ave Donovan had bought Kate and Tess Farrell two rounds of drinks, and Kate was already feeling somewhat light-headed before the Jazz Cellar filled up and a couple of musicians wandered on to the tiny stage to a halfhearted round of applause.

'Nine o'clock opening seems a bit elastic,' Tess said sceptically.

Kate had had to work hard to persuade her to come with her at all, as they were both working the next day, but she had persevered and eventually she had agreed. Kate, as always, was curious to see something new but she did not want an evening alone with Dave who still seemed to nurse some ambitions that they could get back together. She had been surprised to hear from him when he called on her brand new phone. The last she had heard of him was that he had gone back to Liverpool with his tail between his legs, his band still not having landed a recording contract in London.

'You're back,' she had said, surprised. 'How did you get this number?'

'Rang your office and they gave it me,' he'd said. They shouldn't have done that, Kate thought.

'Why are you back?' she demanded, not at all sure she wanted him pursuing her again. 'I thought it was too expensive down here.'

'It is but we've got a session with EMI, a break at last. This could be it, Katie. You've got to be persistent, la. Look where the Beatles are now. It could be us next.'

'Maybe,' she said, trying to mute her scepticism. Donovan and The Ants sounded remarkably similar to the Shadows and looked, in tight denim and leather jackets, like the Beatles in Hamburg; no longer, she thought, a good look. 'The pictures I took for you could come in useful, then.'

'Oh, if we get a contract the record company will do all

that for us,' he said dismissively. So much for appreciating the help she had given him, she thought.

'That's not why I phoned you,' Dave rushed on oblivious to her mood. 'I wondered if you'd like to come to a place in Soho called the Jazz Cellar? I heard someone raving about it the other day.'

Kate thought quickly and had to admit to herself that she was curious about the place where a young girl had been found dead, just around the corner from the Fellows agency. 'I'll come if Tess can come too,' she had said. She waited while he thought about it but he had eventually agreed with ill-grace and later that night the three of them met in the French pub and wandered up through the early evening crowd, mainly tourists ripe for ripping off in the bars and clip joints of the square mile of sinful Soho which were just opening their doors and swinging into gear.

'Isn't jazz a bit old-fashioned?' Tess asked, as they settled themselves at a table. 'I had an uncle who used to play clarinet in a jazz band but I don't think many people ever took much notice of them. They were too old to attract the girls. Don't they make the music up as they go along?'

'It's called improvising,' Dave said loftily. 'They take a tune and weave around it. I just really wanted to hear some muckers who knew what they were doing instead of just strumming three chords on a guitar.'

'Like your lot do?' Kate said tartly. She glanced around the rest of the tables where people were settling themselves in and ordering drinks. Tess was right, she thought. The three of them must be the youngest in the room so far, apart from a group of young men at a corner table who looked like students but even they were wearing tweed sports jackets and cravats and sporting haircuts short enough to pass muster in the Brigade of Guards. The fashion revolution the likes of Tatiana Broughton-Clarke and other designers were promoting still had a long way to go, she thought.

'Here we go,' Dave Donovan said as a clatter of drums and cymbals reduced the buzz of conversation in the dimly lit room, which was already growing hot and smoky. The drummer had led the influx of musicians on to the tiny stage, which hardly seemed big enough to accommodate the entire band. There was a smattering of applause as the trumpet player, middle aged, paunchy and balding, soberly dressed in shirt, tie and waistcoat, edged his way to the front and, without any introduction, launched into a melody, backed by a fast beat from the drummer and bass, which many of the audience appeared to recognize and applauded more loudly.

For more than an hour the music continued, the players, getting visibly hotter, refreshing themselves with beers handed up from the bar and throwing off top layers of clothing as they continued. At last Stan Weston signalled some sort of conclusion with what seemed to Kate to be an impossibly high blast on his trumpet, leading to a crescendo of applause from the audience.

'Ladies and gents,' he said as the noise subsided slightly. 'We'll be back in one half hour when we will be entertaining Mr Gerry Statham, the best jazz singer this country's ever produced . . . Enjoy yourselves. Make yourselves at home.'

'Wow,' Kate said. 'What did you make of that then?'

Dave Donovan and Tess both looked slightly stunned although in different ways.

'Great stuff,' Dave said, but Tess looked dubious.

'It's all American, isn't it?' she said. 'I can't say I like it much. I'd rather have the Beatles or Gerry and the Pacemakers any day.'

'And there's another group on the up as well,' Donovan said slightly gloomily. 'I heard a group called the Rollin' Stones the other night. They were standing in at a club I was at but I thought they were pretty good. I hope they've not going to get in ahead of us with a recording contract.'

'I wonder if they'd let me take any pictures,' Kate said, gazing at the empty stage. 'I'm not sure that Ken knows about this place. But it might be worth a try. I don't really think fashion's going to turn out to be my scene. Ken's only dumped it on me because I'm the only female he's got.'

'Let's go and ask them if they'd like you to snap them,' Donovan said, jumping to his feet. 'Can't do any harm, can it? You hang on to the table, Tess. Don't let anyone take our places.'

Tess pulled a disgruntled face at that but she did as she was told. There would be recriminations later, Kate thought. Not quite knowing where she was going, she went with Donovan to the door beside the stage that the musicians had used and followed him through it when he pushed it open. Beyond was a small room, even more hot and stuffy than the club itself, where most members of the band appeared to be knocking back pints of beer. Stan Weston was slumped in a battered armchair, nursing his trumpet and a pint glass, shirt sleeves pushed up now and waistcoat discarded, but looked up sharply when he saw them.

'Who the hell are you?' he asked. 'This is private.'

'I've just signed up with EMI,' Donovan lied airily. 'Dave Donovan of the Ants. And this is Kate O'Donnell who's taken some incredibly moody publicity pics for us. I though you might like to meet her. She's very good and could take some snaps for you tonight if you like, for you to have a look at. No obligation.'

Kate pulled her precious Voigtlander out of her bag. 'Perhaps you don't have any of the great Gerry Statham at the club,' she said. 'I can focus on him if you like. I could let you see anything I take first thing tomorrow.' If I get up early and do the developing and printing very fast, she thought.

'Could be useful, Stan,' the saxophonist said, tall, grizzled and black, with a distinct American drawl, drawing deeply on a battered-looking cigarette. 'You can't say we've had good publicity this week with a dead girl on the stoop.'

Weston scowled. 'True,' he said. 'I was thinking of talking to Bob Davies on the *Evening News,* see if he'll cover Gerry's gigs.'

'If you could offer him some pics of your singer it might go down well,' Donovan jumped in. 'You've not got anyone else taking pictures tonight, have you?'

'Have a drink, why don't you? What'll it be?' Weston said as he introduced the rest of the band.

To Kate's surprise Muddy Abraham waved his cigarette in her direction but Donovan waved it away impatiently.

'Gerry's not here yet but we'll see what he says,' Weston said. 'I can't see he'll have any objection. But don't get in the way of the audience. They like to concentrate, you know. This isn't pop music. It's a whole lot more serious than that.'

By the end of the evening Kate had shot a roll of film, but her companions were less than happy. She could see that Tess, the convent girl, had been shocked by Gerry Statham's explicit songs and gestures and Dave had stalked off alone at the end, declaring himself furious at the drummer, Steve O'Leary's sleepy-eyed invitation to Kate to spend the night at his place, which the clarinettist, Chris Swift witnessed with a disapproving scowl. Kate had quickly turned the invitation down but smiled at Dave's reaction, not unhappy to see him go. After this rare evening spent together, there was no way she felt inclined to give him any encouragement. The Liverpool they had enjoyed together so recently was rapidly fading away, she thought, and it wasn't going to come back again. There was no way she would contemplate going 'home'. The two flatmates eventually dodged their way side by side towards Leicester Square underground station through Soho streets still teeming with revellers.

'If that's jazz, you can keep it,' Tess complained as they made their way down the escalator. 'It's disgusting. And why did Dave say the American offered you his cigarette, for heaven's sake, and think it was funny.'

'Dave said it wasn't tobacco, it was marijuana,' Kate said quietly. 'Best keep quiet about that, maybe. They seem to be having enough trouble with the police without being raided for drugs.' She didn't tell Tess quite what a real possibility that might be, or that, as she had dodged around the tables and the stage taking her pictures, the distinctive aroma of the drug had grown more intense as the evening progressed, though exactly whether it was coming from the stage or the audience was difficult to pin down.

DS Harry Barnard was taking his usual mid-morning stroll around Soho. The place was barely awake yet: a peep show had lured in a few curious tourists to gape at a couple of girls who promised more than they delivered. A couple of Americans in trademark cowboy hats were staring aghast at a bookshop window, the like of which they had obviously never seen before. And a couple of tarts, pale and gaunt without their make-up, were chatting on a street corner, one clutching a bottle of milk, the other a loaf of bread.

'Morning, girls,' he said. 'Just the people I want to see.' Both women looked less than enchanted by his approach, but they knew better than to scuttle away without at least a reluctant word. Harry Barnard could make life too uncomfortable for them if they tried that.

'I've got a name for the kid who was found dead the other day,' he said. 'Jenny Maitland she was called, up from the East End about a year ago. Now what I want to know is how long she's been on the game and who was running her. Sure as eggs, a kid that age wasn't working on her own. Stands to reason.'

'They don't plan it like that,' the older of the two women said. 'A lot of them now are following the bands, hanging round the recording studios screaming, or else they want to be models and they hang around the photo studios trying to cadge an entry. They all think they can sing, or else they're going to be the next Jean Shrimpton. Since David Bailey, the models seem to have got younger and younger. Barely out of nappies some of them. Skirts up to their knickers.'

'Anywhere particular round here?' Barnard asked.

'Some of the studios take them on and then throw them out as soon as they prove they're no good. There's a couple of kids renting a room below us. They might be worth talking to. They might have known this Jenny Maitland. I'm not sure they're turning tricks but I'm damn sure they soon will be.'

'Right, I'll have a word,' Barnard said. 'What number are you? Twenty-five?' The two women nodded.

'I blame the parents,' one said as they turned away. 'They're out of control, the kids these days.'

'Yeah, yeah,' Barnard muttered under his breath. 'And your lot weren't, out with the teddy boys as like as not.' He strolled round Soho Square, where a few office workers were taking an early lunch hour on the benches, enjoying an unseasonable outbreak of sunshine, and started down Greek Street, when he found himself walking in step with a small weaselly man who might in an earlier incarnation have earned his crust as a jockey. Now, he knew, he worked for Ray Robertson as an errand boy and runner.

'Mick,' he said. 'How's it going?'

'Can we have a chat, Mr Barnard? Somewhere quiet? I've got a message for you.'

Barnard hustled Mick through the half-open door of the nearest pub where the barman looked for a moment as if he would try to throw them out but when he recognized Barnard he shrugged.

'Drink?' he asked.

'Two large Scotches,' Barnard said sitting at a corner table and making no attempt to pay when the drinks were brought.

'So,' he said. 'What's this message?'

'It's from Mr Bettany,' Mick said and Barnard froze.

'Fred Bettany? Ray's money man?' he asked.

'The same. He says he wants to have a chat. He says could you meet him this evening at the Spaniards on Hampstead Heath. You know it?'

Mouth dry, Barnard sipped his Scotch and tried to control his breathing. 'I know it. What time?'

'Six o'clock. He'll pop in on the way home. He's with Mr Robertson at the Delilah all day today, busy with meetings, he said.'

'Tell him I'll see him there,' Barnard said, wondering if Ray Robertson knew about this meeting and fearing even more whether or not he knew about what Barnard feared it was about. He picked up his glass and drained it, putting it down carefully so as not to reveal his shaking hand. 'Is Mr Robertson going to be with him?'

'Nah,' Mick said. 'I don't think this is anything to do with him. Just you and Mr Bettany.' And that, Barnard thought, with a vivid image of Fred Bettany's wife slipping in between the sheets with him, stark naked and infinitely enticing, was what he was afraid of. If Fred had somehow uncovered that secret, a transfer to the Outer Hebrides might not be far enough.

On his way back to the nick he tried the door of the house his contacts had told him a couple of young women were working and to his surprise found it open. When he shouted, a bleary-eyed face peered over the banisters, not one he recognized so he guessed she was a recent arrival. He went up, warrant card in hand and hustled her back into the bedroom where the door was open.

'You on your own, darling?' he asked.

The girl, who was in a loose robe, which she clutched tightly around her, and slippers, nodded. 'I'm not working,' she said, looking anxious.

'Just now, or at all?' Barnard asked. 'Come on, you can tell your uncle Harry. I'm not looking for a trick, I just want some information. You know a girl was found dead the other day just down the street? What's your name?'

'Josie,' the girl said.

'And how old are you, Josie?'

'Sixteen,' she said, although Barnard found it hard to believe. She might look sixteen or more in full make-up and night-time gear, but here and now, shivering on the landing, she could have been twelve.

'Do you have someone looking after you?' he asked.

'Yeah, yeah, of course I have,' Josie said. 'I'm not stupid.'

'Well, we get the feeling that some girls your sort of age are being a bit stupid, taking risks, including the one who died. Did you know Jenny Maitland?'

Josie shook her head dully.

'She came to Soho to be a model and ended up on the streets like you.'

'She's not the only one,' Josie said unexpectedly. 'I heard someone say . . .' She hesitated, obviously wondering if she had gone too far.

'Say what?' Barnard pressed her.

'Say there were new girls, supposed to be models, but it was all a front. They were schoolgirls being groomed . . . My man didn't like it, said he would pass it on to his boss.'

Barnard nodded bleakly. He smelled the beginnings of a war, and did not like it.

Andrei's studio was at something of a loose end. Kate had got in that morning only to find the boss heading out in the opposite direction.

'Got a meeting with the editor at *Vogue*,' he had said breathlessly as he bustled out with Ricky Smart in close attendance and not neglecting to put a casual arm around her waist as he passed. 'Maybe this is our breakthrough. You never know.'

Kate raised her eyebrows, careful that neither man could see her. She hung up her coat and glanced around the studio. There was no one there except Sylvia, looking even more pale and wan than the last time she had seen her.

'I'll make some coffee,' Kate said, filling the kettle and switching it on. 'Are you all right?'

'Not really but I've got the name of someone to go and see,' she said listlessly.

'To get rid of it, you mean?' Kate said cautiously.

The girl nodded and Kate drew a sharp breath. All her upbringing told her that the very idea was terribly wrong but when she looked at Sylvia, little more than a child herself, she could not bring herself to even begin to persuade her not to go ahead with what she was planning.

'Some of these people are very dangerous,' she said quietly. 'Are you sure?'

''Course I'm sure,' she said. 'What else can I do?'

Kate made the coffee silently and handed Sylvia a cup.

'Though I need the cash and I don't know where I'm going to get that from,' the girl said as she took a sip and grimaced. 'I've gone off coffee,' she muttered, putting the cup down.

'How did you end up here?' Kate asked as the two of them perched on high stools and Sylvia opened a packet of custard creams and began to eat them voraciously.

'It seemed better than anything else, didn't it?' she said. 'Where I came from you worked in a shop or a factory, then you got married and had a load of kids. When Ricky turned up outside the school looking for pretty girls to go modelling it seemed like a good idea at the time. He can be very persuasive, can Ricky.'

'He does the recruiting, does he?'

'I think he hangs around some of the schools looking for likely targets. It's been going on for ages. It was only when I got here that I realized that a lot of them don't stay long. Andrei chucks people out as soon as look at them if they don't suit. I expect if he discovers I'm pregnant I'll be out on my ear.'

'And then what would you do?' Kate asked.

'I don't know,' Sylvia said. 'That's why I've got to get rid of it.' A single tear ran down her face. 'There was another girl here from my school. She was the year ahead of me. Jenny Maitland she was called. She seemed to be doing fine when I started, but suddenly she vanished. I asked Ricky where she'd gone, but he told me he hadn't a clue. She just went, didn't she, he said. She's a free agent.'

'Jenny?' Kate said, remembering that the girl who had been found dead behind the jazz club had been called Jenny. 'How long ago did she leave?'

'Oh, I don't know. A couple of months, maybe. I can't remember.' The girl looked at Kate speculatively. 'Could you lend me some money?' she said.

Kate drew a sharp breath. 'I can't do that,' she said quietly. 'I know you're desperate but . . . I can't.' She sipped her coffee as another tear slid down Sylvia's cheek. 'If you're sure that's what you want to do, can't you get Andrei or Ricky to help you? Surely it's their responsibility.'

'If I ask them they'll throw me out,' she said. 'With or without the baby they'll throw me out.'

Kate sighed and then suddenly had an idea. 'Did you realize that the girl who was found dead a couple of days ago was called Jenny?' she asked.

Sylvia shook her head.

'You know the police pay for information sometimes. If I took you to see a policeman I know and you told him about Jenny Maitland and how you were both recruited by Ricky he might think it's worth paying you for. I can't be sure, but it's worth a try. It sounds as if he needs to know anyway.'

'But if Andrei found out I was telling the police things, he might throw me out. He's not going to be very pleased is he? You haven't seen him in a rage.'

'I'm sure Sergeant Barnard wouldn't say where his information came from,' Kate said. 'Why don't you let me ring him, la. I can check it all out if you like.'

Sylvia was silent for a moment and then she nodded. 'Go on then,' she said.

Back at the nick, wondering what to tell the DCI about his anxieties, Barnard picked up the phone at the first ring and when Kate explained what Sylvia knew about the dead girl he sounded immediately interested.

'Meet me at the Blue Lagoon,' he said. 'Coming to the police station will likely frighten your little friend to death, but she'll probably have to come in to make a statement in the end. We'll do a bit of persuading. It strikes me that these people you're working for are recruiting under-age girls, if nothing worse.'

'Ten minutes,' Kate said.

The three of them arrived at almost the same moment and Barnard bought them all frothy coffee in the coffee bar's trademark glass cups before sitting down with them at a Formica table and offering Sylvia a cigarette and lighting it carefully for her. The girl's hand shook and he glanced at Kate sharply.

'Is she OK?' he asked.

'She has some problems,' Kate said.

'All right,' Barnard said. 'We'll make this as painless as we can.' He turned to Sylvia. 'Kate tells me you knew a girl called Jenny Maitland. Is that right?'

Sylvia nodded, her eyes full of tears. 'She went to my school, didn't she?' she said. 'She was a year ahead and was one of those who came up west with Ricky Smart. I knew him when he came back again the next year. We all quite fancied being models, didn't we? If Jean Shrimpton could do it we didn't see why we shouldn't.'

'And Jenny was still working for this Russian bloke when you arrived?'

'Yes, she was there on and off. But I don't think she was very happy. She kept having rows with Ricky. Andrei seemed to quite like her, indulged her, but I expect he was sleeping with her then.'

'That was what generally happened, was it?' Barnard asked.

'That's what usually happened, yes.'

'And when they got tired of them? What happened then?'

'They were soon out the door,' Sylvia said. 'We never saw them again. We never knew where they went. They just weren't good enough, according to Andrei. Not up to scratch, though I always thought that it was the prettiest ones who went. Jenny Maitland was lovely looking.'

Barnard nodded, thinking of the photograph of the girl taken on the mortuary slab. Even in death she had been attractive. But her looks had not been enough to keep her off the streets.

'How about you? Have you had the same sort of treatment?' Barnard asked.

Sylvia looked away, flushed and a tear ran down her cheek. Barnard's lips tightened. 'Right,' he said.

'She's pregnant,' Kate said quietly, and Barnard sighed. 'Is there a chance you can pay her for her information? She needs the money.'

'Won't this Andrei do anything?' Barnard asked.

'He doesn't know yet, but he won't. He'll throw me out on the street. I'm no use to him now, am I? I'll be looking like a balloon in a couple of months,' Sylvia mumbled into her coffee cup.

Barnard flashed a slightly desperate look at Kate. 'Information received?' he said quietly. 'I suppose that's fair.' he turned to Sylvia again. 'What's the going rate for what you want?'

'Thirty pounds,' Sylvia whispered.

Barnard whistled. 'I'll be round to see your boss later,' he said. 'He's got some serious questions to answer about Jenny Maitland. I'll see what I can do about the cash.' He looked at Kate much more seriously than he usually did. 'No promises,' he said. 'Meet me here about five o'clock. I might have some answers then.'

'Make it half past,' she said. 'I'm going to see Ken Fellows at five to see if I can get myself out of Lubin's clutches. I don't think I can bear to stay there another two weeks.'

# SIX

Ricky Smart put an arm around Kate and stroked her left breast and laughed uproariously when she pushed him away.

'What's your problem? By invitation only, is it? You don't know what you're missing, sweetheart,' he said.

'Go away, Ricky,' Kate said. Ken, she thought, had to get her out of here.

'Are all the girls in Liverpool as uptight as you?' Ricky sneered. 'You're all getting above yourselves since the blessed Beatles hit the big time. It won't last, you know. It'll all be over in six months, you'll see. They'll be dead and buried and forgotten.'

'I doubt it,' Kate said. She had got back to the studio before Andrei and Ricky and had time to help Sylvia tidy her hair and repair her make-up before the men arrived. It was obvious as soon as they came up the stairs that their trip had not been a productive one. Andrei had flung his portfolio of photographs on to a chair and pulled the rack of clothes which they were booked to photograph that day into the middle of the floor.

'Kate, will you make a start on this shoot,' he said. 'Sylvia's early but the rest of the girls will be in any minute. We can't waste time. Here, I want them to wear these. I reckon stockings will be obsolete soon.' He dropped half a dozen pairs of tights in plastic packets on to a table.

'Oh, Gawd help us, what will we do without a flash of stocking tops and knickers?' Ricky Smart wailed. 'It's one of the pleasures of a summer day in London. All those girls sitting on the grass eating their sandwiches and showing their suspenders and, if you're lucky, a little bit more than that.'

'Shut up, Ricky,' Lubin snapped. 'Come in here and tell me what we did wrong for that prissy cow at *Vogue*. You realize that was Bailey himself with the models, smirking in the corner. What's he got that we haven't?'

'I told you we were trying to walk before we could run,' Smart said, following Lubin into the tiny space he called his office. 'We haven't got the experience yet.' He shut the door but Kate could still hear the two men's angry voices. 'I think maybe you'd better talk to Tatiana. Maybe take some pics for her after all. She'll know what all the designers are up to, and what the girls are buying. She might be really useful.'

'She's an amateur. She's just playing at it,' Kate heard Lubin object before he slammed the door, muffling the rest of their conversation. She turned her attention to the girls who were drifting in one by one and began to distribute the dresses – more avant-garde than anything she had seen here before – to the models and make sure that they adjusted their make-up to suit the heavy, dark-eyed look Andrei liked. The trouble with this assignment, she thought, was not that she did not like fashion but that she really could not see herself devoting her career to it. The people she had met so far in the rag trade would drive her doolally in a very short time, she thought.

Sylvia, who had struggled into her short dress with some difficulty, grabbed Kate's arm as she spotted DS Harry Barnard walking through the open studio door.

'That was quick,' Kate said quietly.

'I told you I needed to talk to your Mr Lubin about Jenny Maitland,' he said. 'Is he in?'

Kate waved at the closed office door. 'He's in there,' she said.

Barnard squeezed his way through the bustle of semi-dressed girls with every sign of enjoyment, tapped on the door and went into Lubin's sanctum. He closed the door behind him but Kate wondered if he had deliberately raised his voice because she could still hear most of what was being said. It was obvious that both Lubin and Smart resented any suggestion that they should be held responsible for Jenny in any way once she had left their employment. Kate marshalled the girls into their position on the set, and began to take some preliminary shots, positioning herself as close as possible to the office door so that she could still hear the conversation, which seemed to be rapidly turning into a rant on Andrei Lubin's part. He could not be held responsible if girls lied about their age, either to work or to sleep with him, if they were so minded, he said loudly, and a lot of them it seemed, were so minded while they worked at the studio. Kate could just imagine Ricky Smart smirking at that blunt response. But neither of the men, it appeared, had seen or heard of Jenny after Lubin sacked her. They assumed she had gone back home to her family. In other words, they claimed to know absolutely nothing about the last two months of the girl's life.

All three of the men eventually came out of the office. Lubin picked up a camera and strode over to Kate, looking thunderous but intent on taking over the shoot. Smart, with a secret smirk, followed Barnard out and ushered him to the door. But as he turned back he looked less than happy with his interview and did not even glance at Kate.

'I'm sure I'll have more questions to ask you, and your boss, and quite possibly some of your models as the inquiry progresses,' Barnard called out to the retreating Smart, before turning away himself and thundering down the stairs.

Kate arrived at the Blue Lagoon early, her interview with Ken Fellows having been brief and unsatisfactory. She ordered herself a cappuccino and sat stirring the froth idly as she waited for Barnard to arrive. Fellows had actually laughed when she complained about Andrei and Ricky's persistent advances.

'News to me, girl,' he had said. 'I thought they were all poofters.'

'Definitely not,' she had shot back. 'In any case I think I've learned enough about the rag trade. I'm not cut out for that sort of photography anyway.'

'It's another string to our bow, girl, if we can show them some sexy fashion shots,' her boss said. 'You stick it out and we'll put some of your best shots in our portfolio.'

'But we've got Tatiana Broughton-Clarke,' she had argued. 'I'll pin her down to a shoot and if you hold the rights you can put as many of her designs in your portfolio as you like. You won't squeeze the rights to any of Lubin's pictures out of him. You know that.'

'See the contract out,' Fellows had said, irritated now. 'It's not very long. I'm sure you'll fend off his unwanted attentions.

You're not a little girl.' And with that he had picked up his phone to dial a call.

Kate was still simmering with discontent when Barnard finally arrived.

He got himself a coffee and slipped into the seat opposite her. 'You don't look too happy,' he said. 'What's up?'

'I tried to persuade the boss to let me bail out of Lubin's studio,' she said.

'Good idea,' Barnard agreed. 'Seems to me he's running a knocking shop with under-age girls. I'll be paying him close attention over the next few weeks. But it's always the same with these cases: the girls say they were willing, and even if they claim to have been forced it's hard to get a conviction. The juries don't believe them.'

'You're joking,' Kate said.

'It's generally one person's word against another's in sex cases,' Barnard said. 'Pimps and rapists generally walk free.'

Kate stared at him in horror for a moment and then sighed. 'Anyway, Ken doesn't want me to leave,' Kate said. 'He seemed to think the fact that Andrei and Ricky both seem to want to get me into bed was funny. I don't see the joke.'

Barnard smiled. 'Come on, I can see why they'd want to do that,' he said. 'But I'm sure you can look after yourself. You don't seem to have much difficulty fending me off.'

Kate smiled slightly, thinking how very different Harry Barnard was, though there was no way she was going to tell him that.

'Here, this should cheer you up,' he said, fishing in his inside pocket and handing her a sealed envelope. 'That should sort your little friend out, though remember, I know nothing about it. See if you can't persuade her to go home to mum.'

Kate took the envelope and nodded. 'Don't you think I've tried?' she said. 'I'll try again, of course I will. It goes against everything I was always taught . . .'

'Quite apart from being against the law,' Barnard said quietly.

'I know, I know. But I'm frightened of what she'll do if she doesn't sort it out.' Barnard's lips tightened.

'It can be dangerous,' he said.

'Yes, I know,' Kate whispered. 'I know.'

'I have to go,' he said. 'I have to be up in Hampstead in half an hour. Take care, Kate, sweetie. I mean it.'

'I will,' she said. 'Promise.'

Barnard eased his car through the narrow gap leading from Hampstead Heath between the pub and the toll house on the other side of the road in the teeth of a large red bus, and then swung the red Capri left into the car park of the Spaniards. It was just on six and there were only a couple of cars there but he knew that the racing-green Jag belonged to Fred Bettany. He parked next to it and made his way into the wood panelled and almost empty interior. The place was popular with walkers on the heath, especially with families who frequented its famous garden, and was still preening itself after fighting off an attempt to demolish the toll house and widen the road outside. But at this time on a working day it was a good choice for a quiet inconspicuous drink, he thought, with just the smallest tremor of anxiety about why Bettany had summoned him to this totally unexpected *tête-à-tête*.

Running a quick eye round the various nooks and crannies, he found Fred sitting at a tiny table almost invisible from the door with a glass of Scotch in front of him that looked untouched.

'Ah, there you are,' he said, sounding irritated, as if Barnard was late. 'Do you want the same?'

'I'll get it,' Barnard said, but he accepted the pound note that Bettany handed him, bought his drink, and sat down opposite him, dropping the change into his outstretched hand. 'All right?' he asked, before taking a sip.

Bettany nodded but without any great enthusiasm. 'I wanted to talk to you about Ray,' he said eventually. 'I'm worried about him.'

'Why, is he ill?'

'In the head, maybe,' Bettany said lugubriously.

'He seemed a bit down last time I saw him,' Barnard said. 'I was asking him if he knew anything about this girl found dead behind the Jazz Cellar and he went into a long moan about how everything was going wrong for him. Seemed to blame it all on Georgie.'

'I think people are turning his invitations down because they're drawing their horns in after all the scandals, Profumo, Keeler, Ward, all that. Suddenly it doesn't seem quite so smart being seen in the *Evening Standard* diary all dolled up and consorting with criminals. What about your lot? What's the Yard doing about Soho? They can't have been very pleased about Ted Verity.'

'You know they've appointed a God-bothering Scot as my DCI in Vice, and he's beginning to dig himself in,' Barnard said. 'Uptight doesn't begin to describe it. There's a few in Vice thinking of looking for a transfer before the proverbial hits the fan. I don't think it's going to be such a comfortable berth in future. He seems to think he can clean up Soho. As if!'

'And you? Will that affect you?' Bettany asked.

'Nah,' he said. 'I reckon I can outlast anyone Bonny Scotland sends down here. It'll take him at least five years to find his way around the manor, ten to suss out who really controls his patch.' Barnard grinned and drained his glass. 'Another?' he asked but Bettany shook his head and did not smile.

'Ray told me he wanted to do something big,' he said. 'Something to put himself back on the map, as he put it. But what the hell does he mean by big? I think he's going a bit doolally, to be honest. I've never known him in a state like this before.'

'He was really peeved about the Notting Hill disaster, wasn't he?' Barnard mused. 'I told him at the time they'd gang up on him. He'd not be able to get a toe in the water without a major war and he didn't have the clout or the contacts down there to win one of those. And he did say to me some time back he thought someone new was muscling in on the girls and he wanted me to do something about that. But I didn't really take him seriously until we found this little girl dead. I have to say the way Ray and the Maltese carve things up between them makes for a quiet life as far as we're concerned. If someone is trying to disturb that set-up we're in uncharted waters, especially with a new DCI wanting to make a name for himself.'

'And a nice little earner for you lot, too,' Bettany said without rancour. 'What's your take on the tarts? Is there someone new trying to get a toe in?'

Barnard thought carefully before replying. 'This girl we've found dead is an unknown as far as I can discover. She's only been around a short time – in fact she's only been up west a short time – and none of the regular girls seems to know how she got on to the game. If someone new was running her I haven't tracked him down yet. But I will, don't worry about that. She was only a kid. She couldn't have been on the street on her own. Someone put her there. And she didn't deserve to end up like that, dumped like a sack of garbage by the dustbins. Beaten up, stabbed, you name it.'

'Ray doesn't want to run girls,' Bettany said. 'He's never liked that. Says his mother doesn't approve. He's perfectly happy running protection and a bit of gambling. He's not a greedy man. At least he wasn't until he started rambling on about the train robbers and retiring to the sun in Spain when his mother dies. Fat chance. I've never known him take his shirt off even if it hits ninety.' He laughed, a thin, dry sound like rustling paper. But Barnard, who had known Ray and Georgie Robertson's mother since they were all boys together in the East End, never laughed when he heard Ma Robertson's name mentioned, even in passing. She was the glue that stuck her formidable family together and he guessed she was currently extremely busy working on the defence of her younger son. She might possibly have taken her gimlet eye off Ray, though he was sure it would only be temporary.

'Anyway, humiliation out in Notting Hill with his attempted takeover and now in Soho with his social climbing, it's all getting a bit much for Ray,' Bettany said heavily. 'I reckon that's what's provoked him into thinking he can turn himself into another Ronnie Biggs.'

'He's never been any sort of a robber,' Barnard said angrily. 'He's got no experience. I doubt he's even picked a pocket. And he seems to forget that Reynolds and Biggs and the rest got caught. They're going to get twenty years for that little lark even if they did get away with a lot of the cash.'

'I tell you, Harry, he's gone a bit bananas and I don't know what to do about it. This needs someone who's known him even longer than I have. It needs someone like you.'

Barnard shrugged. 'No,' he said. 'He won't listen to me – and to be honest I've known that since way back, if you must know. When we were evacuated he liked having me as one of his gang, as he saw it. Me and Georgie – or Georgie and me, in fact. Family always came first. I made up the numbers against the local lads, and they soon learned to leave us alone, especially when Georgie threw one of his strops. Ray and me pulled him off the local kids a couple of times, or there'd have been a murder back then. But when we came home to Bethnal Green it was different, wasn't it? They were on home turf heading in one direction and I went to grammar school and headed in another. Oh, I know he plays at "East End boys all made good together" with me. But it's only when it suits him, when it fits his book. If he really wants to nick the crown jewels there'll be nothing I can say to stop him, nothing at all; he'll go ahead and steal them and then try to flog them back to the Queen.'

Bettany's lips thinned but he nodded. 'Well, keep an eye on him for me at least, will you Harry? That's the least you can do, for old times' sake. It's probably all just flimflam, Ray in a panic because he feels humiliated, no more than that. But if you hear of anyone trying to muscle in on his charity events, give me a bell. That would certainly grieve him. And if you track down anyone who might be trying to butt in on his agreement with the Maltese let me know. That would cause major problems. Have you got my home phone number?'

Taken by surprise and trying hard not to show it, Barnard shook his head and Bettany wrote a number down on a piece of paper.

'We're ex-directory but don't call me at the office,' he said. 'Any time at home. Shirl will always take a message.'

Barnard tucked the number he could recite by heart into an inside pocket and stood up, hoping Fred could not see how fast his heart was racing. 'Ta for the drink,' he said. 'I'm sure Ray will calm down. The Notting Hill business has shaken him up, that's all. It wasn't what he expected.'

Bettany nodded gloomily. 'I hope you're right,' he said.

# SEVEN

DCI Keith Jackson steepled his hands together under his chin and looked at DS Harry Barnard thoughtfully, his bright blue eyes the colour of ice.

'I want you in on this, laddie. You've already been to the place and can give uniform an idea of what to look for. Go to their briefing at six and then organize a thorough search when they've got everybody out, which should be around midnight. I want all the punters thoroughly frightened – searched at the very least, brought to the station if they're found with anything remotely illegal at all. I want the musicians brought down here and held in the cells to be questioned thoroughly in the morning.'

'That's quite an operation, guv,' Barnard said mildly.

'It'll pay off if I can get the place closed down,' Jackson said. 'I've no time for this disgusting jungle music. These places are hotbeds of drugs and vice and perversion.'

Barnard raised an eyebrow. He had not thought it would be long before perversion revealed itself as at least part of the motivation for this proposed crackdown on the Jazz Cellar. 'Much of that going on there, is there, sir?' he asked dead-pan.

'I have it on good authority that at least one of the musicians is a poofter. And then there's all this racial mixing . . .' He did not finish the sentence, obviously preferring to leave it to Barnard's imagination what horrors that might involve. 'I'm sure we'll find the American supplying marijuana,' he said. 'They're all at it: bohemians, jazz musicians, blacks.' Jackson's lips pursed in distaste and Barnard nodded, he hoped not too gloomily, knowing how easy it was for a DCI sure he would find drugs on a suspect to actually make sure he found them.

'You could make a start by discovering if this Mr Abraham is in the country legally,' Jackson went on.

'He claims to have come over with the American army during the war and stayed on,' Barnard said. 'You know how many US troops were here then. He wouldn't be the only one who decided to stay if he could get away with it. He says he's applied for citizenship.'

'It would be useful to know whether we have the option of deporting him,' Jackson said. 'There are strict controls on American musicians working here. There are always arguments about it being reported in the press. As I understand it they're not permitted to work here at all. So how is he getting away with it?'

'I'll check it out,' Barnard said without enthusiasm. 'In the meantime I've still got more questions for the studio where Jenny Maitland is supposed to have come to work. Now I know a bit more about her it's looking increasingly dubious, the whole set up.'

'Well, you'd better get cracking then, hadn't you? You've got a busy day ahead of you, laddie. With a bit of application we should have someone charged with this killing by this time tomorrow.'

Barnard did not overexert himself to get to Andrei Lubin's studio again before he had visited a few of his regular clients in the bookshops and peep-shows which were open in Soho's narrow streets even at this time of day. And if some of them were properly grateful for the blind eye he turned to their more questionable activities, who was he to object? But when he probed into the chances of any of the jazz musicians putting girls on the street in defiance of the agreements already in existence, he met only shrugs and blank looks. If there was anyone trying to break into the trade in girls and women, no one at all seemed to know who it might be and they all seemed to have a clear idea of what might happen to anyone who did. Either they did not exist or they had covered themselves up more successfully than anyone Barnard had come across in almost ten years of pounding the streets of Soho in uniform and out of it.

He finally tapped on the studio door and put his head round as it was coming up to noon. Inside it looked to him like some sort of pantomime, with a group of girls in bizarre outfits cavorting against a backdrop of gauzy fabrics drifting in the breeze of two powerful fans, and Lubin, in shirt sleeves, with wild hair, ducking and diving with a camera. Kate O'Donnell perched on a stool to one side of this panorama with a slight smile on her lips, though no one else was either looking amused or speaking, the only sound the repetitive click of the camera shutter.

Kate was the first to see Barnard and looked slightly shocked as she slid to the floor and tapped Andrei Lubin on the shoulder. He turned round with what Barnard could only describe as a snarl on his lips until he, too, saw who the visitor was and composed his face into what might pass for a welcome, smoothed down his hair and pulled on a jacket.

'I'm sorry to bother you again but I'd like another word with you and Mr Smart about Jenny Maitland,' he said, in a tone which left little room for argument, although Lubin initially drew a sharp breath to object but then apparently thought better of it.

'It'll be here or at the station,' Barnard added.

'We can't talk here,' Lubin said abruptly. 'Kate, will you finish this session off, please, and Ricky and I will go down to the pub with the officer. It'll be quiet as early as this.'

Barnard nodded his agreement. 'I'll talk to you separately,' he said. 'Mr Lubin first, if you don't mind. I'll phone Mr Smart when we've finished.'

The two men shrugged but did not argue and Lubin set off down the stairs at speed.

Barnard hesitated as he passed Kate. 'A word in your shell-like,' he said. 'Keep clear of the jazz club for a bit. It could be a bit uncomfortable there, even for the audience.'

Her eyes widened but she said nothing, realizing that Ricky Smart was watching them closely, and Barnard turned quickly and followed Lubin downstairs to where he was waiting impatiently on the pavement.

'I've not got time to waste,' he snarled when the sergeant came out of the studio's door and led the way into the cavernous and empty lounge bar of the pub on the corner, which was not yet serving in spite of its open door. Barnard flashed his warrant card again at the barman this time and he shrugged indifferently and waved them in.

'So tell me a bit more about Jenny Maitland,' Barnard said as soon as they had sat down at a corner table. 'When did you recruit her? How long did she work for you? Why did you sack her?' Barnard fired the questions like bullets until Lubin waved a hand to stop him.

'We take on lots of girls,' he said. 'She was no different from a dozen others who've worked for me over the last year. They're all dazzled with the idea of modelling but when it comes to it, very few of them are any good at it. They don't move properly or they get too fat or they lose their looks very quickly. I'll give them a try. Some studios can't be bothered. But you can't always tell at first glance just how good they will be. Sometimes they blossom, you know?'

'How do you find them in the first place?'

'Ricky has contacts in some of the schools. It's generally girls who are leaving when they're fifteen. They're not taking exams and they don't have much choice of jobs. In the East End its factories or shops mainly, until they get pregnant and have to get married, so anything that looks a bit more glamorous they'll jump at. You'll have to ask Ricky for the details. I don't have anything to do with all that.'

'And you pay them?'

'Of course, but only for the sessions they do. They won't get rich on that. But if their face fits, if one of the magazines likes them, then they can do very well in the long run. Look at Jean Shrimpton – she came from nothing to New York in no time at all.'

'But Jenny wasn't one of the ones who did very well, was she?' Barnard said.

'Not really,' Lubin said. 'She was putting on weight and didn't move very well. She was pretty enough, willing enough even, but not right for a model. It wasn't working out.'

'Do you sleep with the girls, Mr Lubin? I'm told there's a very relaxed attitude to sex in your studio, and some of these girls, like Jenny, are below the age of consent. Do you bother about their moral welfare while they're working for you?'

Lubin shrugged and didn't answer.

'Or do you expect favours in return for employing them, taking their pictures?' Barnard persisted.

'My studio is not a knocking shop, if that's what you're asking,' Lubin snapped. 'I don't know what people do in their spare time.'

'But Jenny Maitland got pregnant somewhere, about two or three months ago, according to the pathologist who examined her,' Barnard said. 'She was pregnant, and somebody must have got her that way. Exactly how long is it since she did any work at your studio?'

Lubin sighed dramatically. 'Two, three, four months maybe,' he said. 'We'll have a record in the office of the last time she worked for me. But the baby's not mine, Sergeant, I promise you that.'

'So you did sleep with her before she left?'

Lubin shrugged. 'Long before,' he muttered. 'The baby's not mine. I haven't been with her for months. You'd better ask Ricky maybe. He makes pretty free with his favours.'

'I'm sure he does,' Barnard said, recalling Kate's comments about Smart's unwanted attentions. 'So, when you drop these kids, do you suggest where they might get alternative work, do you check at all if they go back where they came from? Or do you just dump them on to the streets of Soho to sink or swim, these kids of fourteen and fifteen?'

Lubin shrugged again and did not reply.

'So how many of them end up as tarts?' Barnard asked. 'Do you point them in that direction?'

'Certainly not. I wouldn't know what they end up doing. I don't generally see them again. As far as I know they've gone back home to Hackney or Shoreditch or wherever. Ricky's the only one who knows where they all came from, he keeps the records, addresses and things like that. I expect he'll remember. There are no promises in the rag trade. I never tell them I'll magic them into Jean Shrimpton. How could I?'

'And you never saw Jenny Maitland again after she stopped working for you? You're sure of that?'

'Quite sure,' Lubin said. 'I'm a very busy man.'

'I'm sure you are, Mr Lubin,' Barnard said, snapping his notebook shut. 'That'll be all for now but I may need to talk to you again. Can you stay here while I ask Ricky Smart to come down for a chat now.'

Lubin scraped his chair back noisily and watched Barnard call the studio from the bar.

Barnard did not totally believe anything he said, but he reckoned that if anyone was funnelling girls into prostitution it was more likely to be Smart than his boss. A man who regularly trawled the East End for pretty girls for one purpose could just as easily recruit them for another.

Smart kept Barnard waiting and came into the empty pub scowling. 'I don't know why you're still pestering us,' he said, flinging himself into the chair opposite Barnard. 'It's months since this kid left the studio. I've no idea what she's been up to since then.' His eyes met Lubin's briefly before the photographer left the bar, but they did not speak.

'You've never set eyes on her since?' Barnard snapped. 'If she's been working round here I find that hard to believe.'

'I've not seen her,' Smart said flatly.

'Did you sleep with her when she was working here? Could the baby she was expecting have been yours?'

'No I bloody didn't, and no it couldn't. I'd take care not to get young girls pregnant.'

'Could it be Lubin's?'

'Yeah, maybe,' Smart admitted reluctantly. 'He puts himself about a bit. And he doesn't draw the line at kids, either.'

'Where were you last Wednesday, when you weren't at work?'

Smart furrowed his brow and made Barnard wait. 'I was out with a bird as it happens. You can check it out if you must. And she stayed the night at my place. All above board.'

'Let me tell you something, Mr Smart,' Barnard said quietly. 'I've worked in Soho for a long time, and I know everything that goes on here, the good, the bad and the indifferent. I know all the bad boys and I know what they do, even if I can't always prove it. I know who runs the girls on these streets and I know that for the last few years there've been no gang wars. Peace has broken out. The villains have rubbed along together and that's mainly because the big beggars have split the business between them. Now if someone else thinks they can muscle in on some of that trade – running a string of girls of his own, for instance – I would ask them very seriously to think again.'

'What's this to do with me?' Smart asked angrily.

'I don't know that it's anything to do with you. I'm just telling you in case the idea crosses your mind, or Andrei Lubin's for that matter. It's a warning, if you like. You seem to be very efficient at bringing pretty girls up from the East End into Soho to be models, and then equally efficient at losing track of them, or so you say. But you need to be aware that the last man who tried to set up a business that trod on Maltese territory was found floating in the Thames with all his fingers and toes and a few more intimate bits missing. And that was just a very small war. Nobody wants that, Mr Smart, least of all the brass over at the nick. So bear it in mind.'

Kate was so busy with her camera that she was not aware that Andrei Lubin had come back in and was standing behind her as she waved the girls from one pose to another, taking shots in rapid succession while the girls changed position to her instructions. In the end he reached roughly round her and took the camera out of her hand, to continue the succession of shots almost uninterrupted.

'Take a break now,' he said and Kate took her place again on the high stool in the corner, realizing that working at this sort of intensity was more demanding than she had supposed. Eventually even Lubin had had enough, turned off the fans and told the four girls he had been using that they could get changed and take a half hour break for refreshments. The girls clustered like a gaggle of exotic birds behind the flimsy screens where they changed back to their street clothes while Lubin approached Kate, winding the film in the camera to its end and removing it, with a steely gleam in his eye. He handed her the exposed film.

'Get that developed ASAP,' he snapped.

She slid off her stool, annoyed that she seemed to be expected to carry on working while everyone else got a break, but she realized Lubin had not finished.

'Ricky told me that you seemed to know that copper,' he said. 'How come?'

Kate felt cold. 'I met him months ago when my brother was in some trouble with the law,' she said truthfully. 'He's difficult to avoid if you work in Soho. He's around the place all the time. It seems to be his territory.'

'Is he your boyfriend, then?' Lubin persisted.

Kate shook her head vigorously. 'Definitely not,' she said. 'I had a meal with him once but he's not my type. He was just telling me to keep away from the Jazz Cellar. He said there's going to be trouble there. You know Jenny Maitland's body was found out at the back.'

'I don't like these coppers asking all these questions. We haven't seen that little tart here for months. We don't know anything about what she's been doing since she left. So don't you go giving the police any other impression or you can go back to Ken Fellows with a flea in your ear, and he won't get the money back he's paid me either. Understood?'

'Of course,' Kate said. 'I'll get on with the processing now, shall I?'

'Ricky and I will be in the French pub if you've got any problems,' Lubin said turning away and beckoning Smart to follow him.

Kate closed the darkroom door with a bad-tempered bang and pushed her hair out of her eyes. Outside she could hear the girls leaving but to her surprise there was almost immediately a faint tap on the door. She had not yet released the morning's film from its reel so she turned out the red light and opened the door again to find Sylvia standing there, dressed in her everyday clothes and biting her lip.

'I just thought I'd tell you,' she said. 'I'm having it done Monday morning. I'll probably be back at work in the afternoon. Can you tell Andrei I'll be late in? Don't tell him why, for God's sake.'

Kate took her by the arm and hugged her. 'Are you sure?' she whispered, suddenly feeling heartbroken, as if she herself were responsible for what was happening to this girl.

'There's no choice, is there,' Sylvia said dully. 'Don't worry, it'll be fine. I just wanted to thank you for helping me. I may not get another chance.'

Kate sighed. 'What on earth's going on here, Sylvia? Don't you have any idea what might have happened to Jenny Maitland?'

Sylvia hesitated for a moment and then grasped her arm

and pushed her back into the darkroom and closed the door. 'There is something going on,' she said. 'But I don't really know what it is. Jenny told me she had been away with Andrei, somewhere in the country, and had slept with him there. It's not unusual for him and Ricky to get the girls into bed if they can, but it's usually just a quick fling here at the studio. But this was different, she said. There were lots of posh people there, and food and wine and stuff, and she and Andrei had a proper bedroom. She said he asked her afterwards if she'd enjoyed it, and she said she had in a way. It was nice to see how people like that lived, she could get used to it, she said. And he asked her if she wanted to go again, and she said OK, she didn't mind. But it was only a couple of days later that she stopped coming in, and in the end he said he'd sacked her, so he must have changed his mind about taking her away again. You never really know where you are with Andrei, or Ricky for that matter. One minute you're in their good books – and usually in their bed – the next you're not. One minute nothing's too good for you, the next you're out the door. You want to watch out yourself. I've seen the way Andrei looks at you when he doesn't think you're looking.'

'And Ricky can't keep his hands to himself,' Kate said bitterly. 'I tried to get back to my own agency but my boss wouldn't have it. He said I've got to complete the month we agreed.'

'Watch out for yourself then, is all I can say,' Sylvia said.

'And what happens if you're pregnant?' Kate asked.

'You're out, as soon as it shows, and that doesn't take long with the clothes we're modelling, does it?' Sylvia said. 'They don't want to know. That's why I've got to go ahead tomorrow. I've got no choice, have I? I need to work and I can't work in this state. I can't go back home. There's no one there gives a damn about me.' A tear slid down her cheek slowly and she wiped it away with the back of her hand.

Kate glanced at the still undeveloped film lying on the worktop beside her. 'Go and have some lunch with your friends, la,' she said. 'I've got to finish this film by the time Andrei gets back or I'd come with you.'

Sylvia gave her a wan smile and reached up and gave Kate

a kiss on the cheek, before spinning away and opening the door. 'Ta,' she said. 'You've been a help. Really you have. It'll all be all right after tomorrow.'

'I hope so,' Kate said. 'Really I do.'

# EIGHT

At eleven that evening the Jazz Cellar was buzzing, the atmosphere steamy and thick with cigarette smoke and alcohol fumes and more, the band slick with sweat as they pumped out Basin Street Blues and the punters at crowded tables moving rhythmically to the beat as they ate and drank. The noise was so intense that at first no one noticed the uniformed police officers crowding through the main entrance but when a sledge hammer smashed in the fire exit at the side of the stage, sending splinters of wood spraying on to the stage and the audience, the musicians stopped abruptly, instruments trailing into silence, and the audience cried out or gasped in panic as the decibels dropped and the entire room quickly fell silent.

A uniformed officer climbed up on to the stage holding a document in his hand and was immediately accosted by a crimson-faced Stan Weston, trumpet in hand, demanding to know what the hell was going on. By this time some members of the audience were getting up from their tables and attempting to leave the club and were being forcibly restrained by officers manning all the doors. After a couple of men had been unceremoniously handcuffed, most of the rest subsided back into their place, complaining loudly but offering no resistance.

'Ladies and gentlemen,' the officer in charge shouted across the growing murmur of outrage. 'If you will stay in your seats, we won't detain you long. But before anyone leaves we will require your names and addresses and we will want to search you. We may well need to contact you in the next few days.' There was another definite murmur of discontent at that but as people took in the strength of the police presence and the very determined way they were preventing anyone from reaching the doors, they gradually settled back at their tables again, some finishing their drinks quickly as if they might lose them.

'I have a warrant to search these premises for illegal substances,' the officer on the stage continued. 'And that includes every one of you.' Stan Weston made to object again but the officer brushed him away. Standing unobtrusively behind a very large uniformed sergeant in the main entrance, DS Harry Barnard had his sights set on Muddy Abraham, who was pacing anxiously at the back of the stage, puffing soundlessly at his saxophone. He did not look, Barnard thought, any sort of a picture of innocence.

Inspector Dave Lewis, who was in charge of the operation, jumped down from the stage and began to organize his men. One he sent to close down the bar, which led to furious complaints from some of the audience as the shutters rattled down. Four he sent up to herd the musicians into the tiny space backstage, with instructions to keep them there until he was ready to deal with them. The rest he set to searching the punters, taking names and addresses and eventually shepherding them out of the door if there was no reason to detain them. When all this was under way, he nodded to Harry Barnard.

'Do you want to have first pop at the band?' he asked. 'I shouldn't think many of the punters will be carrying drugs, though I can see a few spliffs chucked away on the floor. If there's a supplier here it's most likely to be one of the musicians. And I hear you're looking for other things as well.'

'I'd like all of the band down at the nick eventually,' Barnard said. 'And all of them searched, and all that space round the back. I'm not so bothered about marijuana but I want some evidence that there's been girls using the club as a base for prostitution. Can you get your lads to ask the punters if they've ever been offered sex here? And who did the offering. My guv'nor reckons there has to be a link with the girl they found dead at the back. A night in the cells might concentrate their minds.'

'Ask the lads in there with them to search them and all their music paraphernalia,' Lewis said. 'I can't see the place opening again soon. I hear your guv'nor wants it closed down.'

'So he says,' Barnard said. 'But he has some odd ideas, does Jackson. He seems to think Soho's full of poofters. I reckon he had a nasty experience in the bogs when he was at school. What do you reckon?'

Lewis laughed. 'If you carry on wearing ties like that, Harry, he'll have you on a charge,' he said, eyeing his latest flowery Liberty's creation suspiciously.

Barnard grinned. 'You have to keep up to date, Dave, if you pound these streets. It's a question of credibility.'

'And a hand in the till, maybe,' Lewis said sourly. 'I can't afford to shop in the West End.'

'I'll talk to the Dixieland crew,' Barnard said quickly. 'Can you lay on transport later?'

'I'll see what I can do.'

Kate O'Donnell was up early the next morning, early enough to attract the attention of her flatmate, Tess, who was usually leaving the house to be at school soon after eight just as the friend she had come down from Liverpool with staggered out of bed.

'What's got into you?' Tess asked, stuffing a piece of bread into the toaster. 'Do you want some?'

'I've had breakfast already,' Kate said, waving a hand airily at the open pack of butter on the table and what looked like a very aged jar of jam.

'Where did this come from?' Tess asked suspiciously, picking it up and sniffing it.

'I think the previous tenants must have left it,' Kate said. 'I found it at the back of the cupboard.'

'Eugh,' Tess said, and pushed it away. 'Anyway, where are you going so bright and early? I thought your arty studio didn't get going till midday.'

'Not quite,' Kate said. 'But I'm popping into a different studio on my way. There's this designer who wants me to take some pictures for her. She's Andrei Lubin's cousin but he won't work for her for some reason. Some family feud. She calls herself a princess, so maybe that annoys him. She's married to some lord in the shires anyway, la, for what it's worth. And she designs all this very trendy gear, straight from Paris, she says. And he hates that. Anyway, I've hooked her for Ken Fellows, I think, which should earn me some credit, if nothing else. I'm just going to suss the place out this morning, see how the space and the light is.'

'I thought you said taking pictures out of doors was all the rage now,' Tess said, stuffing a mountain of exercise books that she had spent the previous evening marking into her bag.

'According to Andrei it is. We were fiddling around in Highgate cemetery the other day. But I don't reckon it's compulsory. We'll see.' She put her camera into her handbag and pulled on a jacket and a soft suede cap.

'That's nice,' Tess said.

'Carnaby Street,' Kate said, looking at herself critically. 'We must go shopping soon. We still look as if we're just off the train from Lime Street.'

'Well, we are, la. Anyway, I can't go to school in a skirt up to my knickers. The lads would go doolally and the head would boot me out the door.'

Kate laughed as she opened the door. 'Your little girls will be chopping the hems off their gymslips before long, you'll see, and what will your headmaster do then, poor thing,' she said, and left the flat before Tess could reply.

The tube was packed and Kate had to push her way out at Oxford Circus, a stop before she normally made her exit from a later, less crowded train. At ground level she crossed the road and turned the corner beyond Peter Robinson's fashion store and made her way into the narrow streets behind the major shops where most of the small businesses seemed to deal in the multitude of fancy goods which the rag trade required: buttons and buckles, sequins and braids, ribbons and linings and threads in a multitude of colours and sizes.

Tatiana had given her precise instructions and it did not take long to find the door with a plate advertising Broughton-Clarke Design and a prominent bell alongside. She pushed and waited and it was not long before Tatiana herself opened the door, looking faintly surprised.

'You really did mean it when you said you'd come early,' she said. 'Come in. I'm all on my own just now. My assistant's gone out to get us some breakfast.' She led the way up a narrow flight of wooden stairs and into a room crammed with mannequins in various stages of dress and undress but all

wearing clothes in a unique blend of plain colours and
geometric patterns, which Kate found quite dazzling.

'Wow,' she said. 'These are quite something.'

Tatiana smiled complacently. 'I told you,' she said. 'My
cousin Andrei hates them but I tell him: this is the future. You
only have to look at some of the French designers like
Courrèges to see what is going to happen. No one is going to
be wearing a twinset and pearls any more.'

'So you want to be in at the start of this revolution in
London?' Kate said. 'Well, I can take some pictures for you
but there's not much room to do it here.'

'There's another room at the back,' Tatiana said. 'That's
where we do the cutting, through here . . .' She led the way
again into a room dominated by a large cutting table, swatches
of fabrics and piles of half-finished garments.

Kate looked around again and sighed. 'It's very dark in here
and very cluttered,' she said. 'I think we'd be better out of
doors, though that's more tricky to arrange. You're dependent
on the weather for a start. But it's not impossible. The clothes
you've got in there would look very startling against certain
backdrops. Andrei's not wrong. It can work very well, a shoot
outdoors.'

'Let's do that then,' Tatiana said. 'I'll get some finishing
done and contact you when I think I'm ready to launch myself
on to the world.'

'You'd better leave messages for me at my agency. I don't
think Andrei will appreciate you ringing me at the studio. But
I'm only with him for another two weeks so it shouldn't
interfere with our plans.'

'Has he got you into bed yet, darlink?' Tatiana asked with
a smirk. 'He doesn't usually hang about.'

Kate frowned. 'I find Ricky Smart more of a pain in the
bum,' she said. 'But so far I've managed to fend them off. My
boss wants me to stay the course, but I may need a pair of
steel knickers.'

But before she could squeeze herself across the room to the
door, it was flung open by a tall man in an almost orange
three-piece tweed suit, a country check shirt, stringy woollen
tie and green trilby.

'Ah,' Tatiana said, with an edge of weariness to her voice. 'This is my husband, Roddy. He had to come into town this morning so he drove me in early, before the rush. This is Kate O'Donnell who's going to do some photographs for me, darlink. Some fashion shots for the magazines, I hope. I even wondered if we could do some fashion shots down there, at home. Taking the models out of doors seems to be the in thing just now.'

Kate flinched slightly under the sharp gaze of pale blue eyes in a flushed and ruddy face.

'Jolly good show,' Roddy Broughton-Clarke said. 'Photographer, are you? Unusual for a girl, eh? But that might be jolly useful all round.'

'I already thought of asking Kate to take some pictures at our next party,' Tatiana said quickly. 'I know you don't want to have Andrei take them again.'

'Rather not, even if he is family,' Roddy said. 'Rather fell out with him last time, you know. Seemed more interested in joining in the fun than doing his job.'

Kate raised an eyebrow at that, but Roddy, it seemed, once started was difficult to stop. He fixed his watery gaze on his wife.

'Good idea to invite her down to have a recce, don't you know? A bit much to simply drop her in the deep end when the old place is full of guests.' He turned to Kate. 'Come down tomorrow, why don't you. You don't work on Saturday, do you? Can you get yourself to Amersham on the jolly old Metropolitan line? We'll meet you at the station?'

Taken aback slightly, Kate nodded and Roddy turned back to his wife.

'Just dropped in to say I'm heading back now, dear. Got what I wanted in Jermyn Street. I'll pick you up at the station later.' And with a waft of chilly air from outside, he was gone.

'It's not a bad idea,' Tatiana said thoughtfully. 'His parties are nothing to do with me, but he does like to have a photographer there and if you want to do that it would be best to know your way around. You might enjoy it anyway. Not everyone lives in a crumbling Jacobean stately home. That's why people come, of course. Roddy's very determined to make it work. And when Roddy wants something, he usually gets it. He was in the commandos during the war, you know. He's a whole lot tougher than he looks. So will you come?'

'I suppose so,' Kate said, feeling pressured.

'It is very photogenic, darlink. You might find it useful for my designs too. Andrei would be spitting blood if we did that but I think he's blown it with Roddy. Won't have him at the Hall any more.'

Kate looked at her, wondering how she had got herself into this situation so quickly. 'He didn't talk about how much he's going to pay me,' she said. 'And I'll have to do the developing and printing either in Andrei's darkroom or at my own agency. That will all have to be arranged.'

'Andrei will let you do it,' Tatiana said with more confidence in her cousin than Kate thought was justified. 'He'd give his right arm to get into Roddy's good books again. Come down and have a look, anyway. Here's the phone number. Call us when you get to Amersham station and I'll come and fetch you. It's only about ten minutes away. And you can stay for lunch, and you can sort out all the details about the next party with Roddy. That would be good.'

Kate nodded, wondering how she had been railroaded into something that she was not at all sure she wanted to do. Roddy Broughton-Clarke had not inspired her with much confidence as a possible employer. She would go to the house because it intrigued her, but she would not necessarily take up his commission unless the rewards were very good indeed.

'I'll see you tomorrow then,' she said to Tatiana. 'And maybe you'll know by then how close you are to doing a shoot. In the meantime I'll suss out some other likely locations. Bye for now.'

DS Harry Barnard was at work early that morning, too. He hung up his jacket carefully in an almost empty CID room, picked up a strong coffee from the canteen and made his way to the custody area, whistling loudly.

'The jazz musicians?' he asked the sergeant. 'Still all here, are they?'

'Oh yes,' the sergeant said. 'Complaining loudly, especially

Stan Weston, and the black bastard. But as they found the
darkie with a stash of marijuana he's not likely to be going
anywhere soon.'

'I want to talk to both of them,' Barnard said.

'Feel free,' the sergeant said, handing Barnard two sets of
keys. 'Number five and number ten.'

Barnard peered into each cell in turn and decided to tackle
Weston first. He found him sitting morosely on his bunk gazing
at the odorous lavatory behind the door. He recognized Barnard
and stood up.

'Have you come to let me out of here?' he demanded. 'This
is a complete farce. My club's been running for nearly twenty
years, since the war ended, and we've never had trouble with
you lot. Never. We don't let tarts in, not that many of my
customers are interested. They don't come to Soho for the sex,
they come for the music. We're well known for it, we get the
top artists, Americans go to a lot of trouble to get permits to
play the Jazz Cellar. We're class.'

'I'm sure all that's true, Mr Weston, but the fact remains
that a tart was found dead in your back yard and marijuana
– pot – was found on the premises. At the very least you'd
expect us to ask some questions. But DCI Jackson will want
to talk to you about all that. I want to ask you about your sax
man, Muddy Abraham. How long has he been with you?'

Weston sat down again on the hard bunk with an anxious
look. 'What's happened to Muddy? I heard some shouting last
night, it sounded like him. Is he OK?'

'As far as I know,' Barnard said. 'I'll be seeing him next.
But first I want a bit more background about him. He's
American, obviously, told me he came here during the war,
with the US forces. So how come he's still here? Is he naturalized? Or does he have a work permit? Has he been with you
since you opened?'

'Whoa, whoa,' Weston said. 'Why don't you ask Muddy
himself? It's not my job to tell tales on members of the band.'

'It's your job to tell the police what they want to know in
a murder investigation, Mr Weston. So let's hear everything
you know about your groovy saxophone player, because I
reckon there's more to Mr Abraham than he lets on.'

'He's a nice guy,' Weston said. 'He came over as a GI, fought in Normandy, one of the black regiments – came back here and was supposed to go home but decided he'd be treated better here than in the States. So he went absent and got away with it, married an English girl – that didn't last, apparently – and took up his saxophone again. He's good. I heard him in a club in Manchester in 1950, '51 maybe, and asked him to join the band. That's about it, all I know anyway. He turns up on time, plays like a dream, goes home, never talks about his private life.'

'But he smokes pot?'

'A lot of people around the scene smoke pot, Sergeant. You know that as well as I do. And you know as well as I do that there's no harm in it.'

'So you turn a blind eye?'

Weston shrugged and refused to meet Barnard's eye. 'So do you,' he said. 'I told you. We've never been raided. You've left us alone.'

'Who brings it in?' Barnard persisted. 'Is it Abraham?'

Weston shrugged again. 'He doesn't tell and I don't ask.'

'Well, I reckon the magistrates will take a pretty dim view of that, Mr Weston. And what about Jenny Maitland and girls like her? She's not part of the existing set-up in Soho. So who is bringing her into the area, into the club even? If you're running a club which you claim is squeaky clean, in the heart of Soho, you must know exactly what's going on in your neighbourhood. You must know who's using the tarts, and who's running them on your doorstep, wouldn't you say? It's self-protection, I'd say.'

'Why would I need protection? You must know how that works round here. I pay for it, in fact I pay for it twice, once to Ray Robertson's enforcers and once to the cops. The only good thing about it is that I get no trouble. Until last night, that is. So what went wrong there, Sergeant? Why didn't my protection money work out?'

'Because we've got a new DCI who isn't as readily bought as some. And because this is murder,' Barnard snapped. 'And when it gets that bad, there's nothing can protect you. Sorry. So think, please. Was this girl Jenny ever in your club? Did anyone use her services, or sell her services? Was it one of

your musicians, or even a regular punter? How did she come
to end up in your back yard?'

'I told you last night,' Weston said angrily. 'She's not been
in the club to my knowledge. We don't get tarts bothering us,
not as far as I know. They stay on the street where they belong.
But that's not to say it couldn't have happened, is it? I just
don't know.'

Barnard gave up and left Weston sitting on his bunk again
looking glum and moved on to Muddy Abraham's cell where
the inmate appeared to be asleep on his bunk, his face turned
to the wall. He did not stir when Barnard went in and closed
the door behind him and he crossed the small tiled cell and
shook him by the shoulder. The prisoner turned over very
slowly with a groan and Barnard drew a sharp breath. The
man's face was puffy and bloodstained and he pushed himself
up on to one elbow gingerly.

'What happened?' Barnard asked.

Abraham attempted a shrug and then thought better of it.
'The usual,' the injured man whispered. 'They asked me some
questions and when I didn't give them the answers they wanted
they asked again – harder.'

'About the girl?'

'The girl I'm supposed to have killed,' Abraham said.
'Except I didn't. And there's no way I'm going to confess to
something I didn't do. Especially that – me bein' black and
her bein' white. In my country that gets you strung up from
a tree without the bother of a trial. I'm not sure about here,
but I sure as hell ain't testin' it out.'

'Have they charged you with anything?'

'Possession of marijuana,' Abraham said. 'And that ain't right.
I'm not fool enough to have pot on me in the club, especially
not that amount. But your boss man – what's his name? Jackson?
He more or less said he wanted me deported back to the States.
One way or another he wants me out so I guess he'll push it as
far as it takes. What's he got against me, man? What did I do
to him? But lookin' at him he's a man who usually gets what
he wants. I've come across men like that before in the army.'

'Have you seen a brief?' Barnard asked.

'A brief?' Abraham looked blank.

'A lawyer.'

'Nope,' Abraham said. 'No one like that. I ain't got no money to pay attorneys anyway.'

'You need one,' Barnard said. 'You should have had a solicitor with you when you were questioned. I'll find out what's going on.'

The door behind them opened and the custody sergeant put his head in. 'He's due in court at ten,' he said to Barnard. 'I need you out of here now.'

'Fine,' Barnard said. 'Can you make sure he has legal aid?'

'Your guv'nor gave the orders last night,' he said. 'That wasn't one of his priorities.'

'The magistrates will ask questions,' Barnard said angrily as he pushed his way out of the cell. 'Look at the state of him. I should clean him up before you send him over there if I were you.'

'The bruises don't show on his skin,' the sergeant muttered contemptuously as he passed. 'I shouldn't think they'll even notice.'

Barnard went back up the stairs two at a time to the CID room where the desks were gradually filling up, hung up his jacket carefully and dropped into his chair. But before he could even open the Jenny Maitland murder file on his desk a colleague put a heavy hand on his shoulder.

'The guv'nor was looking for you, mate,' he said. 'You'd better get up there toot sweet.'

'Did he say what he wanted?' he asked.

'Nope, but he didn't look a very happy bunny.'

Barnard pushed his chair back, picked up his file, put his jacket back on and made his way upstairs and down the corridor to DCI Keith Jackson's office and tapped on the door before putting his head round cautiously.

Jackson was sitting at his immaculate desk looking thunderous. 'Where the hell did you get that tie, laddie?' he asked, looking Barnard up and down censoriously. 'You're looking more and more like a poofter every day.'

'Strictly a lady's man, me, guv,' Barnard said. 'Don't worry about that.'

'I hope so,' Jackson growled. He picked up a slip of paper on his desk and handed it to Barnard. 'See this man at the American Embassy,' he said. 'He's got access to records of US citizens who have served here in their armed forces, right back to when they came into the war in 1941. He should be able to track this black bastard down. I've got someone at the Home Office looking for naturalization papers for him as well. With a bit of luck we'll be able to get him out of the country even if we can't pin the Jenny Maitland killing on him.'

'I've not got anything to link the girl to anyone inside the club yet, guv,' Barnard said mildly, glancing at the name the DCI had given him. 'Does this bloke know who we're interested in?'

'Not yet,' Jackson said. 'But apparently there are lists of soldiers who didn't go home when they should have done and it's easy enough to track down the coloured ones because they were in separate groupings. They mostly kept to their colour bar.'

'So I heard,' Barnard said neutrally, not wanting Jackson to know he had gleaned that information from Muddy Abraham himself. He could not recall ever seeing an American serviceman as a boy during the war, let alone a black one.

'Get on with it then,' Jackson said. 'We'll oppose bail at the magistrate's hearing this morning for further inquiries but we can't get away with that for long just on a marijuana charge. We need a confession or evidence for the murder charge and we've got neither so far. He's an obstinate bastard. So chop, chop, laddie. Chop, chop.'

# NINE

Kate O'Donnell clung uncertainly to her seat in the front of Roddy Broughton-Clarke's muddy and dilapidated station wagon in which he had met her, as promised, at Amersham station at the end of the Metropolitan Line. She had been somewhat surprised to discover that in this direction the familiar London tube train headed out above ground into green and wooded countryside far beyond even the suburbs of the city. Roddy, in wellington boots and a waterproof jacket, had met her at the station exit and ushered her into the car where two large, bedraggled and rather smelly dogs occupied the rear, both of them panting heavily in the confined space.

Roddy took off at speed out of the town and into winding country lanes at a rate which Kate reckoned could only lead to disaster if they met anything coming the other way. But the journey concluded quite quickly and without incident as he braked suddenly and swung through open gates, down a winding drive and on to a forecourt flanked by high yew hedges with, immediately ahead of them, the entrance to a four-square stone house with tall windows and a tiled roof and ornate chimney stacks, one of them supported rather precariously by some sort of scaffolding.

'The family pile, Broughton Hall,' Roddy said, getting out of the car and releasing the excited dogs from their temporary captivity. 'Eighteenth-century facade slapped on the front but parts of it unreconstructed fifteenth century behind. Bally nightmare to maintain. The Broughtons never had enough cash to keep it in good nick back as far as one can see. Married into the Clarkes in the hope of doing better but even that didn't work in the long run. Driven to sell off most of the land in the end after the First World War – agricultural depression, you know – leaving my father, and then me, with a whole heap of problems. Still, maybe Tatiana will become dress

designer to the Queen. Stranger things have happened. So
come on in. Come on Robbie, Bruno! Heel!'

The two retrievers fell in behind their master and Kate
followed behind as Roddy opened the front door and led the
way into a chilly stone-flagged hall filled with huge pieces
of dark furniture and with a wide staircase leading into the
dim upper regions of the house. The place felt as if it was
permanently cold and looked dusty and uncared for, although
Kate was sure that the old furniture was genuine and probably
worth serious money. She had never been anywhere like it
before.

'Tat, we're here,' Roddy bellowed and Tatiana appeared like
a genie at the top of the stairs.

'Kate, welcome to the Hall,' she said as she made her way
down. 'His lordship will give you the grand tour while I finish
off the lunch. I don't have any help at the weekends so it's
something fairly simple. Is that OK?'

'Of course,' Kate said.

Roddy's dogs followed Tatiana towards the back of the house
while Kate found herself being steered through the nearest of
the doors off the hall into a huge room furnished not as any
sort of sitting room but with chairs and small tables around
the walls and a small polished area of wooden floor where
people could presumably dance. It was not cheaply furnished
but it was not at all what she had expected of what must once
have been an elegant salon for the resident family.

'When we party, we hold the drinks reception in here to
get them going, then a buffet a bit later when everyone's nicely
warmed up. Later on they can dance in here, if that's what
they fancy.'

'You charge, of course,' Kate said.

'Oh yes, and with a bit of luck I make a profit. People like
to visit old places like this. If they can come and have a bit
of a do laid on they like it even more. And of course, it's very
private. We're not even near a village. If people want to come
with other people they are not quite attached to, if you know
what I mean, they are at liberty to do that. Or maybe meet
people here. We get some single people too. It's all very free
and easy. And very discreet.' He led her through several more

reception rooms pointing out where the meal was served and where people could play cards.

'So people want pictures taken even if they're not with their wives or husbands?' Kate asked.

'They do, they do,' Roddy assured her, leading the way upstairs. 'You don't have any moral objections, do you?'

'Not really,' Kate said uncertainly, wondering what difference it would make if she did. If she was here to snap the visitors she could hardly ask to see their marriage lines in advance, she thought.

Roddy hurried her on. 'But as I said to Andrei, once you've printed them off I do insist on having the negatives back here. Just in case of any embarrassment. I make sure the prints only go to the people concerned.' He flung open a few doors upstairs, revealing comfortably furnished bedrooms. 'Bedrooms are available for a small consideration.' He grinned at her wolfishly. 'You won't be required up here, except by special request.'

From below they heard Tatiana calling them for lunch.

'Come and eat,' Roddy said putting an unwanted arm round Kate's waist and steering her back to the stairs. 'You can talk to her about her fashion shoot. This place might make a good backdrop for that too, don't you think? Do you think she can make some money out of this designing business? Honestly now.'

Kate pulled away from her host and shrugged. 'Her designs are very bold,' she said. 'I'm not sure they'd go down well with the old guard. I don't think I'm qualified to judge whether or not they'll sell to the general public. Fashion's changing so quickly at the moment.'

Roddy grunted.

'Well, we need something to sell,' he said. 'Or this old place will have to go on the market. Which after six hundred years in the family would be a ruddy shame.'

There was, Kate thought, a note of real desperation in his voice.

The following Monday morning, Kate O'Donnell stood on Waterloo Bridge, leaning over the parapet, with the River Thames ebbing swiftly eastwards beneath the arches, and the sun glittering on the panorama to either side. On the north bank, Westminster and its Parliamentary towers stood stiffly alongside the fast running water, its familiar gothic outline very definitely not what she was looking for. While to the south, on both sides of the bridge, a more promising prospect unfolded, not pretty, in fact in some ways deliberately stark, but far more in tune, she thought, with Tatiana's geometric clothes. Better in many ways, she thought, than the old manor house in the Chilterns.

The Royal Festival Hall she had never seen before, though she vaguely remembered that it was all that had survived of the Festival of Britain, of which she had seen pictures when she was at school. She liked its strangely curved roof with the small colourful shield on the left, and the sharp horizontal rows of windows facing the river. The whole modernist structure was oddly complemented by what looked like a much older circular tower or chimney, with small windows running up the side, almost like a decapitated lighthouse plonked down far from the sea.

Across the river itself ran the metal lacework of the Hungerford Bridge across which green trains trundled at regular intervals, and to the east there were tantalizing glimpses of more chimneys and towers, an almost industrial landscape in sharp contrast to Westminster and the dome of St Paul's on the opposite bank of the river. She felt a shiver of excitement. There was grist to her mill over there, she thought. She could do interesting things with Tatiana's clothes against that backdrop. She dropped down from the bridge and took a brief excursion along the embankment and her pulse quickened. This would work, she was sure. This was undoubtedly the place to set her shoot. She pulled out her camera and spent twenty minutes snapping the area from every angle before glancing at her watch.

She did not have much time to get back to Lubin's studio in time for the afternoon session he had planned. She worked her way through the walkways and tunnels that surrounded the Festival Hall and took the underground from Waterloo station back to Oxford Circus and walked slowly down into the narrow streets of Soho, which were relatively quiet as the lunch hour came to an end. She was anxious about Sylvia, who was having her operation today, although she had no idea where. And she wondered if she could persuade Tatiana that she was experienced enough to launch herself on to the fashion sea where the current captains were like cruising destroyers circling anxiously and looking for the chance to blow each other out of the water. Did she stand a chance in that company, she wondered?

The studio was bustling when she arrived and Andrei Lubin soon had her fully occupied organizing the girls and making sure their clothes were just so. She was surprised when half way through the afternoon Sylvia sidled through the door. Andrei glanced in her direction briefly.

'I wasn't well this morning,' she said in little more than a whisper.

'You look like death warmed up,' Lubin said with no trace of sympathy. 'I should get home to bed. You're no good to me looking like that.'

The girl's eyes filled with tears but she turned back to the door and Kate, who had been making coffee, followed her. On the narrow landing outside she put an arm round Sylvia's shoulders. 'How did it go?' she asked.

'OK, I suppose,' Sylvia said. 'She gave me some aspirins for the pain and told me to go home to bed.'

'Then I should do that if I were you,' Kate whispered. 'Don't come in to work until you feel better. If you feel too bad, get yourself to the hospital. These things sometimes go wrong you know.'

'I can't do that,' the girl said miserably. 'It's illegal, what I've done. They'll arrest me.'

'I'm sure they won't if you need help,' Kate said. 'Anyway, go home and go to bed for now. Can you get there by yourself?'

'I expect so. It's not far.' Sylvia said.

Kate looked in her purse and gave her a ten bob note. 'Take a cab,' she said.

Sylvia nodded and turned away and Kate watched her make her way awkwardly up the street towards Shaftesbury Avenue. There would be plenty of cabs there, she thought, and walked slowly back to Andrei Lubin's shoot upstairs. The way these girls were exploited and thrown away like used rags infuriated her but she could not see how she could do anything about it while she was working for him herself. If the commission for Tatiana went well she would tackle Ken Fellows again and try to extricate herself from the current arrangement. But she knew he would not do anything unless she had proved that she could produce fashion pictures on her own that were acceptable to the magazines. Until then she was trapped and she hated it.

She ploughed through the afternoon and once the shoot was finished she developed the shots she had taken on the south bank of the Thames and walked back along Oxford Street to Tatiana's fashion studio. She found Broughton-Clarke in the cutting room, working on a mannequin and lengths of white and black fabric, her mouth full of pins. Tatiana nodded in Kate's direction and held up three fingers, which Kate took to mean that she would be free to talk in three minutes or so. She took her pictures out of her bag and spread them out on the large wooden table and eventually Tatiana joined her, pin-free, and cast her sharp eye over Kate's exhibits.

'The south bank?' she said, slightly doubtfully.

'It's perfect,' Kate said. 'All sorts of ultra-modern buildings in amongst older stuff. Look at this tower thingy. What's that, for goodness' sake? It looks like a lighthouse. Your designs will fit the area like a glove. If you're not sure we could go down there with a single model and take some shots. Set the whole thing up on a small scale and see what it looks like. We don't have to go the whole hog first time out. Take it a step at a time.'

'Mmm,' Tatiana said. 'I've got a couple of dresses we could try out.' She picked up a couple of sketches showing two short shift dresses in geometric shapes of black and white. 'What do you think?' she asked.

Kate shrugged. She did not really know what to make of these new fashions and Tatiana laughed at her non-committal expression.

'You'll be wearing them yourself in six months' time, you'll see. Fashion never stands still and I think it's on the verge of a revolution. I need to be at the front. In the meantime you just take the pictures, dear. That'll be your contribution.'

Kate nodded. 'I'll run these prints past Ken Fellows tomorrow. Show them to him with some of the stuff *Vogue* is using. See what he thinks as well.'

Tatiana shrugged. 'OK,' she said. 'We'll give it a whirl. Midweek some time, maybe?'

'Perfect,' Kate said, well satisfied. 'As soon as you like.' There was a way, she thought, that she could escape from Andrei Lubin's studio, even if it did mean tying herself to his cousin. At least Tatiana wanted her for her skills not her body.

DS Harry Barnard strolled the short distance from the nick through Mayfair, enjoying the weak sunshine and the classy shops that he longed to patronize, across Grosvenor Square to the still stark new American Embassy on the west side of the gardens. He was admitted without much ceremony to the office of a uniformed army officer who got up from his desk when he was shown in and held out a beefy hand.

'Lieutenant Tony Saprelli,' he said cheerfully. 'Glad to meet you.' Taking his hand back, feeling as if it had been put through a mincer, Barnard took the seat he was waved into.

'Good of you to help,' he said.

'From what your boss told us it looks as if we might be helping ourselves,' Saprelli said with undiminished enthusiasm. 'We didn't lose many soldiers on the way home. We made it pretty attractive for them to go back, college places, all that razzmatazz. But there were a few strays, and some of them we have unfinished business with. So tell me what you've got. I've already had a look at our lists and sorted out the coloured guys who went AWOL.'

'Our man is calling himself Muddy Abraham, plays the saxophone in a jazz band, apparently spent some time in Liverpool before coming to London. There's a long-standing black settlement in Liverpool, former seamen mainly, so he could blend in without too much trouble up there in the forties and fifties. He doesn't seem to have got himself naturalized here, not under that name any way, so he's likely still a US citizen.'

'Probably some fancy woman at the bottom of it,' Saprelli said. 'Let's have a look at my list, see if we can pin him down.' He flicked through the papers he had in front of him and underlined a couple of names. 'No one with Abraham as a surname, but two with Abraham as a given name, Abraham Lincoln Stevenson and Abraham Moses Davis. You got a picture of this guy you're holding?'

Barnard took a copy of the mugshot that had been taken when Abraham was arrested and handed it to Saprelli. 'That's him,' he said. 'He's a big man, over six feet and broad with it, a heavyweight, not a man I'd like to tangle with, though our dealings with him have been pretty amiable so far.' He thought it best to glide over the beating the musician had suffered when he was questioned.

'Let's have a look at their files,' Saprelli said. He got up and rifled through a filing cabinet behind him and grunted as he located two dossiers. He flicked both of them open in turn and studied them for a moment, and grunted again. 'This looks like your man,' he said, coming round to Barnard's side of the desk with one file and the police mugshot in his hand. 'A lot younger in our shot of course, but I reckon Abraham Moses Davis is your Muddy Abraham, don't you?'

Barnard nodded cautiously. The soldier in the file was much younger, of course, thinner faced, but the likeness was unmistakable.

'He's the right sort of height too,' Saprelli said. 'Six foot two, in fact. And here – there's a note he played saxophone. There was a lot of music going on in those black units when they got the time. But this one? I guess we'd very much like to see him again when you've finished with him.'

'He has a record?'

'Oh yes. He went AWOL for a very good reason, if you look at it from his point of view. He came back with his unit to this country, prior to being shipped home, hooked up with a white girl, in a village near where the unit was stationed, was warned off – we don't put up with that – and got into a fight with a white sergeant, refused to obey an order, hit the sergeant hard and ran. The sergeant hit his head as he went down and died in hospital the next day. Davis may not even know that, but the US Army wants him on a charge of murder. Believe me, we don't look kindly on negro soldiers knocking off their superiors. I don't suppose you do either.'

Barnard whistled. 'He's not going to want to hear that after all this time,' he said. 'Isn't there some time limit on these things?'

'Not if I can help it,' Saprelli said, his face hardening. 'I'll look into it straight away, but in the meantime I think we'd be grateful if you kept him under lock and key.'

'He's been remanded in custody by the magistrates but he's only charged with possession of marijuana. We won't be holding him long unless something more serious crops up.'

'Well, do what you can,' the American said. 'I'll see how quickly I can sort out a request for extradition.'

'Right,' Barnard said, getting to his feet. 'Thanks for your help, Lieutenant. You know where to find me if you need me, or DCI Keith Jackson. We'll wait to hear from you.'

Barnard walked slowly back to the nick, and reported back to the DCI, with a sense of foreboding. But Jackson was not in his office and his secretary said he had been called to Scotland Yard for a meeting. Barnard shrugged. It would keep until the morning when he could write a report and avoid actually witnessing Jackson's satisfaction at the outcome of his American inquiries.

Kate did not notice Ricky Smart as she walked across an ill-lit Shepherd's Bush Green on the short trip from the tube station to the flat she shared with Tess Farrell. She was deep in thought after her discussion with Tatiana as she walked up the steps to the front door, and was not aware of anyone coming up behind her quietly until an arm suddenly wound itself round her neck and a hand covered her mouth. From the beginning she had no doubt who her assailant was. She had been in close proximity to Ricky too many times to mistake the feel and the smell of him, and even though he only whispered, she still recognized his voice.

'Come on, sweetheart,' he said. 'It really is time we got together. Open the front door, why don't you then we can get cosy.'

Kate pushed back from the door, hoping that Ricky would lose his footing on the worn stone steps down to the street but he only gripped her more tightly and reached for the key that she had already pulled out of her bag.

'Come on,' he said. 'You know you're gagging for it.'

Kate glanced up at the tall Victorian house where none of the windows appeared to be lit. Tess, she recalled, had mentioned that she would be home late as there was a rehearsal for the school production of *Romeo and Juliet* for which she was assistant producer. And none of the other three flats appeared to be occupied. She was on her own and she clung on to the front door key but she was not as strong as Ricky and his hand over her mouth effectively prevented her from calling for help. In spite of her increasingly frantic struggles he got the door open quickly and pushed her inside into the silent and almost dark, cabbage-smelling communal hall, where piles of post for generations of former tenants lay in piles on a table and the payphone hung precariously off the wall. She tried not to panic but her heart thumped painfully and she could scarcely breathe.

'You can thank Andrei for this, sweetie,' he said, holding both wrists now so that she could not wriggle away. 'He asked me to follow you because he didn't believe you were really going to crazy Tatiana's place, and then when you finished there I thought I might as well find out where you lived as well. Ken Fellows wouldn't give us an address.'

'Why on earth do you want to know where I live?' Kate croaked, as he loosened the grip on her mouth enough to allow her to speak. 'What do you want?' she gasped, starved of oxygen.

'Having got so far I thought we ought to finish it off,' he said. 'Which is your flat?'

'Oh, no,' she said.

He rattled the keys he had taken off her, one for the front door and one for the flat, and even in the dim light she could tell he was smiling, a wolfish flash of teeth that terrified her. 'No one seems to be at home,' he said. 'We could just try them all. Find a nice comfy bed. Come on you little tease. I've waited long enough for this.' And he pushed her hands behind her back and her back against the wall and kissed her hungrily, pressing his body against hers and leaving no doubt what the next step was intended to be.

Suddenly he stiffened in a different way, hit her hard across the face and turned to the front door where someone was silhouetted against the street lights outside.

'Hello?'

Kate heard Tess's familiar voice, slightly uncertain as she reached a hand in and switched the light on, then gasping as Ricky pushed past her and leapt down the front steps and disappeared into the street. Kate's knees gave way and she sat down on the stairs, gasping and trying to hold back the tears of relief.

'What's going on?' Tess asked. 'What on earth is going on? Who was that?'

Hardly able to speak, Kate shook her head. 'He followed me from my work,' she said. 'He's been pestering me for days. Ever since I got there, in fact. Thank God you're early. I thought you weren't coming . . .'

'Is this the Russian you're working for?' Tess said, outrage in her voice. 'Shall I call the police? Here, let's get home and see what damage he's done. Holy Mother of God, what's going on in that place you've been going to? You've got to get out of it.'

Tess helped Kate up the stairs and out of her coat, brewed sweet tea, which Kate sipped gratefully, and applied cold water to the bruise on her cheek, while Kate told her haltingly what had happened.

'This time we need the bizzies before it gets out of control,' Tess said soberly.

Kate clutched her hand. 'They won't do anything,' she said dully. 'They don't do anything about these girls on the street who aren't even old enough to be having sex. They don't do much even if you get raped, Harry Barnard says. They don't believe you, do they? And he didn't actually get that far, thanks to you.'

'But you've got to do something,' Tess complained. 'If you don't do anything he might try again. What about your Harry? Do you want me to ring him? He fancies you rotten, you know he does. Surely he'd do something about this, if it's you. You can't ever feel safe if you just ignore it.'

'Maybe I'll tell him tomorrow,' Kate said. 'He's always around. He's got a murder on our doorstep at the moment, a girl who worked for Andrei for a while.'

'Maybe Ricky killed her. He's vicious enough,' Tess said angrily. 'You really ought to get out of that place, you know. It's not safe, is it? Not with someone like that there every day. You're really not safe.'

'Leave it till tomorrow,' Kate said, her head in turmoil. 'All I want now is a bath and some sleep.'

'If you can sleep,' Tess said. 'I'm not sure I'll be able to. I'm only glad he dropped your keys. I picked them up off the hall floor. Otherwise I don't think either of us would ever have slept here again.'

# TEN

Kate had slept fitfully and got up early the next morning still unsure what to do about her previous evening's encounter with Ricky Smart. Tess pressed her over a hurried breakfast to go straight to the police but Kate knew that would effectively put an end to her connection with Andrei Lubin and she did not want to do something so precipitate without discussing it with Ken Fellows first.

'I'll go to see Ken on my way into the studio,' she told Tess. 'I've some prints to show him anyway. I'll try again to get him to pull me out, though I know he wants me to finish the course.'

'He can't expect you to put up with being treated like that,' Tess objected. 'The man should be in jail.'

Kate shrugged, feeling dispirited. 'And I'll talk to Harry Barnard about it,' she offered by way of a compromise, though she wondered if even he would be willing to put much effort into investigating an attack that had petered out without much damage done. He would be angry, she had no doubt, but would he really think he could get a conviction after what he had told her about women and girls not being believed? And when Kate had marched into Ken Fellows' office and explained why she had come in so early and so full of righteous indignation, she found him less than sympathetic.

'There's always some smart-arse who'll try it on, girl,' he said. 'If you want to make your way in this business you'll have to learn how to handle them. Treat it as a bit of fun, why don't you? You sure you didn't give him the wrong idea, lead him on a bit?'

'This was way beyond a bit of fun,' she came back angrily. 'He tried to rape me. And no, I didn't give him any encouragement. I can't stand the man.'

'Well, it may have felt like that, but he probably didn't mean it. He probably just got a bit carried away,' Ken said as if that were a consolation. 'Men do sometimes.'

'He shouldn't have been there. He followed me home,' Kate insisted.

'I'll have a word with Lubin, tell him Smart is being a nuisance, and he should tell him to back off. But I want you to stay there until the end of the agreement. Otherwise what you've done so far will just be wasted, which would be stupid when it was all looking so promising. Come on, girl, I didn't think you were a quitter.'

Kate scowled. 'You know I'm not,' she muttered through gritted teeth. 'But this was serious.'

'There was no harm done,' Fellows said, clearly dismissing the matter. 'So, you said you'd have some prints to show me. What have you got?'

'These are the shots I took in the studio with Andrei, and this is one of the locations I thought would suit Tatiana's designs. Outdoor shoots seem to be the coming thing, modernist and brutal and seemingly the tattier the better, so as soon as she's got enough designs available I'll get the models down there and see what I can do. She's very enthusiastic. She also suggested doing some at her husband's stately home, though when they took me down there on Saturday it didn't seem that stately to me. That's a bit tatty too.'

Fellows studied the prints keenly and nodded. 'You're doing OK,' he said, which was as close to praise as Kate had ever heard him go. 'So get on with it, is my advice. You don't want an idiot like Ricky Smart to mess up your career, do you? Ignore him. And get the shoot with Tatiana organised ASAP. I think we could have a good thing going there.'

Less than happy, Kate collected up her prints and made her way the short distance to Andrei Lubin's studio, which was almost deserted when she walked in. Lubin himself was on the phone and gave her a vague wave before continuing his conversation and there was no sign at all of Ricky Smart. Kate hung up her coat and began to load her Voigtlander with fresh film and check her stock of flashbulbs. 'Right,' she heard Lubin say before he ended his call and crossed the room with a sympathetic smile to put a hand on her shoulder, which he probably thought was avuncular but made Kate squirm.

'That was Ken,' he said. 'He says you've been having trouble with Ricky. I'm sorry about that but please don't feel that you can't talk to me about it if he bothers you again. He's got a day out today to do some recruiting, but I'll talk to him tomorrow. He means no harm but he's sometimes a bit overenthusiastic.'

'This was more than overenthusiastic,' Kate said flatly, slipping out of Lubin's grasp. 'The man's a menace.'

'I'll see to it,' Lubin said, irritated. 'He won't bother you again.'

'Thanks,' Kate said grudgingly.

'I have to go out this morning,' Lubin went on. 'Will you hold the fort here till lunchtime?' It was a question to which he obviously expected no objection and Kate soon found herself alone in the office with little to do. She sat on a high stool with a mug of coffee in front of her flicking through the glossy pages of fashion magazines and wondering how the violent contrasts between the traditional and the avant-garde of high fashion would pan out. Would Tatiana's experimental designs for the young and trendy really triumph, as she so firmly believed? Or would the likes of Hardy Amies make a sneak counter attack, take hemlines down again and waists in and banish shiny boots to the dustbin of fashion history? Lubin seemed to dither while the likes of David Bailey plunged wholeheartedly into the brave new world. Whatever happened, it would be fun to watch, she thought, and maybe, if she was lucky, play her own small part successfully.

Her browsing was interrupted by the sound of the door opening and her heart pounded for a moment in case the new arrival proved to be Ricky Smart. Instead she found herself jumping off her stool to greet Sylvia Hubbard, ashen-faced, and leaning against the wall for support, clutching her stomach.

'What are you doing here again?' she asked the girl, taking her arm and helping her on to a stool. 'You still look terrible.'

'I just came in to look for Andrei to see if he had any work for me next week,' Sylvia whispered.

'You should still be in bed by the look of you,' Kate said. 'Here, I'll make you a coffee.' She busied herself with the kettle, stirred a couple of teaspoons of sugar into the brew, and thrust a mug into Sylvia's shaking hand. 'Did it all really go successfully?' she asked gently. 'You really don't look good.'

'They said there would be some bleeding, but there seems to be a lot,' the girl said. The girl was shaking and Kate shuddered.

'You must see a doctor,' she said. 'Or go to casualty at the hospital. These things can go wrong you know.'

'I can't go anywhere,' Sylvia said flatly. 'They'll arrest me and lock me up.'

'Of course, they won't,' Kate said, although she was not at all sure that what Sylvia believed was not true. Before she went to college and her horizons had broadened beyond the Catholic church's rigid views on procreation, she had not even known that what Sylvia had done was a possibility. 'Look, I have to stay here until Andrei comes back. Why don't you go down to the cafe on the corner and buy us something for elevenses and bring it back. You look as though you've had no breakfast. Something to eat will perk you up.' She gave the girl a ten-bob note and folded it into her shaking fingers. 'I'll come with you to casualty if you like, if you don't want to go on your own when Andrei comes back. You really need to see a doctor, I think. You must.'

Sylvia nodded uncertainly. 'All right,' she said, finishing her coffee and sliding off the stool with a wince of pain. She walked slowly to the door and Kate heard her going down the stairs to the street. She was not surprised that when Andrei Lubin returned after half an hour Sylvia had not.

'You might as well go for an early lunch,' Lubin said, much to her relief, but when she ran down the stairs and hurried up and down the street in both directions there was absolutely no sign of Sylvia Hubbard. Heart pounding she slid into a telephone box on the corner of Frith Street and dialled DS Harry Barnard.

'Can you meet me at the Blue Lagoon?' she asked when she was put through. 'I think I've got problems I can't handle. I need some advice.'

Kate had almost finished her coffee when Harry Barnard arrived, hung up his coat carefully by the door and weaved his way through the crowded lunchtime tables.

'Have you eaten?' he asked, looking at her sharply. She shook her head. 'I'm not very hungry,' she said. 'We'll see about that,' Barnard said. 'I'll get you a sandwich and another coffee.'

'Now,' he said when he brought back a tray and arranged their lunch on the table. 'You look terrible. What's up.'

Kate fought back the tears that had threatened her equilibrium ever since the events of the previous evening, but chose to deal with Sylvia's problems before her own. 'It's Sylvia,' she said quietly. 'She had her operation yesterday and she came into the studio this morning looking like death warmed up. I'm sure she needs to see a doctor but she won't. She thinks she'll be arrested if she goes to the hospital. In the end she ran off again.'

'Do you know where she lives?' Barnard asked. 'She might just have gone back home.'

'I asked Andrei Lubin if he had an address for her but he said he didn't. I'm not surprised. His paperwork is a mess. Ricky looks after it usually but he's not in today. And none of the other girls were in this morning so I couldn't ask anyone else if they knew where she was living. There's no shoot today. The place is deserted. I don't know what to do next.'

Barnard frowned. 'You're right to think she might be at risk,' he said. 'But I can hardly report her as a missing person. She's only been gone for an hour or so. Uniform would laugh at me. Do you have a photograph of her?'

'That was easy,' Kate said, delving in her bag and pulling out a print of Sylvia which she had taken from Lubin's files, the girl looking demure in one of the more traditional outfits he still made space for.

'How old did you say she was?' Barnard asked.

'Fifteen,' Kate said.

'She looks older. Leave this with me. I'll keep an eye out for her and I'll check the hospitals. See if anyone like her has walked into casualty or been brought in by ambulance. And I'll ask one or two uniformed bobbies I trust to keep an eye open too. But you have to accept that we may be too late.'

'She could die?' Kate whispered.

'Of course she could,' Barnard snapped. 'Some of these

backstreet people are butchers. They've got no medical quali-
fications, they're here today and gone tomorrow, from one
address to another more or less overnight. Some of them get
away with something which is very close to murder, and it's
not the babies I'm thinking of. If she was unlucky . . .' He
shrugged.

'But you gave her the money . . .' Kate felt confused.

'She's a child, Kate, and she needed help. Unfortunately
the only place she could get it was in the backstreets. It's the
law that's an ass, but the powers that be – not to mention my
DCI – don't see it that way.' He drank his coffee and pushed
away his plate impatiently. 'I'll do what I can,' he said. 'But
I don't hold out high hopes that it won't end badly. Now, you
said problems. What else is going on? You look like death
warmed up yourself.' He took her hand across the table and
she did not pull away. 'Come on, tell me.'

So, very slowly and haltingly, she described what had
happened the previous night with Ricky Smart. Kate felt the
pressure on her hand increase as Barnard's expression darkened. But he said nothing until she came to the faltering end
of her story.

'Where is he now?' he asked, his face rigid. 'I'll bloody
have him, one way or another.'

'I don't know where he is,' Kate said. 'He wasn't at the
studio this morning. Andrei took it all very lightly when I told
him what had happened. He tended to be a bit overenthusiastic,
he said. Anyway, he said he was out for the day recruiting,
whatever that means. Looking for more girls like Jenny
Maitland and Sylvia Hubbard, I suppose. Andrei says he'll
talk to him tomorrow, though I don't see what good that will
do.'

'Do you want to press charges for sexual assault?' Barnard
asked. 'Did Tess see what happened?'

'She saw that I was being attacked but I don't think she
could identify who it was, not properly. It was dark in the
hallway when she arrived and Ricky went past her like a bat
out of hell. Tess thought at first it might have been Andrei
Lubin.'

'So she couldn't identify him for certain?'

'Not really, I don't think,' Kate said, realizing that this was not the answer Barnard wanted.

'These cases are always difficult, I've told you before,' Barnard said. 'It's almost always one person's word against another and juries have this fixed idea that women make these allegations up.'

'Why would anyone do that?' Kate asked, bewildered.

'Women scorned, pregnancies that need an explanation, all sorts of reasons. I don't know how many allegations of rape are real crimes but the courts seem to assume that very few are. It's just a fact of life. And then you have to ask yourself whether you want to stand up in public and go through all the details. And that's after being grilled by people like me. I believe you, but lots of coppers wouldn't. They'd say you led him on, you're not a "good girl", you'd be questioned on all that in the police station and then in court if it ever got that far.' He shrugged.

'So you're saying I should just let him get away with it? A word in his ear from Andrei, a slapped wrist, naughty boy, don't do it again, and that's the end of it?' Kate pulled her hand from Barnard's grasp angrily.

'I'm just warning you that's how it may end up,' Barnard said. 'I'm sorry, Kate.'

Kate gazed into her empty coffee cup trying to hold back the tears. 'It's a bloody man's world, isn't it, la?' she said. 'You hold all the cards, we get whatever you graciously decide to give us. And if we make a fuss you close ranks, call us liars, cheats, tarts, whatever you like. So I'll leave it to Andrei to sort out, go back to the studio like a good girl and get on with my job. But I did think you might be more use. I thought you would help. Silly me.' She got to her feet and pulled her jacket round her shoulders, pulling her hand away from Barnard's grasp when he tried to deter her.

'Thanks for lunch,' she said over her shoulder, leaving Barnard to pay the bill and try to locate Sylvia Hubbard. Then, he thought, he would begin to work out some way of evening the score with Ricky Smart.

Barnard picked up his red Capri from outside the nick and headed east, down New Oxford Street, across the City of

London, where building sites were still putting right some of the ravages of the blitz. Then the abrupt plunge into the East End and the Whitechapel Road, a multiracial bustle of small businesses and shops and, down a side street, the gym where Ray Robertson had tried to make a boxer of him while he was still at school. It was the traditional way out for a likely East End lad, but Harry Barnard doubted he would have made the grade even if some latent caution had not pulled him away from the Robertson brothers, whom he saw steadily drifting on to the wrong side of the law.

But even now, twenty years on and a police career going as well as he had ever hoped, he still regarded Ray Robertson – though not his brother Georgie, currently banged up in Pentonville awaiting trial at the Old Bailey – as a sort of a mate, and always a useful source of information on the criminal hierarchies of the capital. He locked his car carefully outside the gym although he did not really believe any little toe-rag would touch it while it was in this particular street, and went into the cavernous gym, which at this time of day was almost empty, just a couple of young boys sparring under the watchful eye of a trainer. There was a light visible in the cubicle Ray called an office and Barnard banged on the frosted-glass door before popping his head in and getting a welcoming grin from the boss who ended his phone call and picked up his cigar with a smile.

'How are you doing Harry? Long time no see down in this neck of the woods.'

'I'm OK,' Barnard said. 'But you know I think it's best if we're not seen together too much till Georgie's trial is out of the way.'

'You worry too much about that,' Robertson said. 'Though my ma is still fuming, silly old moo, trying to get the lawyers to rig the jury and God knows what. She's always thought the sun shone out of little bro Georgie's bum. So what's so urgent that brings you down here in spite of all that?'

'I'm trying to get a handle on a man called Ricky Smart who seems to be recruiting very young girls down this way to be models, he says. Very tempting no doubt if all you've got in front of you is a dead-end job in Woolworths. But a lot of them seem to end up on the street in Soho, and at least one of them has ended up dead.'

Robertson flicked the ash from his cigar and looked thoughtful. 'That sort of activity wouldn't please our Maltese friends, would it?' he said. 'The odd freelance they'll put up with, but anything organized, anything which could seriously impinge on business, they'll take measures. What did you say this bloke's name was?'

'Ricky Smart,' Barnard said and waited while Robertson mused, blowing a thick smoke ring at the ceiling.

'Can't say I've heard the name, but I'll put out a few feelers, see if anyone's come across him. Where's he been picking up girls, did you say?'

'Clapton way, chatting them up as they come out of school apparently.'

'Naughty, naughty,' Robertson said. 'I've a few contacts down there. Someone will have spotted him, no doubt. No doubt at all. All I've picked up about girls recently is that someone at the Jazz Cellar was trying to get involved, just like you suspected. I was going to give you a bell about it. I didn't get a name, but whoever it was got warned off by our friends from the Med. And I'm not going to complain about that. I've got an agreement with them and I don't want free-lances muscling in any more than they do.'

'That's very interesting,' Barnard said. 'Can you find out who it was, specifically?'

'I'll see what I can do next time I'm up west for business. Always ready to help an old pal, you know that. I took your advice about the boxing gala, by the way. I'm leaving it until the spring when Georgie's trial will be over. Should go down much better then. But you could keep an ear open for me, as it goes, Flash. Someone told me that some of the nobs I know were being catered for at some place out in the country, special do's for those in the know. All tastes catered for. I'd like to know who's organizing that. Could be a nice little earner if it's as kinky as this bloke thought it was. On the other hand, even if it's straight up, I wouldn't mind an invitation now and then. I don't want to lose touch, do I, just because of Georgie's shenanigans hitting the Delilah Club just now?'

Barnard could not help grinning. Robertson had walked a delicate line between his natural criminal habitat and his social-climbing activities, between the East and the West Ends of the city, since he had discovered that loads of cash could open even the apparently well-defended doors of the aristocracy, now many of them faced straitened times.

''Course not, Ray,' Barnard said. 'London would be a much duller place without your little do's. How could anyone who's anyone miss you off their guest list in return?'

'I like a trip to the country now and then,' Robertson said with unconvincing enthusiasm, knowing only too well how Barnard would remember his dislike of all things rural when they had been pretty unwelcome evacuees together on a Hertfordshire farm. But just what rewards Ray envisaged from wheedling his way into a grand party in the sticks Harry Barnard could not really imagine.

# ELEVEN

DS Harry Barnard responded to the call from Casualty with a deep sense of foreboding. He was met by a young, harassed-looking doctor who nodded bleakly to him and led him into a curtained cubicle where a slight form lay on the bed covered completely by a sheet.

'She died half an hour ago,' the doctor said. 'She was brought in after being found in the street, bleeding heavily. We did our best but we couldn't save her. Can't you do something about these abortionists? That's the third we've had this month, plus a couple we managed to save. This one's just a kid.'

Barnard pulled the sheet away from the dead girl's face and had no difficulty recognizing the body of Sylvia Hubbard, who had sat with him and Kate O'Donnell drinking coffee in the Blue Lagoon a couple of days before.

'Do you have a name?' he asked and the doctor responded only with a brief shake of the head.

'She was barely conscious when they brought her in. There'd been a massive loss of blood.'

'I think I've seen her on the street,' Barnard said carefully. 'I know someone who should be able to identify her for us if I'm right.' Making a positive identification himself was a course that could lead to all sorts of complications, he thought. There were enough other people who could do the job for him.

'She'll be downstairs until someone claims her,' the doctor said. 'The coroner may want a post-mortem, I suppose, to confirm the cause of death, though I don't think there's much doubt myself. The trouble is that if the worst happens you've got no chance of tracking these butchers down. She's probably the only person who knows where she went. And she's not telling us now.'

'Tell the morgue we'll be in touch,' Barnard said. 'The coroner's been informed, I take it?'

The doctor nodded and Barnard made his way out of the hospital wondering how he was going to tell Kate what had happened. She would be distraught and there was no way he was going to ask her to identify the body. He had that task down for Andrei Lubin or Ricky Smart. It was the last service they could do for the girl they had brought to Soho, exploited and then thrown away like so much garbage. The least he could do for Sylvia was to give one or both of them a hard time. But first he had to go back to the nick to clear his lines with the DCI. The second task he knew he would enjoy, the first he guessed he would not.

As the sergeant had half expected, DCI Keith Jackson went into full-scale Presbyterian mode when Barnard told him what had happened.

'The wages of sin,' he intoned, and when he pulled open one of his desk drawers Barnard wondered if he was going to pull out a Bible, although all that appeared was a buff file which he flicked through quickly. 'There are a number of known suspects in the area, are there not?' he said. 'You can start by checking them out. I don't suppose they keep records of who they're dealing with, do they? That would be too risky for them. But you can threaten them with manslaughter charges if they don't tell us whether or not they dealt with this girl.'

'I can do that,' Barnard said. 'Though unless you catch them in the act there's little evidence on the premises as a rule. They tend to provide their services in discreet rented rooms. And there's plenty of demand in an area with so many on the game.'

Jackson's lips tightened in distaste. 'You say you think you know who the dead girl may be? Was she a tart?'

'I don't think so,' Barnard said. 'She'd been working for a photographer as a model, a fashion model. But according to someone who worked with her, she's not been seen for a day or two. I'll check it out. Someone there will be able to identify the body.'

'How do they find these jobs? What are their parents doing about it? That's what I want to know,' Jackson asked.

'There's at least one man going round schools in the East

End recruiting girls to work as models. Ricky Smart, he's called, and he's top of my list of people to talk to if the dead girl really does come from the agency he works for. As far as sex is concerned most of them seem to be under-age, all trying to be the next Jean Shrimpton.'

'Tarts, models, what's the difference?' Jackson snapped. 'I saw a lassie walking down Oxford Street with her skirt hem up to her knickers only this morning. And shiny plastic boots. I've never seen anything like it. If it's not Sodom, it must be Gomorrah.'

'Yes, guv,' Barnard muttered, anxious to placate a man who would inevitably terminate his career if he ever discovered that police funds had helped pay for the unfortunate Sylvia's illegal operation. 'Perhaps we'd better get an identification first?'

'Do that,' Jackson said. 'Then get to work on finding the killer. If I had my way the charge would be murder.'

'Sir,' Barnard said and thankfully made his escape. He had not yet, he recalled as he left, passed on the information he had gleaned at the American embassy about Muddy Abraham but he guessed that Jackson had not been moved to let the American go. Confirming that he was a wanted man in the States would only slam the prison door even more firmly against him, and Barnard felt a certain reluctance to do that, although he knew in the end there was probably no alternative. The Americans themselves would certainly come running now they knew the former GI was not only in London but in police custody.

Kate O'Donnell met Harry Barnard in the street outside Lubin's studio looking anxious.

'I saw you coming,' she said, nodding at the windows three storeys up. 'Is there any news of Sylvia?'

Barnard hesitated for a moment and then concluded that there was no easy way of shielding Kate from the news she would certainly not want to hear but would have to. 'A girl was taken to hospital last night who might be Sylvia,' he said. 'I was just coming to see your boss, and Ricky, to ask them to identify her. I'm afraid she died.'

Kate put a hand on Barnard's arm, as if afraid of losing her balance, her face draining white. 'I told her to go to hospital yesterday,' she said quietly. 'I couldn't drag her there bodily, could I? But I knew she needed help. But she ran off.'

'She collapsed in the street and was taken in by ambulance,' Barnard asked, glancing up at the studio windows above them. 'Is Smart in?'

Kate shook her head. 'I've not seen him this morning yet,' she said. 'But Andrei's up there haranguing a couple of girls who didn't do exactly as he asked them quickly enough.'

'He'll have to do, though I still want to see your Ricky Smart about the other thing,' Barnard said, his face grim. 'What do you think about those two, Kate? Do you think they're recruiting girls deliberately to run them on the street? Is the studio just a cover, do you think?'

Kate looked startled. 'I don't honestly know,' she said. 'Jenny ended up on the street but I don't think Sylvia was doing that. I think she just slept with Andrei, or Ricky, or maybe both, and got caught out. They regard the girls as fair game, both of them. But I think the studio's genuine enough. He's not a bad photographer, Andrei, though he's a bit old-fashioned about the fashion scene. Otherwise he'd support his cousin more. She's a very good designer. I jumped at the chance of taking some shots for her.'

'But Ricky Smart, what about him? From what you've told me about him he'd have no scruples about pimping, would he? Perhaps he put Jenny Maitland on the street.'

Kate shook her head. 'I wouldn't put anything past him, la,' she said. 'He'd put his own grandmother on the street if it suited him.'

Barnard nodded. 'I'll have a serious talk with him later down at the nick,' he said. 'Are you coming back upstairs?'

'I'll go for a coffee,' she said. 'I feel a bit shaky. I don't really want to listen to you grilling Andrei about poor Sylvia.'

'I'm sorry, Kate, truly I am,' Barnard said, kissing her lightly on the cheek. 'We won't know definitely until she's been formally identified, but I guess it's her. I'm really sorry.'

Andrei Lubin looked angrily across the studio as Barnard walked in. He had been talking to a skinny girl who didn't seem to the sergeant to be more than about twelve years old and whose eyes were red-rimmed from crying.

'Get out,' Lubin hissed at the girl. 'You're finished. I don't want to see you again.' He spun towards Barnard, switching on an instant smile that quickly faded as soon as the policeman mentioned Sylvia's name.

'She buggered off,' he said. 'I haven't seen her for a couple of days. They're all unreliable, these girls.' He waved a hand at the trio who were huddled around the one in tears. 'Go and get a coffee downstairs, all of you,' he said, and watched them scuttle away. 'What's this about Sylvia then?'

'We have reason to believe that a girl who bled to death in casualty last night as a result of an illegal operation might be Sylvia Hubbard. We need someone who knew her to identify the body and, if it is her, give us some details about her, where she lived, where she came from, her family.'

Lubin swallowed hard and his face froze. He turned away to riffle through a pile of prints lying on his desk. 'That's Sylvia,' he said, handing Barnard a black-and-white print of a demure-looking blonde in a traditional summer dress.

'And that's definitely the girl in the hospital mortuary. Did you know she was pregnant?' Barnard asked.

'No, I didn't,' Lubin said. 'Silly cow.'

'Were you likely to be the father of the child she was expecting, and tried to get rid of?' Barnard flashed back quickly.

'No I bloody wasn't,' Lubin said.

'Was Ricky Smart?'

'I don't know,' Lubin said, glancing at his watch. 'In fact I don't know where Ricky is. He was supposed to be here at nine this morning and he hasn't turned up yet.'

'Well, I'll want to talk to him but we'll worry about him later. For now I'd like the details you hold on this girl, and then for you to come to the hospital with me to formally identify the body.'

Lubin looked at his watch again. 'Does it have to be me?' he asked. 'I've got an important appointment at twelve. Can't her parents identify her? I've got an address here somewhere . . .'

'I'd like you to come to the hospital now, Mr Lubin,' Barnard said, a touch of ice in his voice. 'You were responsible for this girl, you employed her under-age for sure, and did nothing to prevent her getting into this situation, even if you didn't personally have sex with her. I want you to come with me straight away, no ifs and buts. And if you don't, I'll bloody arrest you for obstruction just for the sheer hell of it.'

Kate did not go back to Lubin's studio that day. She had already arranged to take the afternoon off to do some preliminary shots of Tatiana Broughton-Clarke's clothes that afternoon on the South Bank and when she saw Lubin leaving with Barnard guessed that not much would be happening there for a while. She had already recruited two of Lubin's young models to wear the new designs and when she walked from the tube station at Waterloo towards the Festival Hall she saw Tatiana with the two models by the open back doors of a dilapidated-looking van parked at the side of the building.

'I'm just explaining to the girls that the changing room is a teensy bit primitive,' Tatiana said cheerfully. She waved at the interior of the van where Kate could see an array of clothes on hangers at the back. 'I've promised them that when I'm famous they'll be my first choice of models on the catwalk.' She gave Kate a broad wink and a grin and tossed back her red hair. She looked tiny beside the two tall willowy girls, but she radiated determination and energy and Kate thought it not at all unlikely that she would succeed in the end.

'Come on,' she said to the models as she clambered into the back of the van. She glanced back at Kate. 'Give me fifteen minutes,' she said. 'I even managed to get hold of a spotlight so we can see what we are doing in here.'

The quartet spent the best part of the afternoon on the embankment with Kate arranging the girls in what she hoped were interesting poses that showed off the short skirts and long boots of Tatiana's collection set off against the modern-istic backdrop of the South Bank. Eventually the light began to fade and Kate realized that the two girls were both tired by the constant changes of clothes and poses and chilled to shivering point by the rising wind from the gray river behind them.

'I think we should call it a day,' she said to Tatiana. 'I'll

go back to my agency and develop the film. If you come round about six I should be able to show you some contact prints.'
'Right,' Tatiana said. 'I'll see if I can manoeuvre this old jalopy back to its garage. Come on girls, jump in, let's go.'
'See you later, alligator,' Kate said as she turned back to the tube station, feeling the cold herself although she had never taken off her duffel coat. She fastened the toggles and slid into the river of humanity that was beginning to make its way home from the City across Waterloo Bridge. London, she thought, was just so big it could easily swallow up the young girls who were attracted by the bright lights and glamour of the West End. Jenny Maitland and now Sylvia Hubbard had been seduced by London itself as well as the men who had brought them there and as she worked her way through the unfamiliar passageways to the Bakerloo line she felt an unaccustomed depression as she realized how very easy it was to get lost here.

It took the unexpected enthusiasm of Ken Fellows to cheer Kate up slightly as a couple of hours later in his office they both studied the still damp sheets of prints which were the result of her first solo fashion shoot.

'You've got some good stuff here,' he said. 'I like the modern clothes against the modern backdrop, though if my daughter came home looking like that I'd tan her backside.'

'I think Tatiana's got something,' Kate said, laughing, taken by surprise by the notion of Ken as father figure. 'This is all going to take off. I fancy some of those boots myself.'

'God help us,' Fellows said. 'Anyway, show the contacts to your Russian princess and see what she thinks. It's all a waste of time if she isn't satisfied and doesn't commission you again.'

'She's coming over,' said Kate, glancing at her watch. It had been a long day, but if Tatiana also enthused over her prints and asked her to have a drink before she went home, she thought she had better accept. She had been in the business long enough now to have learned who called the tune.

Tatiana was late and the office was empty by the time Kate heard her clomping up the stairs in her trademark shiny knee-high boots.

'Sorry, sorry,' she said, evidently picking up a sense that Kate would like to have left for home by now, where she knew that Tess was cooking a meal. 'So what have we got? The trouble with doing shoots out of doors, darlink, is the weather. It was bloody cold down there. The girls did nothing but complain on the way back. If we're going to make a habit of it I'll have to get a heater for the van. And what happens if it starts to rain?' She took a stool at the table where Kate was sitting.

'The girls did begin to look a bit chilly towards the end,' Kate admitted. 'They look it in some of the pictures too. We'll have to weed those out. Rain we'll have to think about. Haven't you designed any raincoats yet?'

Tatiana didn't answer and didn't look amused.

'But here are the contacts,' Kate said quickly, sliding the sheets towards her. 'Some of them are quite good, I think. Ken's seen them and was quite pleased.' Kate felt tentative and she realized that maybe she needed more practice in actually selling her work. That, after all, was what Ken was good at and why the agency flourished as it did.

'Yes, well, he can see the financial possibilities, can't he, darlink? I was hoping that Andrei would help me as I'm family, but he's always had a mean streak. Now I'm stuck paying you before I've got anything into the shops and got a bean in return. My husband's not best pleased, I can tell you.'

'I thought he was funding you,' Kate said.

'Well, he is, but he seems to think the profits will come flooding in overnight. He's completely unrealistic and the old place soaks up money like a sponge. He's just found a new hole in the roof. I swear when I married him I thought he was loaded, darlink. But it seems that lords and ladies in this country are generally poor as – what is it – church mice? In fact church mice are probably more comfortable tucked up under the organ than we are in our draughty old barn of a place.'

She turned back to the sheets of prints and grunted now and again though whether in satisfaction or irritation Kate found it difficult to tell.

'Should I mark the ones I think are the best?' she asked eventually.

Kate handed her a pen. 'Just a small mark underneath,' she
said, and watched as Tatiana selected about twenty of the
prints for enlargement.

Eventually she pushed the sheets back to Kate. 'Very good,'
she said. 'How soon can we get them out there?'

'I can print them tomorrow,' Kate said. 'But you need to
talk to Ken about what happens next. That's not really my
business. He makes the contracts.'

'OK,' Tatiana said. 'But have you thought any more about
how would you feel about taking some shots on a private
basis? As he told you, one of my husband's little projects is
throwing parties at our place in the country – it's all for charity,
of course, but he makes a little profit on it too. But you know
how people like to have their pictures taken at parties. Andrei
had been doing it until he and Roddy fell out, and there was
another man in High Wycombe who looked like a possibility
but he's had a car accident and won't be available for the next
one. So we're a bit stuck. If you took a little more trouble
with your clothes and your hair, you'd fit in all right. So long
as you kept that accent buttoned up.'

'Oh thanks, la,' Kate said, trying hard not to show how
insulted that made her feel. 'Will you lend me something of
yours then?'

'Oh I don't think so, darlink,' Tatiana said airily. 'A bit out
of your league. Maybe Andrei would lend you something for
the night. I don't know how well you get on with him. In my
experience, if he does you a favour he always wants something
in return, so bear that in mind. Or you could buy something.
You could try Carnaby Street, or a place called Bazaar. Mary
Quant's place. I'm not the only person doing miniskirts, you
know. It's getting to be quite the thing. People have suddenly
woken up to the fact that young people want their own styles
now. It's beginning to take off.'

'When is this party of your husband's?' Kate asked. 'I might
be interested.'

'I'll get you the details,' Tatiana said. 'But you really will
have to shape up clothes-wise. The 1950s is dead and buried
now.'

Not where I come from, Kate thought wryly, recalling the

congregation at her mother's church in their sensible coats and fur-lined boots and regulation felt hats as they trooped in to Mass.

'Would these pictures just be for private consumption or for the society magazines?' Kate asked. 'Ken would certainly be keen on that.'

'Yes, well, don't try to sell it to Ken just yet,' she said. 'I'll talk to my husband about exactly what would be wanted. Some people like appearing in *Tatler*, and some don't, in my experience. But you know what the backgrounds are like, now you've been down to see us. Leave it with me. Let's talk when I've spoken to Ken and worked out how to use these pictures and get this collection launched.' With that she picked up her voluminous handbag and, draping her coat dramatically round her shoulders, looked as if she was about to leave.

'By the way, have you ever met a man called Ray Robertson?' she said unexpectedly. 'He's a bit of a party-giver himself I hear, and a little bird told us he'd like an invitation to our next do. Roddy thought he might be a useful contact.'

'I have met him, as it happens,' Kate said carefully. 'I was sent to take some pictures at a boxing gala at his club, the Delilah. There were a whole lot of people there – a government minister, actors and actresses, people who obviously had pots of money.'

'That's interesting,' Tatiana said. 'Roddy thought he might be able to pick his brains about what goes down well at these do's. I'll maybe get him to send him an invite. If we don't like him we don't have to have him a second time.'

'You do know he's some sort of gangster, don't you?' Kate said.

'Well, if nobody else is bothered about that, why should we be?' Tatiana said loftily, and clomped across the studio and down the stairs, leaving nothing but a waft of a cloying perfume behind her.

# TWELVE

The Alfa Romeo Giulietta might have remained unnoticed where it had been left at the end of an alleyway close to Berwick Street if a delivery driver who needed to reach the dilapidated double doors leading into the Italian restaurant's delivery bay, against which the Alfa was parked, had not driven up bumper to bumper behind it, and jammed his thumb on his horn before he jumped from his cab in a fury.

'Which effing idiot has left that there?' he asked himself angrily before walking to the driver's door and peering through the glass. The window seemed dirty on the inside, which puzzled him at first until he worked out what it was, looked more closely, and then could barely believe what he was seeing.

'Bloody hell,' he said at last, appropriately enough, and tentatively tried the car door, which opened easily, revealing without any doubt that his eyes were not deceiving him. A man was lying sprawled across the two front seats, his legs still in the footwell, tangled across the pedals, his head and shoulders on the passenger side covered in blood that had splashed and dripped across the leather seats and the windows. The delivery man found himself panting for breath and fighting off nausea. He had absolutely no doubt that the man was dead. He could not, he thought, be anything else with his head apparently half severed. After a moment he slammed the Alfa's door and leaned against the side of his own van until he felt able to stand without support and climb back into his cab. He reversed carefully out of the alley and drove round the block to the restaurant that was expecting his load of fruit and veg.

The place was closed not long after nine in the morning but when he banged on the door a waiter opened it a grudging couple of inches.

'I can't get round the back, some idiot has parked there,' the driver said. 'You'd better take your stuff this way.' Together the two men unloaded the van and carried the crates and boxes through to the kitchens. Only when it had all been signed for did the van driver mention that there might be rather more than just a car in the alleyway.

'You'd better call the police, mate,' he said. 'But don't mention my name, eh? It's bugger-all to do with me.'

The waiter shrugged dramatically, hands waving. 'I wait for the boss,' he said. 'He won't thank me for bringing police.'

And in the end, more than an hour later, it was a young uniformed constable, sent from the nick to take a look at the badly parked and possibly abandoned car causing an obstruction outside a Soho restaurant's back doors who opened the Alfa's door for the second time that morning and had to call in the discovery of a man with his throat cut lying across the front seats.

Within ten minutes it was DS Harry Barnard who was peering at the body and quickly making way for the first arrivals from the murder team, DCI Keith Jackson in the lead, the police doctor and the forensics specialists quickly following behind.

'A bit of a mess,' Barnard said to the DCI as he passed on his way out of the alleyway, which was now seriously crowded. 'Difficult to see without moving the body but it looks as if he wasn't far off having his head taken right off, whoever he is.'

'Check out who the car's registered to,' Jackson said curtly. 'It's Italian, isn't it?'

'Nice little motor,' Barnard said. 'Pity about the mess inside.'

'Let me know who the owner is,' Jackson snapped, and continued his way to make his own inspection of the body before making way for the doctor to confirm, as if he needed to, that the man at the centre of the shambles inside was indeed dead.

'Right, guv,' Barnard said placatingly. 'I'll let you know as soon as.' In fact the answer from the licensing authorities gave him nearly as much of a shock as the sight of the body in the Alfa Romeo had done. The car, they told him, after what seemed like an inordinately long wait, belonged to a Richard Anthony Smart, resident at an address in Tufnell Park, date of birth 1933.

'Well, well, well,' Barnard said to himself as he put the phone down. 'That's a turn up for the books. I wonder who else Ricky Smart has been annoying.' That, he thought, might turn out to be a very interesting question indeed.

Back at the nick himself, DCI Jackson assembled his murder team in the CID office and conducted an initial briefing. 'So, what do we know so far?' he asked. 'We have a pretty firm ID. The victim was carrying a driving licence and some other documents in the name of Richard Anthony Smart, and the car was registered in his name. We already had an interest in Mr Smart, according to DS Barnard here, and knew he was employed by a photographer called Andrew Lubin . . .'

'Andrei, guv,' Barnard said. 'He's half Russian apparently. Ricky Smart was his sidekick, fixer, something like that, and recruiter of young girls who wanted to work as fashion models, including Jenny Maitland, the girl found dead behind the Jazz Cellar, and apparently Sylvia Hubbard who died in hospital yesterday after an illegal operation. I've already talked to Lubin and Smart in connection with those two deaths. It's tricky to see at this stage whether there's any connection with Smart's own death, but it's obviously a possibility. Revenge maybe. We'll need to talk to the families of the two girls. I've already talked to the Maitland family and I can't see any of them being able to find Smart let alone attack him.'

'The post-mortem will be at three this afternoon,' Jackson said. 'It would obviously be sensible if you came with me, Sergeant, as you've already spoken to this man. You can confirm the identification.'

Barnard nodded and Jackson went on to detail other officers to visit Smart's workplace and home address as soon as the ID was confirmed and convene again later in the day for more instructions.

Barnard drove the DCI back from the hospital to the nick, carefully obeying every traffic regulation he could remember and a few extra just in case. Keith Jackson had stood impassively by while the pathologist examined the body of Ricky Smart, his identity easily confirmed by Barnard himself who tried not to let his eyes dwell on the fact that the man's head was only loosely attached to his body. The pathologist had found no other external injuries on the corpse but surmised, when he opened the stomach, that Smart had consumed a considerable quantity of alcohol before he died and almost certainly should not have been behind the wheel of a car.

'From the position of the body he must have driven the car to where it was found,' Barnard said. 'And from the position of the car, in a dead-end alley up against doors that were obviously regularly used, he was either lured there to meet someone or forced to drive there by someone else in the vehicle.'

'The blow that cut his throat most likely came from behind,' the pathologist had offered. 'You couldn't easily get that sort of wound from the side in the confined space of a car. My best guess is that someone was sitting behind him and reached round with an extremely sharp knife.'

'Have we found the weapon?' Jackson asked Barnard, as he drove across Oxford Circus and swung down Regent Street.

'Not to my knowledge, guv,' the sergeant replied. He overtook a bus cautiously, knowing that he must tell Jackson about Kate O'Donnell's involvement with Smart and Lubin and knowing that the information would raise all sorts of questions in the Scotsman's mind. Even so, he reckoned that sooner was very much better than later in this case.

'There is one thing about this case – and the deaths of the two young girls – you ought to know, guv,' he began tentatively. 'There's a young photographer working temporarily in Lubin's studio, a female photographer, who I've known for a while.'

Jackson's bright blue eyes focused on Barnard's, his face impassive. 'And?' he said as the silence lengthened.

'She's called Kate O'Donnell. I met her before your time, guv,' Barnard said. 'Her brother was a suspect in a case I worked on while Ted Venables was still around. She contacted me again recently because she was a worried about what Smart and Lubin were up to with the girls they employed. She's working there for a month to learn about fashion. In fact what she said was very helpful in the Jenny Maitland case. It helped us identify her, and link her to Lubin's studio. She was sure the two men were sleeping with the models, more or less as a matter of course. Some of them were obviously under-age. Kate told me she was having trouble herself in fending Smart off, but she's a lot older and more streetwise so she was able to cope with working there. It was only for a short time anyway.' That, Barnard thought, was as much as he wanted to tell the DCI about Kate's troubles with Smart. He would warn her not to mention to anyone that she had told Barnard about Smart's attack on her doorstep. That would open a can of worms for both of them if Jackson found out.

'Sleeping with the models, even under-age models, is not the same as working the streets,' Jackson said.

'I suspect that happened after the girls left the studio,' Barnard said. 'A lot of the girls Smart recruited were being sacked quite quickly. Some of them only worked there for a few weeks, and I was beginning to wonder if they were being put on to the streets either by those two themselves or someone they were passing them on to. It was looking very nasty. And then Kate contacted me again when a second girl went missing, Sylvia Hubbard, the one who turned up in casualty after a botched abortion. She wasn't strictly speaking missing, she was only away for a day or so before she turned up in hospital. But it made me even more suspicious that something odd was going on. I was on the case with Smart and Lubin before someone else decided to take him out a bit more finally than I had in mind.'

'Are you involved with this young woman?' Jackson asked coldly.

'No, guv,' Barnard said. 'Not that I wouldn't like to be, but the answer from her is no. In this case she is strictly a witness and likely to be a useful one.' He pulled up outside the nick and Jackson opened the passenger door.

'See you keep it that way,' he said, before getting out of the car. 'Briefing at half four.'

Strolling across Regent Street on his way to grill Andrei Lubin about his relationship with Ricky Smart, and hoping for a quiet word in Kate's ear in case Jackson took it into his head to interview her without him, Harry Barnard noticed a Jaguar parked half on the pavement outside the Delilah Club, a stone's throw from Piccadilly Circus. It was a sure sign that the owner of the club, Ray Robertson, was in residence. Although it was only lunchtime and the place would not swing into action for another eight or nine hours, the main doors responded to his push and he made his way through a deserted reception area, across the dance floor and to a small narrow door beyond the bandstand marked simply 'Office'. He tapped and a familiar voice called him in.

'Flash! Come in, come in, I was hoping I might see you. I hear there's been some unpleasantness on your manor.'

'You're well informed,' Barnard said drily. 'It's not in the papers yet, as far as I know.'

'It pays to be well informed, you know that,' Robertson said. 'So inform me some more. Who is this beggar who got his throat cut? What the hell's going on, Harry?'

'I came to ask you the same question,' Barnard said. 'We know who he is. He's Ricky Smart who worked for a photographer called Andrei Lubin, organizing models for him. The worst he'd been accused of as far as I knew was sleeping with under-aged girls and fathering illegitimate kids. But I guess there was a lot more than that going on.'

'You say he was recruiting models? Pretty girls, that'd be, then?'

'Sure,' Barnard said. 'A bit skinny for my taste. Certainly no Marilyn Monroes amongst them. But pretty enough.'

'You think they were tempted to try to put them on the streets?'

'Could be.'

'That would get up Frankie Falzon's nose, for sure,' Robertson said. 'You asked me about the Jazz Cellar and girls, remember? But I couldn't raise a whisper about that place. But I did get a hint that Falzon's not best pleased about something or someone. Maybe it was this bloke Smart, not the jazz fellows, you should have been following up.'

'And Falzon's a man who favours the knife,' Barnard said. 'We know that from past experience.'

'Well, I wish you the best of luck if you're going to try to get anything out of that mob. It takes me all my time to get to see him even if I want to discuss things that are in his best interest. He's not really a businessman, at all. He still thinks he's a clan chieftain hidden in the countryside with his men all sworn to secrecy. Bloody Robin Hood, or who's the other one, the Scottish one – Rob Roy was it? If you can find a chink in his armour let me know. There's a few questions I would like a straight answer to as well.'

Barnard laughed. 'I'm not sure my dour Scottish guv'nor would go with that idea,' he said. 'He's definitely some Scottish version of the sheriff of Nottingham. He'd hang the lot of you, given half a chance.'

Barnard's next port of call was Andrei Lubin's studio where, as he had hoped, he found Kate O'Donnell and Lubin himself working with three young models in various outfits that made no attempt to cover up more than was strictly necessary.

Kate grinned at the sergeant while Lubin's attention was distracted by one of the models complaining that dress was so skimpy it risked revealing her naked breasts.

'If the skirts get much shorter they'll have to turn them into shorts in the interests of public decency,' Barnard whispered. 'Mind you if we start arresting girls for exposing themselves the custody officers won't complain.'

'What do you want, la?' Kate asked in broad Liverpudlian and Barnard reverted quickly to an official look.

'A word with you, honey, but later. Just now it's bad news, I'm afraid,' he said, turning away. 'Mr Lubin, can you spare me a few minutes? I need to talk to you about Ricky Smart.'

Lubin turned impatiently in his direction but evidently picked up on Barnard's seriousness quickly enough. 'Take five and go and get some coffee, girls. You'd better put your coats on or you'll catch your death of cold in that gear.'

After they had all left, he perched languidly on the arm of a chair. 'Ricky?' he said. 'Where the hell is Ricky? That's what I want to know.'

'I'm afraid he was found this morning in his Alfa Romeo with his throat cut,' Barnard said, ready enough to shock Lubin perhaps into giving something away. But the Russian merely looked stunned and sat down in the chair with a thump while

Kate, turning pale, gasped and grabbed hold of the table for support.

'Dear God in heaven,' Lubin said. 'What is going on round here?'

'That's what I would like to find out, Mr Lubin,' Barnard said. 'Do you have any idea why anyone would want to kill Ricky Smart? This is not an area without its criminals but they don't generally target people at random. There has to be a reason for such a deliberate assault on a man inside his own car. This wasn't some random street violence where someone pulled a knife. He seems to have been in the driving seat when he was killed by a single, very violent blow. So I'd like you to think very hard, Mr Lubin, about what that reason might be. Tell me how Smart set about his job of recruiting girls for you, please. Where he went, who he saw, anything you know about his activities in the East End.'

Lubin stood up and then sank into the chair he had been perched on, with a massive sigh. 'He didn't tell me a lot. It wasn't something he did every day of the week. He just said that when we needed fresh talent he went to certain schools, and once he had persuaded one girl to come and work here, it was easier to persuade more. Word went around, you know how young girls chatter . . .'

'But you seem to have a pretty fast turnover of girls, Mr Lubin. How long would you say you employ them?'

Lubin shuffled uneasily in his chair. 'They never turn out to be as good as you expect,' he said. 'You hope you can train them up, but more often than not they don't do as well as you hope they will, or as Ricky hopes when he brings them to me. I take them on a month's trial generally, if they scrub up at all well. But not many stay longer than that.'

Kate drew a sharp breath at this sanitized version of how Lubin and Smart treated their recruits but she knew that she had better keep her version of their procedures to herself for now.

'And where do they go when they leave here?' Barnard snapped. 'Do you make sure that they get home safely again or do you just throw them out on to the street?'

'Ricky dealt with all that,' Lubin said. 'As far as I know he sent them home.'

'Well, Jenny Maitland certainly didn't go back home, did she? She ended up on the game. And the other girl, Sylvia, seems to have been left to fend for herself when she got pregnant. Did you or Smart use these girls for sexual favours?' Lubin made a fairly unsuccessful effort to look affronted. 'Ricky may have done that,' he said, glancing at Kate and flushing red. 'I tried not to get involved.'

'And did Mr Smart also try to trick the girls into prostitution when they left? Was he pimping?'

'That's a disgraceful suggestion,' Lubin protested.

'Not really,' Barnard said. 'You're ideally placed here in the heart of Soho to get into the sex trade. Is that what Ricky was up to? Were you involved in that? Because I can tell you for nothing that some people would regard that as an invasion of their territory, and would think nothing of putting a stop to it with a knife.'

Lubin turned a dirty shade of gray and Kate noticed that his hands were shaking. 'I don't know anything about what Ricky was doing in his own time,' Lubin said. 'But maybe these people will think I did. Am I in danger too, Sergeant? Are they going to come for me as well with a knife?'

'I've no idea, Mr Lubin,' Barnard said. 'In the meantime I'd like you to come down to the police station to give us your fingerprints, purely for the purposes of elimination – at this stage. Have you ever been in Mr Smart's car?'

'No, no,' Lubin said. 'Never.' He hesitated. 'Can't you give me some protection from these people?' he asked. 'Am I safe here anymore?'

Barnard smiled slightly wolfishly. 'If you haven't been doing anything illegal I should think you're quite safe, Mr Lubin. Perhaps we can see you at the nick at four this afternoon? That would be very helpful.' He got up and gave Kate a brief smile before leaving the studio echoing to the sharp slam of the door.

Lubin looked at Kate helplessly for a moment. 'What has that idiot been doing to get us into this mess?' he asked. 'Perhaps I'd better go away for a while, close the studio for a bit, I've nothing planned that can't be postponed.'

'I don't know what Ricky was up to, but you and him have

been treating those girls like so much rubbish, picking them up then throwing them away when you've finished with them. And if Ricky was putting your rejects on the streets maybe he deserved what he got.'

Lubin's jaw dropped in astonishment but he said nothing and Kate was astonished to see tears in his eyes. 'Ricky Smart was the seed of the devil,' he said. 'You don't know half of it.'

But Kate, who reckoned she knew as much as she wanted to, turned away. 'If that's true you should tell the police everything you know this afternoon.' she said. 'The girls who died deserve that much.'

Lubin shook his head and let the tears roll. 'That's easy to say,' he moaned. 'But impossible to do.'

Kate turned her back on him and followed Barnard down the stairs and caught up with him quickly. 'You said you wanted a word, la,' she said, linking an arm in his.

'Yes,' he said. 'Nothing personal, just a quick warning. I think DCI Jackson may want to interview you as a witness. You'll have to tell him what happened between you and Ricky Smart of course, but I'd rather you didn't tell him you'd told me about it. I'm not sure it would do either of us any good if he got the idea we had a particular grudge against him. I don't think he'd imagine that you cut his throat, but it might cross his mind that I did.'

# THIRTEEN

With time on her hands when Andrei Lubin closed up the studio and set off for the police station, telling her to phone him before coming in again, Kate made her way back to the Ken Fellows Agency and told her boss what had happened.

'You certainly have a genius for getting yourself into dodgy situations, girl,' he said. 'Do you really think he's going to close the place down?'

'He's certainly very scared,' Kate said. 'And with good reason. Ricky Smart was my least favourite person, as it happens, but to be killed like that.' She shrugged. 'Someone really wanted him out of the way, and if it's something to do with the girls at the studio, Andrei might be next in line. Closing down for a bit and making himself scarce might be the best thing he can do.'

Fellows steepled his hands in front of his face and looked thoughtful. 'It might also make the police think he had some- thing to do with Smart's death,' he said. 'I'll get on to him in the morning. He can't just dump you and end our arrangement willy-nilly. I've paid good money to have him train you up, and so far you've done very well. So we need to think about how to build on that. If he's packing it in – even for a short time – you'd better follow up with this cousin of his, and we'll see what other contacts you can make. If Lubin isn't taking pictures there'll be a gap in the market which maybe we can fill. You know what they say: one man's disaster is another man's opportunity?'

Kate nodded somewhat wanly. 'Tatiana's a bit critical, of me not the pictures,' she said. 'She says I need to smarten up, buy some more fashionable gear . . . but I'm pretty skint. I lost most of my clothes in the fire at our flat. If you want me to do fashion I can't look as if I just got off the train from Lime Street.'

'Dear God, am I supposed to dress you now? That's a new one. The blokes'll be asking me to buy them flowery shirts and ties next in case they look too old-fashioned when they're out on assignment. They'll want to ponce around like that detective boyfriend of yours if we're not careful – next best thing to a poof.'

Kate shook her head but knew better than to protest about any of Ken's assumptions. 'I certainly can't go to this do Tatiana wants me to cover unless I look a bit smart,' she insisted. 'It wouldn't do the agency's reputation any good, would it? I haven't even got the dress I went to Ray Robertson's boxing gala in, because I lost it in the fire and anyway I can see now it's a bit 1950s. I've learned that much.'

Fellows pulled a sour face but reached into his back pocket and peeled a couple of ten-pound notes off the roll of cash he brought out. 'See what you can get for that,' he said grudgingly as he handed them over. 'And don't think you can do this again in a hurry. There'd better be a lot of commissions coming in to make it worthwhile.'

Kate gave Fellows a flashing smile. 'I'll see if I can get a bargain or two,' she said. 'Perhaps I can go shopping in the morning before I come in? Carnaby Street is supposed to be good. Or Bazaar.'

'Be here by lunchtime,' Fellows said. 'I should have sorted Lubin out by then and then we'll see where we go next.'

Smiling broadly, Kate made her way through the main office, where a few of her male colleagues were packing up for the day and looked at her curiously as she passed by their desks, but they made no comment. Most had still not come to terms with the idea of a female photographer in their midst and she knew from their expressions even now that some of them never would.

On her way down Frith Street she passed the open door of the Jazz Cellar just as Stan Weston and Chris Swift were coming out, neither of them looking very happy.

'Hi,' she said. 'I'll have some pictures to show you from the other night as soon as I've developed them. Sorry I've taken so long over them but I've been a bit busy with one

thing and another. Can I bring them round tomorrow maybe?'
Weston looked at her for a moment as if he did not quite
recognize her. He looked tired and seriously worried, dark
bags under his eyes. 'The photographer girl,' Swift said. 'You let her take pictures
the other night. You remember, before we got done over by
the Old Bill.'

Weston nodded and offered Kate a faint smile. 'Oh yes,
course,' he said. 'Tomorrow'll be fine. Hopefully we'll be back
to normal tomorrow.'

'You're not normal yet?' Kate asked, surprised. 'No one
got hurt, did they? You should see the way the bizzies wade
in on a Liverpool Saturday night when they've found something
– or someone – they've taken a dislike to. They chuck them
into the paddy wagons like sides of beef when they've finished
with them. Half of them are unconscious by the time they get
to the bridewell.'

'Depends on whether you think getting arrested is the same
as getting hurt,' Swift said tartly. 'They kept me there all night
for no reason at all that I could see, and Muddy Abraham's
still there.'

Kate was slightly surprised by the vehemence Swift showed.
He had seemed the least talkative of the band members when
she had been taking photographs of them, almost to the point
of avoiding her lens if he could. She had wondered if he was
one of those people who really hate having their photograph
taken.

'We can't put on a normal show, not with Muddy Abraham
still banged up,' Weston said angrily. 'People come a long
way to hear him. We're on our way to see a brief to see if we
can get him out. They've only charged him with possession
of marijuana, that's not enough to be remanded for days at a
time. I don't know what the hell's going on.'

Kate could see how worried the band leader was. 'I may
know someone who does know what's going on, but I've no
way of contacting him just now,' she said. 'I know he's in a
meeting. I'll see what I can find out later and tell you when
I bring your pictures in tomorrow. See you later.' And she
swung on down the street wondering why she felt distinctly

elated by the idea of putting in a call to Harry Barnard, even if it was on someone else's behalf.

But when she finally made contact at the station with Barnard the sergeant did not sound particularly pleased to hear her voice and sounded exceedingly reluctant to explain why exactly Muddy Abraham was still languishing in a cell.

'Something else dodgy has come up with Abraham,' was all he would say over the phone.

'This is another case of you lot trying to pin things on a black man because you don't like the look of him, is it?' she asked angrily. 'Like in Notting Hill?'

'Not me, darling,' Barnard came back quickly. 'This is nothing to do with me, honest to God, believe me.'

But Kate had already hung up without saying goodbye.

'Damn and blast,' Barnard said to himself after he listened to the crackling of the dead line for a moment before he realized Kate had gone. He had been distracted from the Muddy Abraham case when Ricky Smart's body had been discovered but he knew he had also been curiously reluctant to pass on to DCI Jackson what he had learned about Abraham's history at the American embassy. But his instinct for self-protection kicked in hard now and he carefully inserted a sheet of paper into the typewriter on his desk and painstakingly began to type up his report on the American musician with two fingers, aiming for it to be on the DCI's desk before complaints from the Jazz cellar's lawyers hit the same spot.

Kate succeeded in prising Tess out of school for a couple of hours the next morning when she had free periods from teaching and they made their way to the Kings Road in arty Chelsea where it was immediately obvious that fashion had moved into a whole new dimension just a couple of under-ground stations from where they shared a flat in Shepherd's Bush.

'If they wore their skirts much shorter they'd get arrested,' Tess said as they followed a couple of skinny girls in very short skirts and patterned tights into Mary Quant's Bazaar emporium, the first shop she had opened in the mid-fifties long before she became well known as the leader of the fashion revolution.

'I must have one,' Kate said, her eyes gleaming with excitement.

'They wouldn't let me into school in one of those,' Tess said. 'They're already bringing out a tape measure when some of the girls hitch their uniform up round their knickers. I can just guess how this is going to go down with the nuns at St Aloysius back home. Not that I really want to look like a tart, anyway.'

'Oh, come on, la, this is just a bit of fun. I'm going to get a skirt and some boots, and then see if I can find a slinky top to go to this do Tatiana wants me to take pictures at.'

'Will that do?' Tess asked doubtfully. 'What a pity we lost so much stuff in the fire. You could have worn that lovely green dress you got at Bon Marche. You looked really great in that.'

'Even if I still had it, it's just the sort of thing Tatiana hates,' Kate said. 'She's aiming to be the next Mary Quant. Her hero is some French designer who's gone all geometric, black and white and long shiny boots. I wouldn't go that far, but I do want her to think I've made an effort to get into the groove. Come on. I'll try some boots. Come and help me choose. Let's live dangerously for once.'

In the end she came away with a black miniskirt that ended mid-thigh, some patterned tights and a pair of knee-high black boots and, as an afterthought, a soft peaked cap, which she immediately put on and pulled down rakishly over one eye.

'You look like a barrow-boy,' Tess complained, laughing. 'You'll never get away with all that when you go home to see your mam.'

'Don't you believe it,' Kate said. 'I bet you the kids in the Cavern are into all this gear. Those wretched beehive hairdos and massive skirts were disappearing even before we left. This is the sixties.'

'Maybe you're right,' Tess said. 'But if the head of Fifth year is tearing a strip off girls who've shortened their school skirts by rolling them over to make them shorter, what are they going to say to the staff? They'll be measuring us with tape measures too, la, if this goes on.'

'Nothing less,' Kate said. 'Now I must get over to Tatiana's studio to show her this lot, and I'll have a look around Oxford Street to see if I can pick up a good blouse to go with them. See you later, alligator.'

'In a while,' Tess muttered gloomily as she looked for a bus to take her back to Holland Park and the confines of school. She was, she thought, just a little bit jealous of her friend.

'Mm, that's not bad,' Tatiana Broughton-Clarke conceded when Kate displayed her purchases with undiminished enthusiasm an hour or so later. 'You say Ken Fellows helped you out? That's a coup anyway. He's not known for chucking money about.'

'He's frightened that Andrei will close the studio down after this murder. Andrei seems to be wondering if anyone's coming for him next. So Ken's looking for new ways into the fashion scene.'

'Andrei always was a scaredy cat, even when we were kids,' Tatiana said. 'It was Ricky who was the driving force in that set-up, the one with the ideas and the energy to get things done. Andrei provided the contacts but Ricky did the work. Andrei won't be able to cope on his own.' She looked thoughtful for a moment, as if trying to work out the implications of her cousin's predicament for her own business.

'So put your new gear on then,' she said eventually. 'Let's have a look at the new you. You can change behind that screen if you're shy.'

Kate did as she was told, ran a comb through her dark curls and stood for a moment before a full-length mirror, liking what she saw.

When she emerged, Tatiana agreed. 'Not bad at all,' she said walking round her and pulling the outfit straight there and there. 'I think that'll do for Rupert's next little gathering. After all, you're going to be working. aren't you? You're not going to be one of the guests as such. No need for couture or anything. So tell Ken that I'd like to go ahead with that idea. And I'll be in touch when I've got some more designs ready to launch. In the meantime he should tout you round the fashion houses. You're not half a bad little photographer, you know.'

After he left the nick that evening, having given up on the passing fancy that he might persuade Kate O'Donnell out for a meal a little later on, he took a detour back to his manor and peered into the murky bar of one of the less fashionable pubs in the area, which he knew was an occasional haunt of some of the Maltese who lived and worked off the back of local prostitutes. It was early and the bar was almost empty but he did spot one familiar figure hunched over a half-drunk pint at a corner table. He pushed open the swing door and put a none-too-gentle hand on Joe Inglott's shoulder.

'Long time no see, Joseph,' he said. 'But you're just the man I need to talk to.'

The dark eyes in a thin, walnut face popped and Inglott wriggled out of Barnard's unwelcome grip.

'Come on, Joe,' Barnard said easily, taking the seat across from his victim in such a way that he could not easily move from his own seat. 'A little chat is all I want. You've done well enough out of me over the years to help me out when I badly need it. I want to know what's going on with your man and the girls. It looks to me as if someone's been trying to muscle in and we both know Mr Falzon won't be very happy about that.'

'I don't know anything about anything like that,' Inglott insisted. 'The Man is in Malta, I heard. Gone to see his mother who is ill, dying maybe.'

'So what are you saying? He's too far away to know what's going down on his patch? I don't believe that for a minute. He has eyes and ears here and I believe international phone calls are much better than they used to be.'

'I don't know anything about things like that, Mr Barnard, I swear to God I don't.'

'A girl who was obviously on the game, very young, was found dead, you know that. Was she one of yours?' Barnard snapped. 'Did she annoy your boss in some way? Was she punished for stepping out of line, or was she being organized by someone else entirely – Ray Robertson maybe – wanting in on the trade, or someone completely new?'

Inglott buried his face in his nearly empty glass and shrugged helplessly. 'I heard she was a new girl, someone we didn't know, that's all I heard, honest to God.'

'So are we on the edge of a gang war, here, Joe? Or just a minor skirmish to warn someone off? My boss is very anxious to know. You know I'm not mean if the information is good.'

'I'll keep an ear open for you, Mr Barnard, I promise,' Inglott said, his face chalk white and the hands holding his empty glass trembling visibly.

'When is your boss likely to be back from Malta?' Barnard asked.

'No one knows that,' Inglott said. 'I think he doesn't know that himself. It is his mother, you understand.'

Barnard sighed heavily. 'So I have to rely on you, Joe. You need to come up with the goods. Understand?' He got up from his seat and gave Inglott's shoulder another heavy squeeze. 'Let's meet again,' he said. 'This time the day after tomorrow. It will be worth your while if you can tell me something useful, I promise.'

'I try, Mr Barnard, I try.'

# FOURTEEN

K ate O'Donnell looked at DS Harry Barnard with a mixture of fury and incredulity.

'He what?' she asked, putting down her coffee so hard that it slopped over her desk at Ken Fellow's agency and threatened to spoil a batch of contact prints she had been working with. Looking embarrassed, and closely watched by a couple of Kate's colleagues who were sitting at the far end of the photographers' room, Barnard dug a handkerchief out of his pocket and made an attempt to mop up the spilled liquid.

'Here, give it to me,' Kate said impatiently, completing the task quickly and handing him back a sodden white handkerchief now stained brown. 'So why on earth does DCI Jackson want to see me in such a hurry?'

'Lubin has locked up the studio and disappeared,' Barnard said. 'You're the only person we knew of who we could contact. I know it sounds pathetic but I did call his cousin, what's her name? Titania?'

'Tatiana,' Kate said crisply. 'Doesn't she know where Andrei has gone?'

'He could be anywhere from New York to Venice, apparently,' he said. 'Anywhere, in fact, except Russia.'

'No, he certainly wouldn't go there,' Kate said feelingly. 'You should hear him ranting about Khrushchev and Fidel Castro and the mess they got us into last year.'

'Well, they did nearly start World War Three,' Barnard said feelingly. 'They're worth a rant. I'm not one to panic but I did go to bed that night not sure I'd still be here next morning.'

'Yeah, it was scary. A lot of the students at college stayed up all night singing stuff, as if that would make nuclear bombs go away.'

'Anyway, Lubin has bolted, the place is locked up and Jackson reckons you're the person who might help us with our inquiries and he wants to talk to you right now, no ands or buts or excuses. I didn't want to send some uniformed clod over to bring you in and let you think you were under arrest so I came myself.'

'Well, thanks,' Kate said unconvincingly. 'Does your boss know I have some history with you people?'

'I filled him in,' Barnard admitted. 'Judiciously,' he added. 'Though as he has me down as a queer because I choose to wear the odd Liberty's flowery tie, that may have been a mistake. As he will happily tell you himself, he doesn't like poofs and nancy boys. He wants them all locked up.'

'I'll bear that in mind,' Kate said drily, thinking of her brother. 'Come on then, let's get this over. I've got work to do.'

They walked together to the police station through the bustling streets of Soho, past Berwick Street market which always attracted crowds of shoppers to its overflowing fruit and vegetable stalls, set up just a stone's throw from the city's main shopping arteries. At the end of Marlborough Street, where the magistrate's courts were just beginning to pull in defendants and lawyers for the day's business, Kate steered Barnard into Carnaby Street.

'Tatiana reckons I need to splash out a bit if I'm going to become a fashion photographer,' she said. 'Let's see what they've got down here.'

Barnard glanced at his watch. 'Five minutes,' he said, humouring her. 'The DCI's not a patient man. He really wanted to send a plod to fetch you. I can just imagine how you would have felt about that. I had to work really hard to talk him out of it.'

Kate shrugged. "Let's get it over with then,' she said. 'It shouldn't take long. I really don't think I can tell you much about Andrei or Ricky that you don't know already. You realize I'll have to tell him that Ricky attacked me.'

'That's fine. Just keep my name out of it,' Barnard said.

He took Kate to an interview room and brought her a cup of coffee before reporting back to DCI Jackson.

'Do you want me to sit in, guv?' he asked.

'You can take notes,' Jackson said frostily. 'But I'll ask the questions as you know the girl.' He led the way back to the interview room and sat down opposite Kate, waving Barnard to a hard chair by the door.

'Good morning, Miss O'Donnell,' Jackson said. 'I understand you've been here before.'

Kate nodded warily. Her brother's brush with the law was not something she wanted to go over with this unsmiling, pink-faced Scot, especially after what Barnard had told her about him. 'How can I help?' she asked.

'How long have you been employed at Andrei Lubin's studio?' Jackson asked.

'I'm not strictly speaking employed there,' she said. 'I work at the Ken Fellows Agency, but I'm at Lubin's place for a month to learn something about fashion photography. I'm in the middle of my second week.'

'So your impressions of what has been going on there are extremely limited,' Jackson said with some irritation.

'It's a very small set-up,' Kate said. 'Just Andrei taking pictures and Ricky doing most of the admin and fixing, and recruiting the models, of course. That seems – seemed – to be his speciality. There's a part-time secretary called June, who pops in and out, and the girls come in as and when they're needed.'

'The girls?' Jackson said. 'Jenny Maitland was one of the models Lubin used, I understand? And she seems to have ended up on the street before she was killed. Did anyone know how that happened.'

'I never heard anyone suggest how that might have happened,' Kate said. 'I never met her, of course, and I'm not sure how many of the other girls knew her personally. She worked there months ago, apparently, and the turnover is very high. I never picked up that anyone had seen her recently. But there was another death as well as poor Jenny. Sylvia Hubbard, who died after an abortion, and was working there until a few days ago. It was Sylvia who told me that Andrei and Ricky Smart used the girls themselves for sex. I was horrified, some of them were very young. I tried to get out of the place, but my boss was very keen for me to stay till my time was up.'

'Did this girl say that one of the men at the studio was the father of her baby?' Jackson asked, not hiding his distaste.

'She said either of them could have been,' Kate said quietly.

'And did she know Jenny Maitland?'

'She did,' Kate said. 'She was very upset by her death.'

'And did she offer any explanation for why Jenny Maitland ended up as a tart? Do you think either of these men at the studio put her up to it?'

'They could have done, I suppose, but I've no way of knowing if they did. Sylvia didn't say anything about that.'

'And did either of the men make advances to you, Miss O'Donnell?' Jackson asked.

Kate flushed slightly and glanced at Barnard who was studiously gazing at his notes. 'Andrei didn't but Ricky always had his hands on anybody female who got close enough. The girls – anyone, really – learned to avoid him. But you had to be fast on your feet.' Kate, her face pink, glanced at Barnard again before going on, wondering what he was thinking. 'He followed me home two nights ago and tried to barge into the flat,' she went on. 'I don't know what he'd have done if my flatmate hadn't turned up minutes behind me. Ricky ran off . . . I think he'd have raped me if he could.'

'Have you reported this officially?' Jackson snapped.

Kate hesitated and then decided she could not dodge the question. 'I told my boss but he told me it would be impossible to prove unless my friend Tess could identify him. It was dark and she didn't get a good look at him as he barged past her. He hadn't done me any serious harm so I decided to take Mr Fellows' advice and not report it. I was going to tackle Ricky about it the next day, but he never turned up while I was there and the next thing I knew he was dead.'

'I should think you were quite pleased to hear that, weren't you, Miss O'Donnell?' Jackson asked.

Kate gasped. 'That's a terrible thing to say,' she said angrily. 'I wouldn't go to his funeral if you paid me, but I'd never wish anyone dead, not even Ricky Smart.'

Jackson swung round in his chair. 'What do you think about that, Sergeant?' he asked.

Barnard sighed. 'I think Miss O'Donnell's boss was right,' he said. 'We might believe her but you know as well as I do how hard it is to make an allegation like that stick if there's no cast-iron witness to back up what she says, and how unpleasant it can be in court for the victim.'

'That's because so many stupid girls think they can get back at their ex-boyfriends by crying rape,' Jackson said flatly, as if there was no room for argument. 'It's the easiest allegation in the world to make and the hardest to prove. It happens all the time.'

'I'm not a liar,' Kate said, still fuming. 'It happened, exactly as I told Ken Fellows, and my flatmate saw it happening, but she doesn't know Ricky Smart and it was too dark for her to identify him even vaguely.'

'So let's move on, shall we?' Jackson said, turning his attention back to Kate, his blue eyes hard. 'I'm told that Smart trawled the East End schools for likely girls to model for his boss. Can you be sure that was all he was recruiting them for?'

'None of the girls I met at the studio seemed to suspect that there was anything more to it, though they knew that Andrei might try to get them into bed and then chuck them out at a moment's notice. I just assumed that most of them went home again. They were very young to be in the West End on their own. But obviously Jenny didn't do that, so maybe Andrei, or Ricky, had other plans for them all along. I just don't know. I can't tell you. I've known them all less than two weeks . . .'

'Did the models ever talk about meeting Smart for the first time?' Jackson asked. 'Did you get the impression it had always happened at a school? Outside the gates?'

'I know Jenny Maitland and Sylvia Hubbard went to the same school but Sylvia was a year behind Jenny. She told me that.'

'We've identified that school,' Barnard offered from his chair by the door.

Jackson glanced at him with some irritation. 'Did any of the girls mention anywhere else they might have been recruited?' he asked.

Kate shrugged. 'I don't think so,' she said. 'There wasn't much time for chit-chat. Andrei worked them very hard while they were at the studio. They were glad to get out of the place when he'd finished with them, I think. They didn't hang around.'

'Do you know where any of them were living?'

'No,' Kate said. 'I did think it was odd because I know how difficult it is to find places to rent, and they can't have been earning much from Andrei's efforts. But I didn't get the impression they were going home to mum every evening.'

'Never mind,' Jackson said. 'We'll get a search warrant for the studio and break in if we have to. There must be records in there of who was employed and where they lived, if only for the Inland Revenue.'

'June did all the paperwork,' Kate said. 'I do remember her saying that she lived in Lewisham and came in on the train. She was quite chatty. She'll tell you far more than I can if you can track her down.'

'Right, Miss O'Donnell, I think that will be all for now,' Jackson said. 'Sergeant Barnard will show you out.' And with that he collected up his papers and walked out.

Barnard walked back to Soho with Kate. She refused his offer of a coffee at the Blue Lagoon and they parted at the door to the Fellows Agency with a kiss on Kate's cheek that seemed tentative on both sides. Barnard left her with a sigh and took a stroll round his manor, without his usual enthusiasm, then headed back towards the nick by way of the Delilah Club, where he thought he might catch Ray Robertson for a chat, in the hope that his more exotic criminal ambitions might have been abandoned by now. But as he turned the corner towards the club's main doors he drew back. Ray Robertson himself was coming out of the swing doors with another man, both similarly dressed in heavy camel coats and turned-down trilbies, and looking similarly pleased with themselves. They were heading towards Robertson's Jag, which was parked outside. Barnard froze, pulling his own hat low, but not so low that he could not watch what was going on from under the brim.

What spooked him entirely was that he recognized the man who was ushered into the back of the Jag before Robertson followed. His name was Reg Smith and he ran one of the biggest crime enterprises in London, but strictly south of the river, well away from Robertson's fiefdoms in Soho and the East End. But if he and Ray were having

friendly meetings, Barnard thought angrily, then maybe Fred
Bettany was right to be worried about what his boss was up
to. Having been rebuffed in Notting Hill, Ray might be
responding like a spoilt child who's had his toys taken away.
Barnard had seen him do that as a twelve-year-old boy, and
had no doubt he could do it again, with devastating conse-
quences for someone, quite possibly Robertson himself.

He crossed Regent Street and found a phone box and called
Fred Bettany's home number where his wife picked up the
phone quickly.

'Harry,' she murmured. 'How nice to hear from you. Are
you free to come round?'

''Fraid not,' he said. 'I'm at work, babe. But I need to talk
to Fred urgently. I've just seen Ray schmoozing the biggest
crook in south London and I need to know what the hell he
thinks he's up to.'

Barnard heard Shirley draw a sharp breath. 'I knew Fred
was worried about something,' she said. 'He's been very jumpy
for weeks. Do you want me to get him to call you?'

'At home this evening, if he can,' Barnard said. 'Before Ray
ends up in the next cell to Reynolds and Biggs and the rest
of them. I reckon he's trying to bite off a whole lot more than
he can chew.'

'Oh dear,' Shirley said doubtfully. 'I'll get him to call,
darling. But don't be a stranger. Please.'

'I'll see you soon,' Barnard said and hung up quickly, the
pleading in her voice touching an unexpected nerve. But
however unhappy Shirley Bettany was with Barnard's long
absence from her bed, she was as good as her word in passing
on his message and at eight o'clock that evening the sergeant
took a call from Ray Robertson's accountant and told him
succinctly who he had seen him coming out of the Delilah
Club with that lunchtime. He heard Fred draw a sharp breath
at the other end of the line.

'Jesus wept,' he said. 'I told him he was crazy to think he
could get involved with that maniac,' he said. 'Ray's never
been on the right side of the law, as far as I know, but he's
not a killer and he's not greedy. He's made a good living
sticking to what he knows. But ever since the train robbery,

even after most of them were arrested, he's been moaning about how many millions they got away with, and how he'd like to retire to the sun in Spain or somewhere and relax. I ask you? What would a born-and-bred East End boy like him do in Spain, for God's sake.'

'He'd hate the oily food,' Barnard said. 'He's a pie-and-chips man, is Ray, through and through.'

'He'd never get as far as Spain in any case,' Fred said. 'That bastard Smith would run rings round him, use him up and throw him away.'

'Given the things Smith's being investigated for Ray wouldn't last a week working with him. The latest thing, apparently, is a bloke who got on the wrong side of him and was found nailed to the floor like Jesus bloody Christ before he was shot. Ray's not in that league for violence or – to be honest, Fred – brain power.'

'So how do we stop him?' Fred asked. 'I've tried to talk him out of it. But I tried to persuade him not to try to move into Notting Hill and that didn't work. Even now he knows I was right about that he's still not listening to my advice. I've been seriously thinking about getting out and moving on myself.'

'Don't do that, Fred,' Barnard said, hoping that his voice would not betray quite how fervently he did not want the Bettanys to move on anywhere. 'Ray would be lost without you.' And so would I if you took Shirley away, he thought. He hesitated for no more than a moment. 'I'll go and see him again myself tomorrow, if I get the chance,' he said.

'He'll be at the Delilah in the morning,' Fred said. 'I do know that. You could catch him then.'

'Fine,' Barnard said. 'I'll see what I can do.'

# FIFTEEN

'The best thing for you to do until Lubin comes back is to see if you can get any more work out of his cousin,' Ken Fellows said, putting an arm round Kate's shoulders as she sat at her desk the next morning at a loose end. She pulled away irritably. 'Tatiana did say that there would be more when she'd completed her next set of designs,' she said. 'I could stroll round there and see how it's going. She may know when Andrei's likely to be back as well.' Anything to get out of the office where her premature return from her fashion studio assignment had been greeted with a certain amount of derision by her colleagues who seemed to regard the sight of a woman with a camera as some sort of aberrant mutation. Their contempt did not seem to be diminishing with time, however much her pictures met with the boss's approval. But since she had come back to the agency she was undoubtedly bored and glad of any excuse to get out of the office.

She strolled down Oxford Street slowly, window-shopping as she went, before turning into the side streets behind the big stores with their shiny Christmas displays and weaving her way to Tatiana Broughton-Clarke's cramped studio. She could see lights inside and Tatiana's assistant opened the door and waved her up the narrow staircase. If anyone dropped a match in one of these old buildings, Kate thought, the whole block would go up like Liverpool's docklands in the war. She had been regaled as a child with stories of the bombing of the port, something blitzed Londoners seemed totally unaware of. But then, she thought, it seemed to her that they had always thought they were the centre of the world, if not the universe. Nowhere else existed.

Tatiana did not seem too surprised to see her and took the pins out of her mouth to acknowledge her arrival with a smile.

'I'm at a loose end with Andrei gone,' Kate said. 'Ken Fellows wondered how another shoot would suit you. If you've got anything ready to show, of course.'

'Well, not quite yet,' Tatiana said waving a hand at the parts of various garments she was working on, none of which seemed to have been sewn together yet. 'But come in and have a coffee, darlink. I want you to tell me all about what's been happening with poor Ricky and Andrei. Ricky was a spiv but a useful spiv, in some ways. I'll miss him.'

'It looks as if someone had enough of him,' Kate said.

'Surely the police don't really think Andrei is the murderer, do they?' Tatiana said. 'Surely that's a crazy idea? He likes to pretend to be some dashing Cossack but the truth is he's a damp squib, completely useless in a crisis. Roddy took him out shooting once and he dropped his gun in a bog. Took them hours to clean it up.'

'They certainly want to talk to him,' Kate said. 'And so does my boss. And I do too, as it goes. I left some stuff at the studio that I want to get hold of if he's not going to open the place up again. I've no idea where the girl who came in to do the typing lives. In any case she probably hasn't got a key. In spite of what you say Andrei did seem to be running a fairly successful business,' Kate complained mildly as Tatiana poured coffee into two mugs and made space amongst the clutter for them to sit down.

'Don't you believe it,' Tatiana said. 'Ricky is – was, excuse me – the driving force there, believe me. Andrei will be completely lost without him. Not that I think Ricky would have stayed there much longer. I happen to know he had a lot of irons in the fire, as it goes. He was keen to make the big time.'

'Yes, I suppose that makes sense, Andrei did rely on Ricky. He'll be lost without him,' Kate conceded, remembering how Andrei himself did little more than take the pictures, leaving all the rest to his energetic – and unscrupulous – assistant.

'Was he really killed in that rather nice Alfa Romeo he was driving?' Tatiana asked. 'What a shame. I rather fancied that car when he'd finished with it, if I could persuade Roddy to disburse of course. Until I get my own money coming in I'm rather dependent on him. I'd really love my own car. At the moment I have to take the underground to Amersham and get Roddy to pick me up there. His family may have once owned a chunk of Buckinghamshire, but the land's mostly gone now and Roddy's as tight-fisted as a Russian peasant with winter coming on.'

Kate sipped her coffee slowly. 'So when do you think you might be ready for another shoot?' she asked eventually. 'If Andrei's moved on permanently my boss wants me to build up my own contacts in fashion. There should be a few of Andrei's clients looking for a new agency, shouldn't there?'

'Oh, Andrei will be back,' Tatiana said airily. 'I don't suppose for half a minute he had anything to do with Ricky's nasty death. I know he doesn't like the sight of blood. He was not at all keen on Roddy's shooting party even before he dropped his gun. Squeamish, Roddy said he was. If the police want to talk to him he'll either realize himself that he'd better get it over with, or they'll track him down. He's got a little place somewhere on the coast in Suffolk that his mother left him. That's where he'll be.'

'Is he on the phone there?' Kate asked. 'My boss would really like to talk to him.'

Tatiana laughed and shook her head. 'It's just a fisherman's hovel. He hardly ever goes there. His mother was a shop-girl his father took a fancy to. She grew up out there – what's it called? Southwold, I think. Some fairly scruffy seaside place. Her father worked in a brewery or something. He'll never tell you all this. He likes to pretend he's a Russian count. It goes down well with some of those society women he takes photographs of. But he's really no more than a peasant on his mother's side.'

Tatiana looked critically at Kate's outfit. 'I like the little cap,' she said. 'Did you buy some other new clothes as well?'

'I did,' Kate said. 'I got another miniskirt and some boots in Carnaby Street. And the cap.'

'Mmm,' Tatiana said. 'I'll see if I can run you up a blouse, something silky and on trend, black and beige, maybe, and let you know the details for Roddy's next little do. Andrei's definitely not going to do the snaps any more. He said something to Roddy the last time he came to our place. I don't know what it was about but Roddy said he wouldn't have him there again. They've never really got on. Pity

really. It would be better to keep it in the family but you'll
have to do.'

Kate bit back a sharp retort at that. 'Do you know Andrei's
address on the coast?' she asked. 'If he's not on the phone I
suppose Ken Fellows could write to him and ask him to get
in touch. Or I could.'

Tatiana reached into her capacious bag, which was flung
amongst the patterns and fabrics on the table, and pulled out
a notebook. 'There you are,' she said, copying out a few lines
on to a scrap of paper. 'I'm not sure he's there but it's the
obvious place for him to hole up for a few days. But I'm sure
he'll be back soon, anyway. He's built up something of a
business I suppose, and he won't want to lose it, whatever's
happened to Ricky. Perhaps he'll offer you a job, but I warn
you, you'll end up doing all the work for very little of the
money, just like Ricky.'

'Ricky never seemed short of a bob or two,' Kate said.

'Ah, well, Ricky had a lot of irons in the fire, didn't he?
He was a very enterprising chap, was Ricky and didn't have
many scruples if there was money in it. Surprising really that
he didn't get on better with my Roddy. They'd have made a
good team. But it looks as if one of Ricky's schemes has gone
a bit awry and annoyed someone very nasty. We'll probably
never know. Now I must get on. Nice to see you, dear, and
I'll let you know when the next designs are ready. And about
the party. Promise, darlink. You can tell your boss that.'

Kate strolled slowly back along Oxford Street wondering
whether she should try to contact Andrei Lubin herself or leave
it to Ken Fellows. And should she, she wondered, tell Harry
Barnard where Andrei Lubin could be holed up? Perhaps she
would leave that decision to Ken.

It was lunchtime before DS Harry Barnard found time to chase
up Ray Robertson. When he had hung up his coat in the CID
office that morning, and parried the usual raucous ribbing
about his latest tie, he had found DCI Keith Jackson breathing
down his neck.

'This report you left me about the American jazz player,'
he said. 'We need words.'

Barnard followed the DCI back to his office and took the hard chair he was waved into.

'Right,' Jackson said. 'It's very clear that the yanks want him back pretty badly. The man you saw, Saprelli?'

'Lieutenant Saprelli,' Barnard said. 'He seems to hold some sort of a watching brief for GIs who never went home. You wouldn't think they'd bother after all this time, but apparently they do. They certainly want Muddy Abraham back, or whatever they think his real name is.'

'They've not wasted any time. They've written to the Yard asking permission to interview Abraham, with a view to his eventual extradition to face a murder – or, as they call it, a homicide – indictment. And remember it's still a capital offence over there. I want you to liaise with Saprelli and Brixton Prison and sit in on the interview. You'd better make sure he has a brief as well. We don't want to be accused of any infringement of the rules when it comes to court. By the book on this one, Sergeant. Strictly by the book. I don't want any bleeding-heart lawyer getting him off somehow.'

'Guv,' Barnard said, his face impassive. 'I never asked Saprelli whether the incident happened in this country. Would that make a difference?'

'The American forces over here were responsible for their own military law. It wouldn't make a blind bit of difference to Abraham's situation. If they can prove he's who they think he is and provide *prima facie* evidence at an extradition hearing, he'll be on his way. If he's an American and his victim was an American, and they were both US soldiers, then the trial will be American. So let's get the process started, shall we.'

Jackson's expression was implacable and Barnard knew there would be no budging him. He knew his prejudices and they ran deep.

'I'll get straight on to it, guv,' Barnard said and had set off to do just that, silently aware of how reluctant he felt to consign a black Muddy Abraham to US military justice and a possible death sentence. I must be getting softer than I thought, he told himself as he picked up the phone back in CID and dialled the American embassy's number.

It was almost lunchtime by the time the arrangements had

been finalized for Barnard and Saprelli to interview Abraham
at Brixton the next day. Only then could Barnard put on his
hat and coat again and make his escape from the nick, and
stroll through the pale winter sunshine to the Delilah Club.
He found Ray sitting in his comfortable executive chair behind
his huge desk, smouldering cigar in one hand, a beatific smile
on his face and his eyes closed.

'G'morning, Flash,' he said, without opening his eyes in
spite of being obviously aware of Barnard's arrival. 'Take a
seat,' he said. 'Have you arrested any likely gangsters this
morning? Doing your job of protecting the great British public
from the likes of me, are you? Or are you more interested in
getting your own sticky fingers into the till?'

Robertson's eyes suddenly opened wide and his blue eyes
flashed without any sign of warmth. What's bugging him?
Barnard wondered, not expecting to have moved from one
antagonistic environment to another.

'How's tricks?' Robertson asked grudgingly, before opening
a desk drawer and pulling out a bottle of Scotch and two
glasses into which he poured generous measures and pushed
one across the desk to Barnard.

'Not too bad, thanks,' Barnard said as Robertson settled
back in his seat again. 'Cheers.'

'Someone seems to be annoying my Mediterranean buddies
and I don't like it. Have you got any idea who?' Robertson
asked.

'We did have a couple of possibles but one's scarpered and
the other's got his throat cut, possibly by the first fella,' Barnard
said lightly. 'We're working on it.'

'That would be Ricky Smart,' Robertson said. 'I'd had heard
some whispers about him, as it goes. Picking up girls for modelling. As if. What are their pathetic parents thinking of? So maybe
Falzon's solved the problem without my help. Do you reckon?'

'Could be,' Barnard said cautiously. 'I'll keep you in the
picture. That wasn't why I popped in, as it happens.'

Robertson took a sip of his drink and smiled the smile of
a tiger sizing up dinner. 'Out with it then,' he said.

'I saw you yesterday with Reg Smith,' Barnard said cautiously.
'I just happened to be passing as you came out of the club.'

'Yeah, I thought you did,' Robertson said unabashed. 'I caught a glimpse of you as we got into the car. And so?'

'And so,' Barnard said. 'What are you plotting with that toe-rag? By rights he should have been hanged years ago when it was still an option, but no one will testify against him. Half of London south of the river is terrified of him. What the hell are you up to?'

'We're just having a friendly exchange of views,' Robertson said. 'Nothing for you and your DCI to get worried or upset about.'

'I think I need to get worried, Ray. The sort of thing Smith is into gets the whole weight of Scotland Yard thrown at it. It'll not be just the vice squad. They're still pursuing him for that armed robbery in Lewisham where two cashiers were shot. This isn't the sort of thing you want to get involved in, is it? If it is, you can't count on me to help if the Yard come sniffing round, poking their noses into your affairs here up West or in the East End. This is big time, nothing to do with vice in Soho. It's way over my head. Just remember how quickly the great train robbers came to grief. Not so great in the end, that lot. They'll spend the rest of their lives banged up.'

'You're a good lad, Flash,' Robertson said. 'But life doesn't stand still, you know. Things move on. You have to be ambitious in this life or you start to slide backwards. I've got one or two new projects on the go at the minute, business and pleasure. You should be doing the same yourself, going for Inspector, moving onwards and upwards, as you do. Getting a ring for that pretty little girl you've been chasing. I'll be all right, Harry. I can look after myself, always have, always will.'

'But better not with Smith,' Barnard said. 'Believe me.' He sighed. There was a limit to how far he could push Ray without provoking a fit of rage that, while it would pale in comparison to his brother Georgie's outbursts, was still not to be ignored. Telling him that Smith was a force of nature he would be unlikely to cope with risked an eruption that he really did not want and quite possibly could not handle.

'Don't blame me if he takes you for a ride,' he said quietly. 'Don't say you weren't warned.'

'It's good of you to worry, Flash, but you really don't need to, boy.' Robertson stubbed out the glowing end of his cigar and sat up straight in his chair. 'There's really no need at all. I'm moving up a league, that's all. You should do the same. We've both been stuck in a rut too long.'

Kate O'Donnell got back to the flat early that evening and helped Tess cook a meal before her friend settled down to a pile of exercise books to mark. Kate was restless. She watched the television news on their newly acquired black-and-white set and smiled faintly at pictures of the Beatles being mobbed outside the Cavern by a crowd of young girls on one of their increasingly rare trips back to Liverpool. But it only occupied half her mind, which returned again and again to the fate of Ricky Smart and Andrei Lubin's disappearance. Was it guilt or fear that had driven him away from the studio, she kept asking herself? Had he killed Ricky or did he fear that he would be next? She wondered whether to ring Harry Barnard, who would probably be at home by now. She was sure that not telling him where Andrei might be probably constituted some sort of crime and she was sure that the police would be able to track him down in a small seaside town. But still she hesitated, partly because she did not want to give in to her own secret desire to see the importunate policeman again, and partly because she was anxious to talk to the photographer again herself before he possibly disappeared into police custody for good.

She was still debating with herself when the phone rang, still able to make her jump with its unfamiliarity.

'I'll get it,' she said to Tess. The fact that it was Andrei Lubin's voice, slightly muffled, at the other end, set her heart racing.

'Andrei, where are you?' she asked. 'Do you know the police are looking for you?'

'I know, I know,' Lubin said. 'But they're not the only people looking for me, so they'll have to wait. What are you doing tomorrow?'

'I don't know,' Kate said. 'I don't think Ken has anything lined up for me because he didn't know I would be there . . .'

'Well, you can do me a favour then,' Lubin went on quickly, not giving her a chance to interrupt. 'Call in sick or something.

Then I want you to get a train to a place called Diss – D.I.S.S.'
He spelled it out. 'Liverpool Street station, or maybe Kings
Cross, you'll have to check. Get there as near midday as you
can. There's a sort of lake in the town centre, the Mere I think
it's called. I'll meet you there. You can't miss it. There are
seats and ducks and things, mothers with kids, no one will
think it's odd of you to hang around. There's no station where
I am so I'll drive there. I've been trying to get hold of June,
because she has a key to the studio, but she's not on the phone,
silly cow, so you'll have to help me. I'll give you my key. I
want you to go to the studio and sort out a few things for me.'

'I wanted to get into the studio myself because I've left
some of my stuff there,' Kate said faintly. 'But won't the
bizzies – the police – have been in already?'

'They will have had to break the door down,' Lubin said.
'I don't see why they should have done that. Whatever Ricky
was up to – and I'm sure he was up to something – is nothing
to do with me or the studio.'

'So why did you run away?' Kate asked.

'I haven't run away,' Lubin snapped back. 'If you just sort
a few things out for me – nothing to do with Ricky, I promise
– I'll get in touch with the police and tell them anything they
want to know about him. Come on, Kate. I've done a lot for
you. This is just a small favour. And if anyone sees you, you
just say you went in to fetch some stuff of your own. That's
a perfect cover. Come to Diss in the morning and I'll give you
the key.'

Kate sighed. 'OK, OK,' she said. 'I'll meet you in Diss, la.
But don't blame me if the police turn up at the studio. I'm
not going to lie to them if they do. I don't want to end up in
a cell, ta very much.'

'Just tell them you're picking up your own stuff,' Lubin
said. 'You don't need to say you've seen me. That's perfect.'

In the end, and against her better judgement, Kate agreed
to meet Lubin in Diss, promising herself that if he didn't talk
to the police on his own initiative she would tell Harry Barnard
what she knew and leave it to him to track him down. When
she hung up she found Tess staring at her across the room
with a worried expression on her face.

'Was that who I think it was?' she asked. 'What on earth have you agreed to do for him?'

Kate told her the gist of the conversation, which only seemed to increase her friend's anxiety.

'If the police are looking for him you must be crazy to meet him without telling them,' Tess said. 'You'll end up getting arrested yourself.'

'It'll be fine,' Kate said. 'I'll tell Harry Barnard that Tatiana knows where Andrei is when I get back to London. Even if he doesn't keep his promise to get in touch with them, they'll soon find him if they know where to look. I really want to get back to the studio to pick up my own stuff. Amongst other things, I left the film I shot at the Jazz Cellar there. I never got round to developing it, I'd so many other things to do.'

'I think you're taking a crazy risk,' Tess said. 'Why don't you talk to Harry Barnard now, tonight?'

'Tomorrow,' Kate said. 'I promise. After I get back.'

# SIXTEEN

DS Harry Barnard had met the American officer, Lieutenant Saprelli, in smartly pressed uniform, outside the jail at eight thirty that morning, a raw dark November dawn only just working itself into daylight. They were signed in and led through locked doors and down long corridors to an interview room close to the governor's office where Muddy Abraham was already sitting at a table with a warder on duty just inside the door. He looked up as the door opened and although his expression did not change as the two officers came in, Barnard noticed that his fists clenched slightly as if prepared to defend himself.

Saprelli thumped his file of papers on to the table and sat down and the warder left the room, telling them to knock on the door when they were finished.

'So don't I get a lawyer?' Abraham asked Barnard. 'Ain't I entitled?'

'Apparently this interview will be conducted under American army regulations,' Barnard said. He had argued with Saprelli over this point but had been overruled by the DCI who seemed determined to ship Abraham out of the country on the next available flight. 'I'm only here to observe,' he said with a shrug.

'Right soldier, let's get sorted out just who you really are,' Saprelli snapped. He pulled the photograph that he had shown Barnard at the embassy and showed it to Abraham. 'Do you deny that's you – Abraham Moses Davis – AWOL since October twenty-seventh, 1945. Last sighted that evening in the village of Edershaw, five miles from the transit camp where you were awaiting a flight home and where you unlawfully struck Sergeant Gary Strang when he approached you to remonstrate about you consorting with a white girl. That you, soldier?'

Abraham shook his head. 'No, sir,' he said. 'That ain't me. No way.'

Saprelli did not argue but pulled some more papers out of his file. 'This is your signature, taken from your army record,' he said, slapping a sheet of paper down in front of Abraham. 'And this is your signature taken from the receipt you signed here for your belongings when you were brought in. Abraham Moses Davis and David Abraham – Muddy not being a given name anyone would accept, I guess. You can say that they were signed nearly twenty years apart, but you made the mistake of using part of your name again. Abraham – it's identical.'

Abraham still objected. 'Not me,' he said. 'I ain't that man.'

'Well I'm sure you are and I'm telling you now I'm applying to have you sent back to the US of A to have you face the homicide indictment you should have faced in 1945.'

'Homicide?' Abraham said, clearly shocked. 'Who said anything about homicide? I thought you said this man Davis hit the sergeant . . .'

'He did and Strang hit his head as he went down,' Saprelli said. 'He died in hospital two days later.'

'Jeezus, man,' Abraham said, flashing a glance at Barnard whose eyes were fixed on his notebook. 'Can they do that to a British citizen?' he asked.

'We can't find any record of naturalization papers in your name,' Barnard said quietly. 'Though I suppose it depends which of your names you used.'

Muddy Abraham shook his head like a baited bear. It was obvious that if he had taken out naturalization papers in another name his denials that he was the man Saprelli wanted were a waste of breath. 'This is crazy,' he said. 'This is nearly twenty years ago we're talking about.'

'Sergeant Strang is still dead,' Saprelli said. 'Why should the United States Army forgive or forget that, soldier? The witnesses are still alive and willing to testify and get some justice for Strang's family. He had five kids.'

'Jee-e-ez,' Abraham breathed into the silence. 'Sergeant Barnard, can I have a private word with you?'

Barnard glanced at Saprelli who hesitated for a second and then nodded.

'I'll wait outside,' he said. 'But don't imagine anything you

can say to Sergeant Barnard is going to make a difference to
your situation, soldier. Uncle Sam wants you and nothing you
say's going to change that. You're going back home and you'll
fry.'

When the American officer had gone Barnard took his seat
opposite Muddy Abraham.

'If I help you can you help me?' Abraham said bluntly.

Barnard shrugged. 'You've got some time,' he said. 'And
if you help me I could maybe get you a bit more as a witness
we need to keep tabs on for a murder trial. But in the end,
they'll probably get their extradition. It has to go to court here,
but I can't see a court refusing the request even after such a
long time. Murder is murder. And America is our ally.'

'I had no idea he was dead,' Abraham whispered, and then,
realizing that what he had just said amounted to a confession,
he said no more, his broad shoulders sagging. 'I didn't hit him
hard.'

Barnard waited, lighting a cigarette and offering Abraham
one.

The American took one and lit it slowly, dragging the smoke
deep into his lungs like a drowning man drags air on his last
visit to the surface. 'OK,' Abraham said at last. 'Your dead
girl. When we talked about her I wasn't tellin' you
everything.'

'I didn't think so,' Barnard said. 'So what did you leave
out?'

'The little girl who died? I saw her a couple of times with
Chris Swift. Once outside on the sidewalk, once inside the
club. I reckon Chris was doing a bit of business with some of
the girls on the game – sleeping with them, maybe, but maybe
more than that. I think he may be their pimp.'

'This is Chris Swift we're talking about?' Barnard said.
'The man who says he'd like the Jazz Cellar to be pretty well
anywhere but in Soho where there are all these tarts around?
The man who sounds like he should be running a bloody
Sunday school?'

'That's the man,' Abraham said. 'He's a good actor, I'd say.
And a good liar. But he has a temper. I've seen him lose it a
couple of times when the music's not going as it should. And

once with the girl. The next time I saw her she had bruises, a lot of bruises.'

'And you'd be prepared to give evidence against him in court, if it came to that? If we find enough evidence and can charge him?'

'Sure thing,' Abraham said. 'And there's more. I don't think he was running these girls on his own. I think he had a partner.'

'Was he working for the Maltese?' Barnard asked quickly. 'They control most of the tarts in Soho.'

'No, I don't think the man I saw him with a couple of times was Maltese. He was called Ricky, a man called Ricky, who had a smart car, an Italian car. But every time I saw them in the club they seemed to be arguing.'

Barnard held his breath for a moment but said nothing about Ricky Smart's death. 'OK, that may be very useful,' he said at length. 'Running girls is not a major crime, even under-age girls, unless we can link Swift to Jenny Maitland's murder, so I shouldn't build your hopes too high. But it might buy you a bit of time if we can pin something on Swift and keep you here as a witness. The other thing that might help you is to prove you're British and get a lawyer. You should be entitled to legal aid.'

'I filled in the forms in my natural-born name,' he said. 'And signed them, of course, which tells Saprelli all he needs to know.'

Barnard sighed. If he was honest, he could see no way out for Abraham. 'If you help us in court, if we ever get to court, I'll do all I can,' he said gloomily.

'Sure you will,' Abraham said, with no conviction at all.

Later, Barnard stood in a doorway outside the Valetta restaurant in Charlotte Street smoking his fifth cigarette on the trot and hoping he was not as conspicuous as he feared he was. He pulled the brim of his trilby down and his coat collar up, and waited, stamping his feet occasionally against the November chill. A muffled phone call at the nick – almost as soon as he had got back from seeing Abraham – from an anonymous caller who Barnard had no difficulty identifying as Joe Inglott, his Maltese informant, had told him that 'the Man' had returned to London and would be having lunch at the Valetta that day. When he had arrived at the restaurant soon after noon he had opened the door and taken a quick look round the interior where tables were set for lunch but very few were taken. He nodded to a couple of waiters lounging by the bar and went out again, content to wait until 'the Man', Frankie Falzon, turned up.

The Maltese, who controlled most of the prostitution in the square mile, did not often turn up in person in Soho. Barnard knew that he had a large luxurious house in Mill Hill and that he left the day-to-day running of his lucrative empire to lieutenants who were generally members of his own large family or trusted friends from the Mediterranean island. Something important must have brought him to the area for lunch and the sergeant wondered if it had anything to do with the two recent murders on his patch.

By the time a long American car pulled up right outside the restaurant door and deposited Falzon and a couple of heavyweight minders outside the door, and raised a cacophony of angry car horns behind, Barnard's feet were frozen and the chill made it almost impossible to light his sixth cigarette. He watched and waited as the limo pulled away, allowing several irate taxi drivers free passage up the narrow street again. He did not move for a few more minutes to give Falzon time to settle himself at a table before he opened the door again and went in, pushing his hat to the back of his head, holding his warrant card in one hand but keeping his hands well away from his pockets.

Frankie Falzon was not a tall man, but broad and muscular, his tanned face shadowed even after what looked like a close shave and his dark hair just beginning to silver, certainly not a man with whom you would want to pick a fight on a dark night, Barnard thought, but so elegantly dressed in a dark suit with silvery tie that it was obvious he had no need to bloody his own hands any more. Barnard had met him before but never in a confrontational situation. Falzon had no criminal record in his adopted country and although a handful of his associates had been charged and a couple imprisoned for vice offences, Barnard assumed that their boss's contributions to

various police charities and individual senior officers' pension
arrangements, in the West End and at Scotland Yard, had until
now protected him from legal embarrassment and would
continue to do so unless the man was discovered by at least
a dozen officers from another force *in flagrante delicto* with a
murder weapon in his hand. And that, Barnard knew, was not
going to happen any time soon.

He approached Falzon's table slowly, the eyes of the two
bodyguards watching his every move.

'Mr Falzon,' he said. 'Detective Sergeant Barnard from Vice.
Can I have a quick word with you.'

Falzon dark eyes flashed but after a second's hesitation he
waved Barnard into a chair. 'Bring us a bottle of Chianti, and
two glasses,' he barked at a waiter. 'You have five minutes
before my guests arrive,' he said to Barnard. 'No more.'

Barnard did not waste any time. 'We are concerned about
the appearance of some very young girls on the streets in
recent weeks,' he said. 'One of them was found dead, dumped
like garbage behind the Jazz Cellar. This is something new,
something we didn't associate with your business operations.
Can you shed any light on who's putting them there?'

Falzon's face darkened and Barnard was aware of the more
aggressive stance of his minders. 'I have been away,' Falzon
said. 'Family business. I have just buried my mother. But I
was told about these events when I came back. I have no idea
yet who is organizing these intruders, but I intend to find out.'

Barnard waited patiently for a moment. 'Are you worried
about your relationship with Ray Robertson?' he ventured.

'Should I be?' Falzon snapped back.

Barnard shrugged slightly.

'He's an old business acquaintance, as you obviously know,'
Falzon said. 'He has seemed a little restless lately but I don't
suspect him of interfering with any of our previous arrangements.'
He shrugged. 'What I think is that he has other ambitions. As
for the girls on the street? I think this is more likely to be some
newcomer who has not yet learned the rules.'

'A man called Ricky Smart, maybe?'

But Falzon's expression did not flicker.

'Or Chris Swift?'

'Them I don't know,' he said flatly. 'I think maybe you should turn your attention to the Jazz Cellar, Sergeant Barnard, if that's where the dead girl was found. That African music is not good for young people, it's primitive, harmful. The church condemns it. That place might be more fruitful for your inquiries. I am told you are already taking an interest there.' His eyes flickered to the door where several people were handing their coats to the *maitre d'*.

Barnard nodded with only the faintest smile at hearing the most successful pimp in London complain about a style of music.

'My guests are here now, Sergeant. I don't think I can be of any more help to you.'

And with that Barnard had to be content.

Frustrated, he took his usual daily stroll around his manor, gleaning whatever he could from the motley collection of shopkeepers and bar and cafe owners who kept him posted about what was going on in the tangle of narrow streets between the big stores to the north and the theatre district to the south. Very little in the tangle of sex, entertainment and commerce which was Soho could be taken at face value and a copper here was only as good as his contacts. And Barnard reckoned he was very good. A judicious mixture of threats and bribes generally kept the information flowing in his direction and if contacts who felt grateful for his protection were moved to offer the odd thank-you present, who was he to complain.

He had a quick lunch at a pub in Wardour Street, glanced in at the open doors of the Jazz Cellar but could see no one except cleaners tidying up after the night before, and then strolled down west towards Berwick Street market which was crowded with eager shoppers as usual. Stepping cautiously round a pile of discarded vegetable debris which had spilled on to the pavement, he glanced down the alleyway where Andrei Lubin's studio was situated and was surprised to see a figure he recognized going into the building.

'Now what are you up to now, Katie, my sweet?' he said to himself as he turned to follow. He caught up with her at the top of the last flight of stairs where they both stood for a moment catching their breath.

Kate flushed pink although Barnard was not sure whether
it was the exertion or embarrassment that caused her blush.
'Well, well, what are you doing here?' he asked. 'Do you
have a key?'

With the key Andrei had given her in Diss in her hand, she
could hardly deny it. She nodded. She knew her cheeks were
flaming, perhaps betraying something more than the embarrassment of being caught out. 'I was going to come round to
see you later,' she said, still slightly breathless. 'But I need to
get some stuff I left here first. I didn't want you lot taking my
undeveloped films if you decided to search the place. I need
them.'

'And can I ask where you got the key from?' Barnard asked,
taking it out of her hand and opening the door and ushering
her inside. 'I think we won't talk on the landing where anyone
can hear us. I think you've a bit of explaining to do, don't
you?' He ushered her inside and locked the door behind them.

'Now,' he said. 'You can make us both a cup of coffee –
I'm sure you know where everything is – and then you can
tell me what the hell is going on here.'

Kate did as she was told meekly, too meekly, Barnard thought
although he was not bothering to hide the fact that he was
furious with her. But the very fact that she did not seem to
want to fight back told him that she knew she was in the wrong.

'There's no milk,' she said, putting two mugs of black coffee
and a bag of sugar on to the worktop in front of him.

He took a stool and waved her into another. 'Now, let's hear
it. What on earth have you been up to?'

So she told him how she had got up early that morning to
take a train from Liverpool Street to Diss in Norfolk and how
she had found her way through the small market town to the
Mere and met Andrei Lubin more or less as planned. They
had sat on a wooden bench together in pale sunshine watching
the swans and ducks, almost like a couple of lovers, she said,
though it was obvious that Andrei was an extremely worried
man.

'He's scared,' Kate said quietly. 'He's very scared and I
don't know exactly why. He wasn't very explicit but it must
be something to do with Ricky's murder, mustn't it?'

'Don't you think he killed him?' Barnard asked harshly. 'Didn't it cross your mind that you might be going out there to meet a murderer?'

'No, of course not,' Kate snapped back. 'I'm not so stupid.'

'What you did sounds very stupid to me,' Barnard said. 'Not to mention illegal. If the DCI hears about it he could have you in a cell for any number of offences up to aiding and abetting murder, if Lubin was charged with that.'

'I don't believe for a moment Andrei killed Ricky. He cut his finger one day in the studio and nearly passed out at the sight of blood. He's a pussy cat. If you suggested the other way round I might wonder, but not Andrei.' It was only now, when Kate looked back on the two men's relationship that she realized that Andrei might have been the boss in name at the studio but Ricky was the boss in fact.

'So why exactly did he want you to rush off to this place in Norfolk anyway? Is that where he's holed up?' Barnard persisted.

'No, his cousin says he's got an old cottage on the coast, Southdown is it, no, Southwold. She gave me the address – here.' She handed Barnard the scrap of paper Tatiana had given her for her cousin's cottage. 'There's no phone. And no railway either. It sounds like the back of beyond. He met me in Diss because I could get there easily on the train. He used his car to get there. I don't know how far away Southwold is, do you?'

But Barnard shook his head irritably. 'But when he called, you went running? So why? What did he say on the phone to persuade you?'

'He said he wanted me to come to the studio and find some documents for him. When I'd got them he said he would come back to London and talk to the police,' Kate said. 'If he didn't come back I told him I would give all the documents to you anyway.'

Barnard laughed but there was no humour in his eyes. 'My guess is that he's planning to contact you again and persuade you to meet him again with the documents. He's got no intention of coming back to London at all if he can avoid it.'

Kate shrugged. There was nothing she could say to prove that she had been right to trust Lubin. 'The other thing was that I wanted to get in here myself anyway. I really didn't want to lose the films I'd left here . . .' Kate trailed off miserably realizing what a risk she had taken, not least from Barnard's stony expression.

'Right,' Barnard said. 'This is what's going to happen. We were planning to search this place anyway so you can leave me the key Lubin gave you, and his documents, when you've found them, and then you can take your own rolls of film and make yourself scarce. And we'll ask the local bobbies to pick Lubin up in Southwold. I expect he's gone back to his cottage. Even if he's not there I shouldn't think he'll be difficult to find. As far as you're concerned I never found you here. If the DCI wants to talk to you again later you can tell him about your trip or not, it's up to you. But stick to what happened with Lubin and not a word about us meeting like this or I'll be for the high jump. I should report you. So be very careful. Jackson's got a reputation for sniffing out the truth from the most innocent-looking hidey-hole.'

Kate nodded miserably and turned to the door. Barnard did not say goodbye.

# SEVENTEEN

Kate walked slowly back to the agency. She felt humiliated by what had happened and guessed that Harry Barnard's obvious annoyance would be hard to dispel. How was it, she asked herself, that he and she constantly edged around each other at cross-purposes. Why, she wondered, was nothing between them straightforward?

Back at the agency the photographers' room was empty, everyone out on assignment, so she set about belatedly developing and printing the photographs she had taken at the Jazz Cellar. They had turned out quite well, she thought, considering the dark and smoky atmosphere she had had to work in and she took the sheets of contact prints in to show Ken Fellows just before lunch.

'I should think Stan Weston might like to buy a set of these for his publicity,' she said, dropping the sheets on Ken's desk. 'They've come out better than I expected.'

Ken glanced at them unenthusiastically. 'Print a dozen of the best and drop them round to the Jazz Cellar. It can't hurt. There might even be a bob or two in it. You're not exactly bringing in much any other way at the moment, are you.'

'Tatiana Broughton-Clarke may come up with something quite soon,' Kate said defensively.

'Have you heard anything from Lubin?' Fellows asked. 'Is he actually going to reopen his studio or do we have to call it a day for you there? You did OK but I'd have liked you to stay a bit longer.'

'I don't know,' Kate said. 'I bumped into Sergeant Barnard and he said the police were still looking for him but hadn't found him yet. I just don't know what's going to happen.'

'Do you think he killed what-his-name, Ricky Smart?'

Kate shrugged. Everyone, it seemed, wanted to know her views on Andrei Lubin as a likely killer. But the more she thought about the man, the more she reckoned it was impossible.

'I can't see him saying boo to a goose, quite honestly,' she said. 'I don't like the man but calling him a likely murderer is something else, isn't it? But running away won't have helped, will it? It makes him look as if he's got something to hide when I think in fact he's terrified he'll be the next to be attacked.'

'It won't have helped, not with the police or his clients,' Fellows said, with some satisfaction. 'Well, I can't complain if the opposition shoots itself in the foot, can I? I'll give some thought to how we can pick up some more fashion work. I don't want the cash I've spent on you wasted, do I?'

There's always a ready reckoner behind Ken's eyes, Kate thought. I suppose that's how you get on in business. But Andrei Lubin wasn't like that. It was Ricky Smart looking out for the main chance all the time, almost taking the decisions for him. Maybe that had been his undoing.

She printed a dozen of her Jazz Cellar pictures and then sat with a coffee looking at them critically, thinking back to the evening she had spent there with Tess and Dave Donovan. The place had been packed, the musicians on a roll, and it had been hard to believe that the body of Jenny Maitland had been found dumped at the club just a week or so before their visit. With the pictures now blown up faces were more clearly visible and on one shot, taken while the musicians were having a break and some of them had come into the main room seeking refreshment, she drew a sharp breath when she recognized someone she did not expect to see in the crowd. Behind a shot of Muddy Abraham talking to two intense middle-aged men, she picked out the face of Chris Swift, the clarinettist, seemingly in animated conversation with a young girl Kate recognized.

'What on earth were you doing there, Sylvia?' Kate muttered under her breath, knowing with a sick feeling that there was no way of asking her and quite probably no way of ever finding out. Sylvia could not have been there in the audience for the whole evening or she would have seen her, she thought. She must have come in during the interval, presumably to talk to Swift specifically. Could he be the father of her baby, she wondered? Or was there some even more sinister reason for their intense discussion?

She sat at her desk for a long time wondering what to do next. When she'd made her decision she went back into the darkroom and printed a duplicate set of photographs and put them into two separate envelopes. One she addressed to Stan Weston at the Jazz Cellar, the other to DS Harry Barnard with a note to identify the slightly fuzzy image of Sylvia Hubbard. Perhaps Swift was the father of Sylvia's unborn child, she thought, or perhaps there was more to it than that, but this time, she thought, she would leave it to Barnard to find out. She really did not want to talk to him again today. She would simply deliver her pictures to him and to Stan Weston and leave it at that.

Her first call was at the Jazz Cellar where she didn't really expect any of the musicians to be around at lunchtime. But when she pushed at the half-open main door she saw Stan Weston by the shuttered bar on the other side of the room, deep in discussion with his drummer Steve O'Leary. She made her way across the room with her envelope of photographs in her hand.

'Hello,' she said. 'I didn't think you'd be here so early in the day.'

'We're having a rehearsal with a new saxophone man,' Weston said curtly. 'A stand-in until Muddy Abraham gets back.'

'If he gets back,' O'Leary added, his expression gloomy. 'I called his lawyer and he seems to think they want to send Muddy back to America. Deport him, that is. It seems completely crazy. He only had a spliff. What's it all about?'

'He told me he was naturalized British,' Weston said. 'Can they do that to him? He's been here since the war, for God's sake.'

'I've no idea what they can do,' Kate said. 'I do know some London bizzies don't like black men, so maybe they don't like Muddy. Why don't you ask Sergeant Barnard what's going on? He'll know.'

'Maybe I will,' Weston said. 'So anyway, what can we do for you?'

'I just popped in to bring you some prints of the pictures I took the night I was here with my friends,' she said. 'I think some of them might be quite good as publicity pics if you want to buy them off the agency I work for.' She handed him the envelope of prints.

'God, I'd forgotten all about that,' Weston said. 'What with the police raid and Muddy still banged up, it went right out of my head.' He pulled the photographs out of the envelope and looked at them critically, one by one, with O'Leary looking over his shoulder.

'They're good,' he said slowly. 'We could certainly use some of them. Can you blow them up a bit bigger?'

'Yes, easily,' Kate said.

'We won't want to use the ones with Muddy in until we know he's coming back,' Weston said. 'But the ones of Gerry Statham are good. I'm hoping to have him back soon. Leave them with me and I'll get back to you. Is that OK?'

'Of course. The address and phone number are in there.' She turned away and realized that Chris Swift had come into the club behind them and was heading their way.

'Look at these, Chris,' O'Leary said. 'There's a couple of good shots of you.'

'Let me know what you want. You've got the agency number on the back,' Kate said, as she headed for the door quickly, wondering if perhaps she had made a mistake in bringing the pictures to the club before showing them to Harry Barnard. She did not particularly want to be around if Swift saw himself and Sylvia in the background. She hoped she had not got it wrong again.

She hurried through Soho and across Regent Street, packed with shoppers already eagerly thinking about Christmas presents, and made her way to the police station. The sergeant at the front desk looked her up and down admiringly when she asked for DS Barnard and kept on giving her the odd wink while she sat on a hard chair opposite him waiting for the sergeant to emerge from the interior of the building. He kept her waiting and she wondered if it was deliberate. If only she could sort out her own feelings about the good-looking sergeant she might be able to sort out their fractious relationship too, even end it, as her friend Tess was constantly telling her to do.

'Let's go and have a coffee,' he said, when he eventually emerged. He had his coat and hat on and obviously wanted to get out of the building as soon as possible.

'Nice one, Flash,' the desk sergeant called out with a knowing leer as they made for the doors. Barnard ignored him and led her to a coffee bar in one of the side streets behind Regent Street, sat her at a table away from the windows and went to the counter to order. He did not seem particularly pleased to see her, Kate thought and wondered if her consistent rejection of his invitations was beginning to get to him. The trouble was, she still could not decide from day to day whether she really meant them or not. When she was out of his sight it seemed logical not to get involved with him more deeply. When she was with him, even when she was fighting with him, she found it very hard indeed to resist his charm. Today though, she realized, the charm was very firmly turned off.

He put a cappuccino in front of her and sat down opposite. 'I think I'd rather you didn't come calling at the nick,' he said. 'You're a witness and my boss won't approve of us socializing.'

'I didn't come to socialize, I came to do a bit more witnessing,' Kate said lightly, taking a sip of her coffee and wiping the foam off her top lip with a finger. 'I came to give you these.' She passed her second envelope across the desk. 'I thought you might find one of them specially interesting.'

He flicked through them quickly at first but slowed to a halt when he found the one she knew would grab his attention. 'There, in the background, behind Muddy Abraham?' he said. 'Is that what you meant? It's Sylvia Hubbard, isn't it? And the man she's with is Chris Swift, the clarinet man? They seem to be having a bit of a ding-dong.'

'Right,' Kate said. 'I can't say I noticed her at the time, I was concentrating on getting a good shot of Muddy in the foreground. There were lots of people milling about behind him. But it's definitely her. What she was doing there I can't imagine. I didn't see her myself, so I don't know how long she was in the club, but I thought you'd be interested.'

'You thought right,' Barnard said, relaxing slightly and brushing his fingers over hers. 'They've all being denying the street girls worked inside the club ever since Jenny Maitland's body was found in the back yard. But they can't deny this. Muddy Abraham's already hinted that Swift had contact with Jenny. I think we can talk to him and Swift again now with much more to go on, thanks to you. That's great.'

'You think Sylvia was working on the street?'

'I think Ricky Smart was recruiting the girls as models, as far as that went. He took them to the studio but we know none of them stayed with Lubin long because he got tired of them and chucked them out. Then Smart found them work elsewhere, almost certainly as tarts. I've no doubt it was a lucrative little business while it lasted. But unfortunately he picked the wrong streets. He was muscling into territory where some very powerful people have the trade sewn up. They don't like intruders.'

'Dear God,' Kate said softly. 'Poor kids.' She shuffled through the pictures again but what the club had been used for tainted her memories of a good night out. She picked out Muddy Abraham's face. 'What's happening to the American?' she asked. 'Is he still locked up?'

'It turned out he'd been on the US Army's wanted list for years for something that happened at the end of the war when he should have been on his way home. They want him sent back to the States, deported, and I can't see any way we can stop that. My boss is very keen to see him go.'

'What do they want him for?' Kate asked.

'Murder,' Barnard said quietly. 'He could go to the electric chair. I'm trying to slow the process down but I don't have high hopes that I can stop it.'

'I'll never understand why people come to a place that seems to hate them so much,' Kate said. 'I've always wondered that about my Irish ancestors coming to Liverpool. The locals hated them, because they were Irish and Catholic and dirt poor.'

'I guess, as Muddy Abraham says, some places are better

than other places, even if they're not perfect,' Barnard said. 'He seems to believe England is better for him than America.'

'But not much better, as it turns out,' Kate said. 'Can't you do anything for him?'

'We can hang on to him as a witness in two murder cases, but even if we can file charges eventually, that won't last forever. My DCI might not even go along with that much. He doesn't like black men, he doesn't like drugs and he doesn't like jazz musicians – or any musicians come to that. He's not exactly part of the rock and roll generation, is he? You only have to look at him. He'd close half of Soho down if he could. And the American army officer who's in charge of this sort of thing is very determined to have Abraham back. I'm not sure whether it's because he's just keen or whether Abraham's colour has anything to do with it. He's supposed to have killed a white sergeant, though he says he never even knew the man had died.'

'Will he get a fair trial?' Kate asked.

'Depends where he's taken for trial, I suppose,' Barnard said. 'It'll be a military court I expect and I don't know how they work or how prejudiced they might be.'

Kate sighed and Barnard thought he could see a tear in her eyes.

'Come on, cheer up,' he said. 'You can't solve all the world's problems. If you're at a loose end come out for a meal with me tonight. No strings, I promise. I'll pick you up and run you home afterwards.'

Kate looked at him for a long time and then nodded. 'All right,' she said. Why not, she thought, and if she ended up at his flat in Highgate so be it. You couldn't go on saying no for ever.

Harry Barnard walked back to the nick feeling absurdly pleased, like an eighteen year old looking forward to his first date. He did not understand how this little Scouse newcomer, ten years younger than he was himself, broke down his defences so easily and completely but she did. He went up the stairs to CID two at a time and knocked on the DCI's door. Jackson was behind his desk with a single file open in front of him, fountain pen lined up to one side ready for action.

'Ah, Sergeant, I was wondering where you were?'

'Inquiries, sir,' Barnard said easily. 'Two quite useful leads as it happens, one that could possibly give us a motive for the deaths of the girl Jenny Maitland and Ricky Smart. And links it to the Jazz Cellar, which I know you always thought was suspect.'

'Tell me more, laddie,' Jackson said, his eyes taking on a zealous gleam. He drank in avidly Barnard's description of his interview with Muddy Abraham, the sax player's admission that at least one of the street girls had connections with Chris Swift and Kate O'Donnell's unexpected production of a photograph which clearly showed Swift having an animated conversation with the second dead girl from Lubin's studio, the unfortunate Sylvia Hubbard.

'I knew that place was a den of iniquity,' Jackson muttered half under his breath as if aware that such old-fashioned condemnation would not necessarily gain him credibility around the nick, and certainly not with the sharp young sergeant in front of him who was obviously enjoying 1963.

'I think we need to hang on to Muddy Abraham in this country for the time being,' Barnard said, trying to keep his expression neutral. 'We're going to need his testimony if we're going to pin Swift, or any of the others at the Jazz cellar down. One fuzzy photograph won't do it.'

'The American army won't like that. We owe it to them to give him back as soon as we can,' Jackson objected. 'It's a capital charge he's on.'

'They've waited for nineteen years to settle the score,' Barnard said. 'I'm sure a few months waiting for a trial here won't hurt. They owe it to us for picking him up, after all. That was all down to your raid on the Jazz Cellar. I bet you never expected a catch like that, guv. Quite a feather in your cap.'

Jackson's thin lips offered an apology for a smile. 'I suppose you could say that, Sergeant,' he said. 'Let's hang on to him for the time being then and hope for a result at the Bailey, if we get that far. So let's get on with it. Don't hang about. One less vice ring in Soho can't be a bad outcome to what looked just like another wee tramp who picked the wrong fellow to sell her services to. Bring Swift in and see what he knows. If there's a link to Ricky Smart we've cracked it.'

# EIGHTEEN

Chris Swift didn't even look particularly surprised when Barnard arrested him an hour or so later. Barnard guessed that he had seen Kate's pictures and realized that he might be incriminated by them, though he seemed not to have reckoned that the police would turn up so quickly. It was Stan Weston who objected most vociferously as the police made their intentions clear and his rehearsal with his new saxophone player was rudely interrupted.

'How the hell am I going to open tonight without a clarinet?' he demanded. 'You've already got Muddy banged up, what more do you want? I'm going to have to close the club at this rate. We're going to be out of business.'

'You should be more careful about what you allow to go on on the premises,' Barnard had said unsympathetically. If the club closed at least DCI Jackson would be happy, he thought. There's always a silver lining for someone. 'Anyway, you have some questions to answer yourself about what's been going on here.'

He sent Swift back to the nick in the patrol car he had come in and then settled Weston down at a table close to the stage, leaving the rest of the band kicking their heels at the bar, where the shutters were firmly down. The man clutching a saxophone looked severely disenchanted.

'Right,' Barnard said. 'Let's get the relationship between the Jazz Cellar and girls on the street sorted out, shall we? Once and for all?' He slapped the incriminating photograph down on the table and let Weston look at it for a moment.

'I don't know what you mean by relationship,' Weston blustered, before deciding that some sort of honesty might be the better course. 'It was absolutely nothing to do with me, or the club. They came in sometimes with Chris, as you evidently know by now. And he was often with another guy, whose name I don't know. The girls came and went with the two of them. It was all perfectly innocent as far as I was concerned, inside the club anyway. They weren't soliciting in here – there's not much space for that sort of thing – but I guess I saw blokes following them outside. What happened after that I don't know, but I expect we both have a good idea.'

'Did you see Swift with the girl in the photograph? Sylvia Hubbard, she was called?'

'No, not that night, but other nights, other girls and often the other bloke as well. They obviously all knew each other.'

'Did you see the murdered girl, Jenny Maitland, ever? In the club? Anywhere?' Barnard pressed.

'Once or twice, maybe,' Weston admitted.

'And you didn't think to tell us this when she was found dead in your back yard?' Barnard did not try to hide the contempt in his voice.

'I was afraid we might be closed down if any of this came out after the murder,' he said. 'This place opened before the war. I took it over when I was demobbed. It's not much to look at but we've had them all here, the greats, even Americans in the thirties. Louis Armstrong dropped in when he played a concert in London, might even have played a few notes here but you couldn't let the Musicians Union know, couldn't advertise the fact. Now the ban's been lifted I've been working on some exchanges – our lads in New York, the Yanks coming here. The place is going to take off, believe me. I couldn't see all that go to waste . . .'

'Because of some little tart, who became a dead little tart, right outside your back door? You must have suspected there was a link to Chris Swift and his partner.'

'She was nothing to do with me, nothing to do with the club, nothing illegal went on here. Why should we be blamed for what goes on outside? There's more little tarts out there than I've had hot dinners.' Weston looked haggard.

'I want you down at the station,' Barnard said, his eyes bleak. 'Say five o'clock. I want a complete statement, every detail, signed and sealed, and then we'll think about whether there should be any charges. Don't be late.'

He left the band leader slumped in his chair with his eyes

closed, ignored the rest of the band who watched his exit in total silence, and slammed his way out into the fresh air, leaving the doors swinging wildly.

Back at the nick, with Chris Swift waiting in a cell to be questioned, he put his head round the DCI's door and brought him up to date with developments.

'Do you want to sit in, guv?' he asked, but the Scot shook his head.

'Find me a definite link between Swift and Ricky Smart,' he said. 'We know Smart was doing the recruiting and Swift seems to have been in on the pimping. Maybe they fell out, or maybe someone else took exception to what they were up to. Swift could lead us to much bigger fish if we handle him right.'

'Right,' he said, glancing at his watch. 'Softly softly then, guv, if that's what you want.'

He had promised to pick Kate up at seven thirty. That gave him three or four hours to grill Swift and then leave him to stew in a cell overnight. That should concentrate his mind on the advantages of helping the police with their inquiries, he thought. There was no great hurry. They could put him on a holding charge of living off immoral earnings and get him remanded in custody if they chose while they pursued the murder charges, or let him out and keep him under observation to see where he led them. That might be even more useful, Barnard thought as he went down to the cells to have Swift brought up.

'Right Mr Swift,' Barnard said when he and DC Ross Staples had him settled in an interview room. The musician looked pale and deflated, smoking compulsively from a crumpled pack of Gauloises on the table in front of him. The ashtray was already half full.

'Let's start with your relationship with young Sylvia Hubbard, shall we?' Barnard said. 'No doubt you've seen the photograph taken in the club last week when you probably spoke to Sylvia for the last time. Were you the father of her child?'

Swift shrugged. 'I could have been,' he said. 'Though I wasn't the only man she was sleeping with. She came in that night trying to get me to pay for an abortion. I'm sure I used some protection when I was with her.'

'Did you know she was only fifteen?' Barnard asked.

'No, I bloody didn't, she looked much older. They all do these days don't they? They're dancing around, plastered in make-up and high heels by the time they're twelve, a lot of them. Jailbait my ma would call them. Asking for it. They shouldn't be working in Soho at that age, calling themselves models. We all know where that ends up.'

'We also have evidence that you knew the murdered girl, Jenny Maitland, which is something you could have told us earlier. Did you have sex with her too?'

'No, I hardly knew her. I . . .' He hesitated, obviously debating the best way of extricating himself from the deep pit he had fallen into. 'This was not my project, not my business, I got into it almost by accident because I fancied Sylvia and then I met the man who was behind her, and Jenny and God knows how many others.'

'And that would be . . .?' Barnard prompted.

Swift sighed. 'The bloke who brought them all to Soho in the first place, of course. Ricky Smart. He was in the club with Jenny Maitland and Sylvia months ago. It was obvious he was pimping them and when I got involved with Sylvia he persuaded me to help, to bring them into the club so they could look for clients. It didn't seem like much and he paid me well. I kept the girls out of Stan Weston's way. I think he guessed and just chose to turn a blind eye. Maybe he was in on it too. Ricky always seemed to have plenty of cash in his pocket. He could have bought more than just me. He looked sometimes as if he could have bought the whole club, lock stock and barrel. I don't know.'

'Do you think Ricky Smart has set up this organization on his own, or is he working for someone else?' Barnard asked.

'He never told me anything like that,' Swift said miserably. 'I'm not stupid. I know there are gangsters in Soho who control these things. But Ricky never seemed to be worried about anything like that. He never seemed worried at all, come to that. He was what you might call a cheeky chappie, a spiv.

He never said he'd been in the forces but I can imagine he'd
have found himself a comfy little berth if he was.'

'Did he kill Jenny Maitland, Mr Swift?' Barnard snapped.

'No, of course not,' Swift said. 'He always seemed quite
fond of the girls. He was shocked when her body was found.'

'Did you kill her?'

'No, no, of course not.' The musician looked genuinely
horrified at the idea.

'And you didn't kill Ricky Smart, either?'

Swift moaned faintly. 'No, no, no.' he said. 'Why on earth
would I have done that? I was making money out of him.
Playing clarinet every night isn't a big earner.'

Barnard glanced at Ross Staples and then at his watch and
got to his feet. He wasn't going to let any of these bastards
interfere with his night out, he thought. 'We'll talk again in
the morning, Mr Swift,' he said. 'Give you time to reflect
whether you've told me the truth, the whole truth and nothing
but the truth, won't it. And then we'll think about charges.'

Leaving Swift pale and shaking he went back to CID and,
back at his desk, he noticed a scribbled note asking him to
call the Suffolk police in Southwold.

'What now?' he said to himself as he dialled and, on a bad
line, made contact with a sergeant at the other end.

'Oh yes,' the voice said in a strong country accent. 'You'll
be the one wanting someone picked up at Clarence Cottages.
A Mr Lubin?'

'Have you got him?' Barnard asked impatiently.

'No, I'm afraid not,' the sergeant said. 'We went down there
soon as you rang but the cottage was empty. Someone further
along said a man had been there but he'd seen him put suit-
cases into a car very early, seven o'clock yesterday morning,
and drive off. Reckons it was the son of the old girl who used
to live there. She died a couple of years back and it's been
empty since. Shame that, when there's youngsters looking for
places to live. Married a Russian, so I believe, but came back
here a widow.'

'Yes, yes, so have you been back for another look?' Barnard
snapped.

'I've asked the beat bobby to keep an eye open but no one's

been back as far as we know. And the neighbours will notice. Everyone knows everyone in a little place like this. Nothing interesting has happened here since the war. I waited to see if he turned up before I phoned you back. But there's been no sign.'

'Blast,' Barnard said. 'Keep an eye on the place for me, will you, mate, though I doubt he'll be back.' Lubin must have decided to leave the cottage the previous day, making an early start and stopping off in Diss to talk to Kate O'Donnell, he thought. If she had told him in advance what she was planning, they could have picked Lubin up then and there. The DCI would not be best pleased when he learned how she had kept that crucial rendezvous to herself.

# NINETEEN

K ate O'Donnell pulled on her new boots, her very short
skirt and a black polo-necked sweater.
'What do you think?' she asked Tess who was
watching her critically. 'It's very short.'

'You can get away with it. You've got good legs, you might
as well make the most of them.'

'Mmm,' Kate said, gazing at herself critically in the bedroom
mirror. 'The tights are definitely better than stockings. If I was
wearing a suspender belt I'd be wondering what people could
see.'

'That's why the lads like suspender belts,' Tess said, with
a grin. 'If you spent all your time with steamy adolescents
like I do, you'd know exactly why the girls are turning to
tights and the lads are looking glum. And why the head wants
skirts strictly on the knee.'

Kate pulled the curtains back and glanced out of the bedroom
to the street below. 'He's here,' she said, as the Ford Capri
pulled into the curb outside the front door and she picked up
her coat. 'I must say it's nice to be picked up, and he says
he'll drop me off again so you don't need to worry if I'm a
bit late.'

'Have a good evening,' Tess said. 'And if you can't be good
be careful.'

Kate was still smiling when she opened the front door to
Harry Barnard, slinging her coat round her shoulders.

'You look good,' he said, giving her a peck on the cheek.
'Do you like Greek food? I've booked us a table at a little
taverna in Charlotte Street.'

'I've never had Greek food, la,' Kate said lightly. 'Is it like
Italian?'

'Not really,' he said, as he opened the passenger door for
her. 'But you can get lots of small dishes to start with, so if
you don't like one you can try another.'

'Sounds OK,' she said as he got into the car and pulled away from the kerb with a roar.

'Do you mean to tell me you don't even know what a kebab is?' he asked, laughing.

'You forget I'm from oop north,' she said. 'It's still meat and two veg up there, none of this fancy foreign muck you're introducing me to. So what's a kebab when it's at home?'

'Meat – lamb usually – cut into chunks and grilled on a skewer, with chunks of vegetables. Very nice.'

'Mmm,' she said non-committally.

Barnard concentrated on the traffic on Holland Park Avenue as he headed back to the West End. But waiting for the traffic lights to change at Notting Hill Gate he turned to her with rather less enthusiasm. 'Andrei Lubin's scarpered again,' he said. 'He didn't go back to the cottage in Southwold after he met you. DCI Jackson's not going to be happy that you didn't tell us what you were planning before you went waltzing off to see him.'

Kate shrugged slightly. 'He said he would come back. He even said he'd talk to you. You lot may imagine he cut Ricky's throat but when you do see him you'll realize he's genuinely scared of getting his own throat cut. Andrei's not a killer, Harry, believe me. He's a pussy cat.'

'Maybe,' Barnard said. 'But we still want to talk to him.'

'Well, I'm sorry you didn't get him today, but he's bound to contact me again if he wants the stuff he asked me to get out of the studio for him, isn't he?'

'And this time you'll tell us when he phones, won't you, and where you're going to meet him? No ifs, ands or buts, no messing about.'

'Of course,' she said sweetly, though she knew how serious a threat DCI Jackson would pose this time if she didn't cooperate. She sighed. 'Tatiana might have some idea where he's gone this time,' she suggested. 'She might even have taken him in, I suppose. She's supposed to have this big place in the country with her husband, though Andrei's fallen out with Roddy, apparently. I met him at her studio briefly. I can't say I liked him very much. As soon as I opened my mouth he looked at me as if I was something the cat brought in. But they gave me a guided tour of their place in the country and they're giving me some work taking pictures at their next party instead of Andrei so I really can't complain. It's a great barn of a place that looks as if its about to fall down. I don't think throwing a few charity parties out there is going to save it. Ray Robertson's do's at the Delilah must be more attractive, though I suppose he's doing it for the status rather than to make money.'

Barnard glanced at her as he waited at the lights on Oxford Street, which was still crowded long after the big stores had closed. 'I don't know how you do it,' he said.

'Do what?'

'Prise all this information out of people. I swear you'd get a confession out of Sweeney Todd if you bumped into him in Fleet Street.'

'I didn't get much out of Roddy Broughton-Clarke, and it's a long shot to think Tatiana might have taken her cousin home with her, but she might have heard from him. I'm going out there on Thursday strictly as a photographer, strictly professional.'

'Worth a chat the morning after if you pick up any more useful nuggets of information,' Barnard said swinging round Soho Square until he found an empty parking place up against the central gardens and thinking that there was another reason for contacting one of the Broughton-Clarkes. An invitation for Ray Robertson to one of these parties at their stately pile in the country, perhaps even the one upcoming, might be just the thing to distract him from his crazier schemes. He might talk to Tatiana Broughton-Clarke about that.

'But for now let's relax and enjoy ourselves,' he said to Kate. 'Have you ever drunk ouzo?'

Kate shook her head. 'You're in for a treat then,' he said, helping her out of the car with a grin. 'Come on, let's go.'

The phone beside the bed rang and roused Harry Barnard out of a deep and satisfied sleep. He moved carefully away from his unexpected guest and picked up the receiver.

'Barnard,' he said quietly, expecting it to be some sort of summons from the nick at three in the morning only to hear

a voice at the other end of the line which he only half
recognized.

'Fred?' he asked. 'What the hell's going on. It's the middle
of the night.'

'I need your help,' Fred Bettany said. 'You know what we
were talking about at the Spaniards the other day. We've hit
a crisis. Ray and Frankie Falzon are head-to-head at the Delilah.
If someone doesn't talk them down you're going to have a
gang war on your hands in Soho, even right across London if
Ray sticks to his plan to branch out with Reg Smith. And if
Smith gets involved you know there'll be all hell let loose.
There'll be war. You know that.'

Barnard swung his feet out of bed and glanced at Kate
O'Donnell, who was now awake and watching him with ques-
tioning eyes. 'I'll be there in half an hour,' he said to Fred
and hung up.

'I'm sorry, sweetie,' he said to Kate. 'I'll have to leave you
for a bit. Someone I know has hit a crisis. With a bit of luck
I'll be back for breakfast.'

He left her looking bemused and he wondered whether it
was because she had been rudely wakened in the middle of
the night or because she could not remember clearly how she
had come to be in his bed in the first place. She had drunk,
he thought ruefully, almost certainly more wine than she had
ever taken in before, plus a glass of ouzo, and only then had
she seemed enthusiastic for his advances. But she had been
enthusiastic enough, he told himself with a faint smile of
satisfaction, once they were in bed together.

He dressed quickly and left the flat quietly. The roads were
almost deserted and he made record time into the centre of
London and parked outside the Delilah Club, on the edge of
Soho, where Ray Robertson's Jag and a Mercedes he did not
recognize were lined up. The main doors were unlocked and
he found a huddle of men sitting round a table close to the
bar, a half-empty bottle of malt whiskey in the centre and used
glasses all around, with a fug of cigar and cigarette smoke
lingering overhead. Ray Robertson and Fred Bettany faced
Frankie Falzon and a couple of heavy men Barnard did not
recognize. If they had been talking before he came in they

were not talking as he wove his way through the empty tables to join them. Ray offered Barnard no more than a grim smile while Falzon turned in his chair, his expression carved from stone.

'Take a seat, Flash,' Robertson said waving a hospitable hand, but his eyes were angry. For a moment there was silence, broken eventually by Falzon.

'I like certainty, Sergeant,' he said to Barnard. 'I do not like people who do not keep their agreements. It makes life more difficult than it ought to be.'

Ray Robertson bristled at that but, glancing warily at Barnard, seemed to decide to bite back his objections to Falzon's barely veiled accusation.

'I suggested to Mr Falzon that you were the person who probably knows as much as anybody about what is going on in Soho at the moment, with these unfortunate killings,' Fred Bettany broke in smoothly. 'Mr Falzon has been abroad recently and is not as fully in touch as he normally is. We – or Ray, I should say – thought you might be able to help.'

Fred talked as though he was smoothly addressing some boardroom meeting in the city instead of what looked like a dangerous stand-off between two of London's most successful and dangerous criminals, Barnard thought. He had no doubt that there was at least one murderer around the table, and possibly more, and that his chances of ever proving that were virtually nil. In which case simply helping to keep the peace on the streets looked like a sensible option.

Robertson found an unused glass and poured Barnard a drink, which he sipped slowly for a moment giving himself time to think. 'Let's look at the problem from the beginning,' he said quietly. 'There have been some new girls on the street recently, very young and not obviously working for the usual people. We've noticed them, and obviously now he's back in London, Mr Falzon has noticed them too.'

Falzon nodded and made an angry growl in his throat. 'My boss was not too bothered until one girl was found dead, murdered, and then, naturally, we took an interest. She was badly bruised and battered, half strangled and killed by a stab wound to the heart from a very sharp knife.'

Barnard paused to accept Robertson's offer of a cigar which he took his time to cut and light and draw on thoughtfully, watching Robertson and Falzon closely. But neither Robertson's blue eyes or Falzon's dark ones gave anything away.

'Jenny Maitland was a fifteen year old from Clapton,' Barnard began, 'who was recruited by a man called Ricky Smart to work as a model at Andrei Lubin's photographic studio where Ricky himself was a general fixer for Lubin. Lubin eventually got rid of Jenny and she ended up on the streets, although quite how that happened we don't know. But she wasn't the only one. A succession of girls seem to have taken exactly this path: brought to the West End by Smart, employed for a short time by Lubin as models, and then on the game soon afterwards. So we naturally began to ask who's running them? Was it you, Mr Falzon? Were you using Smart as an efficient recruiter of fresh new blood?'

The Maltese stiffened and shook his head angrily.

'Or was it you, Ray, deciding not to leave prostitution to Mr Falzon, as you'd agreed for years?'

Ray Robertson snorted. 'I've other fish to fry,' he muttered.

Barnard nodded at the two of them with a faint smile that he hoped was placating. 'Or the third possibility. Was Smart trying to set up in the business on his own account, perhaps with some help from the people at the Jazz Cellar where some of these girls seemed to hang out? We were looking at all these possibilities,' Barnard went on. 'Then someone upped the ante. We had made very little progress on the Jenny Maitland case, even after my DCI insisted on raiding the jazz club. All we got out of that was a black musician with marijuana stashed away in his saxophone case. But then things got really out of hand when someone slit Ricky Smart's throat – another very sharp knife, perhaps the same sharp knife – and the DCI began asking why, and who might be next? Was this the end of something or just the beginning of something very much bigger and bloodier?'

Barnard leaned back in his chair and drew on his cigar again and waited. It was Falzon who broke the silence and Robertson who remained quiet, glowering at the Maltese and at Harry Barnard with indiscriminate fury.

'It is Ray who is disturbing the peace, maybe with these girls, maybe not,' Falzon said. 'But I know he wants a bigger slice of the action. I know he talk to this man Smith who has left us alone for years, keeps himself south of the river. Ray doesn't deny this. I don't want this man Smith in Soho disturbing the peace we have had for a good few years now. And I don't expect you do, Sergeant.'

'What I do with Reg Smith will have nothing at all to do with our arrangements in this neck of the woods,' Robertson said flatly, facing Barnard, his face red. 'Nothing at all. I keep telling Frankie this. He's way out of line. And these new girls and Ricky Smart are nothing to do with me either. I don't know the fellow and if Frankie doesn't then he must have been working on his own.'

'And if so, if he was muscling in, which of you gents had Smart's throat cut and messed up a very nice Alfa Romeo?' Barnard asked. 'A real shame, that.'

'Not me, no way,' Robertson said. 'You know that's not my style, Harry.'

'This has been going on while I was away,' Falzon said. 'I never heard of this man Smart until I got back from Malta. I knew nothing at all about him. Absolutely nothing.'

Barnard glanced at Fred Bettany and shrugged. Though DCI Jackson would probably call him a fool, he tended to believe the two men's protestation of innocence, though that was not a word that anyone would usually associate with either of them.

'I'm sure these two gents can get back on to amicable terms without my help,' he said to Fred. 'I reckon Ricky Smart was a freelance who thought he was on to a nice little earner recycling Andrei Lubin's cast-off models. But I doubt he would be working alone: maybe he misjudged one of his associates, or even one of his girls, or her family.'

He turned to Ray Robertson. 'Whatever you decide to do with Reg Smith, Ray, Mr Falzon here won't be the only one pleased to hear you'll keep him out of Soho. I'll second that. There'd be mayhem and all the allowances that have been made for you would be put at risk. DCI Jackson would be like the avenging angel, I promise you. He would take no prisoners.'

'You believe them?' Bettany asked Barnard, looking startled. 'About the murder, I mean?'

'I believe them, for now,' Barnard said. 'We've other leads to follow. But if they turn out to be dead ends, I may be back.'

Sergeant Harry Barnard's suspicion that DCI Jackson might want to talk to Kate again very quickly proved true. They had got up early so that he could drive Kate home to Shepherd's Bush where she could change for work and he was back in the West End and at the nick well before nine. But the DCI was even earlier: canteen gossips had bets on whether anyone could ever be in CID before him and so far no one had succeeded. The consensus now was that he had no home to go to and he was sleeping underneath his office desk.

Barnard reported to the DCI's office as requested and faced the steely eyes across the gleaming wood of the almost bare desk with a discomforting and rare pang of nervousness.

'No trace of this Russian, Lubin, I take it?' Jackson said.

'Not so far, guv,' Barnard said. 'My first task this morning was to go to see his cousin, Lady Broughton-Clarke. She was the one who suggested that he might be hiding out in a cottage in Southwold, but if he was he'd scarpered by the time the local plods got round there to check. I thought she might have ideas where he could have moved on to. If she's too evasive we could perhaps get a warrant to search her place in the country. It's not impossible he's persuaded her to give him a hiding place.'

'Who's her husband? Isn't he Lord something or other?' Jackson asked.

''Fraid so,' Barnard said.

'Well, let's leave him to stew for a bit. Stick with the known criminals for now. What about this man Swift? Have you enough to charge him?'

'Not really, guv, the only thing he's admitted is sneaking some of Ricky Smart's girls into the Jazz Cellar against Stan Weston's instructions. Ricky apparently paid him to do that. But there's no evidence that he had anything to do with either of the killings. You could get him on living off immoral earnings at a pinch but I'm more inclined to let him go and keep a close eye on him. He might lead us somewhere interesting. The other possibility is still the Maltese. Frankie Falzon says he was out of the country while all this was going on, back home in Malta, but it's quite possible that one of his lieutenants took exception to what Smart was doing. He could have got rid of the girl as a warning to Ricky, and when that didn't work, went for the man himself. It was a vicious knife attack.'

'And we know the Maltese like knives,' the DCI said. 'It would be good to pin something on Falzon after all this time he's had building up his criminal interests more or less without let or hindrance as far as I can see. Would that be a fair summary of what's been going on in Soho, Sergeant?'

'To some extent, guv,' Barnard said. If Jackson was going to make it his mission to clean up the corruption that was rife in the square mile of Soho he would have his work cut out, he thought. He would be fighting not only the criminal gangs but a large part of CID as well. When push came to shove, he did not give much for his chances. If it was ever to be done it would be done by someone with much more clout and resources and credibility than a mere DCI in Vice.

'And what about this O'Donnell woman?' Jackson asked. 'You say you knew her before her involvement with Lubin. Can we believe what she says or is she likely to be covering up for him?'

'She didn't like Lubin. She was trying to get her boss to pull her out of his studio,' Barnard said carefully.

'So why did she agree to meet him, running all over East Anglia to some secret tryst like a lovesick teenager? What was that all about?' Jackson snapped.

'Well, for a start she didn't seem to think we were looking for him, and she had her own reasons for wanting to get back into Lubin's studio. She had left some of her own films in there when Lubin closed the place down so suddenly. She had an ulterior motive for helping him out, if you like. She's a bit naive, she's not been in London long, and she's very keen to please her real boss at her own agency. When Lubin offered her a key she jumped at the chance.'

'That's what she told you, is it?' Jackson said sceptically. 'I'll want to talk to her myself to hear about her little escapade at first hand. Especially if we don't get our hands on Lubin himself for an interview very soon.'

'Right guv,' Barnard said uneasily. 'Shall I get on to Lady Broughton-Clarke now, then? I reckon she might tell us where Lubin is holed up.'

'What are you waiting for, laddie?' Jackson snapped.

# TWENTY

Harry Barnard had decided to take Keith Jackson's instructions very seriously. After his interview with the DCI he had called Tatiana Broughton-Clarke to press her on Andrei Lubin's latest whereabouts but she had indignantly denied knowing where her cousin was holed up.

'It struck me that you have this big house in the country and you might have found a room there for him,' Barnard pressed her. He knew DCI Jackson was right, he did not have enough hard evidence to justify a search warrant for Broughton Hall but he was sure that Lubin could not disappear so totally without someone's assistance and his cousin seemed to be the most likely source of help.

'Ha!' Tatiana had exclaimed dismissively. 'My husband had a furious row with him. Roddy wouldn't have him over the doorstep, darlink, especially now he seems to have gone on the run. In any case we have a big party tonight. We'll be far too busy to bother with Andrei and his problems. Surely you don't really think he killed Ricky Smart, do you? It's quite absurd, you know. They've worked together at that studio for years.'

'We need to speak to him,' Barnard said, sharply. 'Kate O'Donnell is your photographer tonight, isn't she? She mentioned it when I was asking her some questions earlier at the Lubin studio.'

'We hope she lives up to expectations,' Tatiana said. 'She's not got that much experience, so we're taking a bit of a chance. She should be on her way out here very soon. I must go now, Sergeant. I'm sorry I can't help you find Andrei, but I have a lot to do here.'

Barnard let her go, fairly sure that she was telling the truth, and turned his attention to the other line of inquiry open to him and what he was beginning to believe was a more likely suspect, if Muddy Abraham was to be believed. He drove into the heart of Soho and stopped outside the Jazz Cellar. The place appeared deserted, and gave no indication that it was going to open tonight, but as he sat outside wondering what to do next he saw a dark car edge its way out of the alley leading to the yard at the back of the club where Jenny Maitland's mutilated and bedraggled body had been found. The driver was Chris Swift.

Barnard followed him, wishing he was driving something a bit more inconspicuous than the red Capri, but as he headed west along Oxford Street Swift seemed oblivious to the fact that he was being followed. He turned north at Marble Arch and followed the Edgware road into Kilburn where he eventually pulled up outside a tall, dilapidated house and went inside. Barnard glanced at his watch. It was half past six and he was feeling hungry. He would give it another half hour, he thought, and then call it a day.

Swift came up trumps. Ten minutes later he came out of the house accompanied by three very young women, long legs bare beneath the coats they clutched around themselves, hair and make-up, even in the semi-darkness, looking impeccable. Swift settled them all in his car and set off at a fair lick back towards the main road with Barnard in close attendance.

'Gotcha,' he muttered to himself as Swift swung round Marble Arch and headed west. 'I don't know where you're going, my lad, but I'll have you when you get there. And if there's any evidence that Jenny Maitland and Sylvia Hubbard took the same ride, I'll bloody well find it.'

By the time he had followed Swift through Amersham and into the narrow Buckinghamshire lanes beyond, Barnard had a good idea where he was heading. He hung back and switched his lights out as he parked and watched Swift's car swing through the gates of Broughton Hall, and the musician usher the three girls up to the front door. He watched them all being sent round the back of the house with a sense of disbelief. Well, well, he said to himself, knowing that there was only one reason why scantily dressed young women would be taken to the charity party here, the charity party to which Ray Robertson had apparently wheedled an invitation and where Kate O'Donnell was probably already taking photographs. He had, he reckoned, a couple of hours to see all the guests arrive, not long to assemble the troops he needed to make sure that by the time the party was in full swing behind those venerable old doors there were enough police here to sort the innocent from the guilty and make sure absolutely nobody got away.

Kate O'Donnell arrived at Broughton Hall in a taxi from the underground station in Amersham. Tatiana had explained somewhat brusquely that she did not have the time to pick her up; she and Roddy would be too busy with the preparations for the party, she said. Kate paid the driver somewhat irritably and clomped up the steps to the main doors in her still unfamiliar boots, feeling the sharp wind beneath her short skirt. It was just gone seven, an hour before any of the guests were due to arrive, but Tatiana had somewhat ungraciously offered to let her eat with what she called the servants in the back regions of the house before she needed to start work.

Kate had almost decided not to come. As she was getting dressed the phone had rung and she recognized Andrei Lubin's voice again. Her heart sank.

'Where are you, Andrei?' she asked. 'Have you been to the police yet?'

'Not yet, but I will,' Andrei had said. 'Did you get the stuff I wanted out of the studio?'

'No, I didn't,' Kate said. 'The police were there when I arrived. They wouldn't let me take anything except my own belongings, and even that was a concession. You must talk to them, Andrei. They seriously think you killed Ricky.'

'That's ridiculous,' Andrei said. 'But I will talk to them. I think I know who might have killed Ricky, which is another reason why I called you. When I rang Tatiana she told me you were going to the Hall tonight to take photographs.'

'That's right,' Kate had argued. 'I'm standing in for you, aren't I? Roddy sacked you.'

'You shouldn't go, my dear,' Andrei said. 'The place is not safe for you. There are things going on at Roddy's parties which you don't want to know about.'

'What do you mean?' Kate had asked, her mouth dry.

'The little girl who died, Jenny. I hardly remember her, you

'Crikey,' he said.

'So show me where this buffet is being served, then,' she said. 'I need to know where everything is before the place fills up.'

She spent the next half hour wandering around the house taking occasional shots of the extensive array of food being laid out in the dining room and the bar in the main reception room to the left of the front door, where the band was frantically at work setting up for the evening. There was no sign of either Lord or Lady Broughton-Clarke and she imagined that they were still dressing somewhere upstairs on one of the long corridors of bedrooms she had seen on her last visit. The catering staff ignored her for the most part although when she saw the waiter she had sat next to in the kitchen once or twice he grinned at her and broke into a tuneless chant of 'She loves you, yeah yeah yeah.' Kate ignored him.

At a quarter to eight she was in the entrance hall when Roddy and Tatiana Broughton-Clarke came down the stairs, Roddy in evening dress, red faced and perspiring although the house was not particularly warm, Tatiana in what Kate guessed was one of her own designs, a short white dress with a single satin stripe from neckline to hemline, with a long, straight black coat over the top, reaching well below the top of her high-heeled patent boots, in some glittering, floaty fabric Kate could not identify. Roddy strode past Kate towards the back of the house without any acknowledgement leaving Tatiana to greet her.

'Are you all right, darlink?' she said. 'Have you got everything you need? People will start arriving soon, although they're not usually on time.' She patted Kate on the arm proprietorially. 'I must have a look at the food,' she said. 'Caterers are so unreliable.'

Roddy Broughton-Clarke came stomping back from the back regions of the house. 'The bloody band have only just arrived,' he said to Tatiana. 'I told them seven o'clock, to give them time to set themselves up. We don't want all that going on while people are settling in.' he glanced into the reception room. 'At least the bar's in place.'

'No one who's anyone is ever here before nine,' Tatiana said soothingly. 'After all, they stay late.'

Kate wondered if she imagined the angry look Roddy flashed at Tatiana before he turned to her.

'You came on the train,' he said, more statement than question. 'I'll get the caterers to run you back to wherever you need to go to catch a late service. You don't need to stay until midnight. Most people will be too far gone by then to want their picture taken.' He laughed. 'You never know, you might get an invitation yourself if you keep your mouth shut. You're a pretty little thing.'

An invitation for what, Kate wondered as Roddy turned away again to harangue an elderly man in a slightly mildewed black suit who Kate guessed was some sort of butler, no doubt in charge of opening the front door to guests when the time came. She smiled to herself. Tatiana had hinted clearly enough at Roddy's struggle to keep this old place going but the reality was obvious. And unless he was making a fat profit on these parties, which seemed unlikely, he was losing the battle. Broughton Hall looked well on the way to falling down.

She wandered back towards the kitchen, passing Jim, the waiter she had sat next to at supper on her way.

'Have you brought your nightie?' he whispered as he passed.

She grabbed his arm, nearly causing him to drop the dish of trifle he was carrying. 'What?' she said. 'I'm not thinking of staying the night.'

'Lots do, I hear, if the price is right.' And the waiter went on his way whistling to himself.

Slightly bemused by that remark Kate took refuge in the main reception room and sat down near the door, idly watching the band finish setting up at the other end of the room, with much crashing and banging and whining of feedback. A couple of men came in looking harassed and began stripping the cushion covers off a couple of long sofas against the wall, revealing brown stains that could have been anything from coffee to wine, gravy to blood. They fitted clean new ones, put them back and plumped them up before retreating with the old ones into the back regions of the house again. It was all a bit hit and miss, Kate thought, like an elderly woman with poor eyesight trying to make up her face like a teenager. If the guests were as important – distinguished even – as

Tatiana had said they were, Kate could not see how they would be taken in by Broughton Hall for a moment. She could not see the attraction. Maybe, as Andrei had suggested, there was more going on here than was immediately apparent.

She jumped when the front doorbell eventually rang and the butler tottered slowly across the hall to open it, admitting two men in evening dress who handed over their coats and hats brusquely and made their way past Kate, unobtrusive in her corner armchair, to the bar. She got up and checked the film in her camera for the tenth time. She did not want the Broughton-Clarkes to see her lounging about when it looked as if work was about to begin. She knew Roddy resented the fee she had asked for the evening and she wondered if maybe Andrei had done the same chore for nothing to please Tatiana for some reason. If Andrei had holed up here at Broughton Hall in one of the innumerable bedrooms upstairs, he could have kept out of sight for weeks, she thought. The row with Roddy must have been serious to make that impossible.

The doorbell pealed again and this time Kate thought she recognized the voice of the next visitor, but even when she positioned herself near the door she could not be sure, although she did hear the butler explaining quite clearly that he should take the young lady – or possibly ladies – to the kitchen door where they would be shown where to change. Perhaps there was to be some sort of entertainment later, Kate thought, wondering at yet another expense Roddy had incurred.

Within half an hour the house was buzzing, the band was playing endless quicksteps and foxtrots, which were mostly ignored, the bar was doing a brisk trade and people were beginning to filter into the dining room to attack the buffet supper. Kate began by taking some general shots of the dining room but as people settled into groups at tables she wandered round the reception room offering to take pictures of couples or groups of friends and explaining that the pictures would come back to Roddy Broughton-Clarke within days and he would make them available after that.

By nine o'clock, Kate had used up a roll of film and went into the hall looking for somewhere away from the crowds to switch to a new roll. She had just about finished when the doorbell peeled again and the butler admitted a new arrival who took her completely by surprise. Ray Robertson and another expensively dressed man she did not recognize handed their coats over and looked around them curiously as if neither of them had been to Broughton Hall before. Robertson spotted Kate almost immediately and strode over to her with a look of surprise.

'What are you doing here, young lady?' he asked. She explained the job she had been hired to do and he smiled knowingly.

'Well, good for you,' he said. 'I'm sure you'll do a good job for his nibs. I thought for a minute you might have that boyfriend of yours with you. Does Roddy know you go out with a copper?'

'Why should he?' Kate said, bemused by the question.

'Well, I'd keep stum about it if I was you,' Robertson said. 'Fred and me, we're here to talk a spot of business with his lordship and it's not anything Flash Harry should know about.' He tapped the side of his nose meaningfully, took Fred Bettany's arm and moved away towards the bar. Within a minute he was joined there by Roddy Broughton-Clarke himself, and to Kate's even greater surprise, the clarinettist Chris Swift from the Jazz Cellar. Kate turned away quickly, as she realized that it was his voice she had half recognized as he arrived at the front door and been redirected round to the back of the house. She still wondered why.

As the evening wore on she noticed that a steady stream of men were having a word with Broughton-Clarke and then making their way upstairs. Her curiosity piqued, she waited for a quiet moment and then went quickly up the stairs herself and found herself at the end of the long corridor where she knew there were bedrooms. She hesitated to open any of the doors, guessing from the procession of men who had been coming up that some of them would be occupied, but as she stood hesitantly close to the stairs she heard a muffled scream somewhere at the end of the corridor, which stopped abruptly as if someone had put a hand over a mouth to muffle the noise and she knew she had to act.

She walked slowly down the corridor, her heart pounding,

listening at every door until she came to one where she could hear the sound of an angry voice and the muffled sobbing of a girl. Without thinking, she banged on the door, which provoked an instant loud curse inside and then complete silence.

'Is everything all right in there?' she asked quietly. The silence continued until suddenly the door opened and an angry red-faced, half-dressed man peered out.

'What the hell do you want?' he asked.

'I thought I heard someone call for help,' Kate said.

'So what?' the man demanded. 'We're having a bit of fun. That's what I've paid for. So sod off, will you, you nosy little tart.' He made to slam the door and then hesitated, looking at Kate sharply. 'You're the photographer aren't you? Well keep your camera well away from me.' At this, he slammed the door hard and Kate hurried away to the stairs, trying to blend in with the party again. But she watched for the man to come down again and when he did she unobtrusively made sure that he appeared in the background of as many of her shots as she could manage. But it was pretty soon obvious that the man was not going to let the matter lie when she saw him deep in angry conversation with Roddy Broughton-Clarke who immediately glanced in Kate's direction, but he did not move towards where she was taking a shot of a group of fairly merry revellers making the most of a bottle of champagne. But she could tell from his expression that he knew she was a threat, and she felt suddenly cold. Maybe, she thought, it was time to go.

A few minutes later Broughton-Clarke seemed about to head in her direction when he was waylaid by the elderly butler who whispered something in his ear. The look of shock on Broughton-Clarke's face was evident even from where Kate was standing on the other side of the room. He stood stock still for a long time, looking suddenly haggard and ill, before eventually coming to a decision and she watched as he approached the band and waved them into a ragged silence. As the music stopped the conversation also drifted to a halt as people became aware that their host was standing on the band's platform wanting to speak.

'Ladies and gentlemen,' he said, his voice slightly hoarse.

'I regret to inform you that I have just been told that the president of the United States, John Kennedy, has been shot and has died in hospital.'

Kate gasped, as did everyone else in the room, and then for a moment there was total silence. Roddy, she thought, looked bewildered but struggled on.

'I hope this will not spoil your evening,' he ventured although one or two groups were already getting to their feet. The collective shock was palpable, the party atmosphere dissipated in seconds. 'There is a television in the dining room if you wish to follow developments . . .' Roddy faltered. More of the company got to their feet and made a beeline for the dining room and Roddy began to look desperate. Behind him the band looked as if they were about to pack up for the night. 'Please do continue to enjoy your evening if you can,' Roddy went on before petering out.

Tatiana appeared suddenly and stood by his side looking distraught as the trickle of people moving out became a rush. Kate felt tears pricking her eyes and a sense of outrage as she followed the crowd into the dining room where a black-and-white television was showing flickering film of the events in Dallas that had ended in tragedy a couple of hours earlier. Her mother, she thought, an Irishwoman with immense pride in Kennedy, would be in pieces. Roddy Broughton-Clarke's party, she knew, was effectively over.

After a few minutes she turned away, too upset to watch any more, only to find her path was blocked by Broughton-Clarke himself, with Chris Swift close behind.

'I want a word with you, young lady,' Broughton-Clarke hissed and took hold of her arm. Between them the two men marched her towards the back of the house and into a small stone flagged alcove close to the kitchen. They were far too strong to resist, and as she looked around she realized no one else had noticed her plight.

'What the hell were you doing upstairs?' Broughton-Clarke asked. 'No one asked you to go up there, least of all knocking on doors and making a nuisance of yourself.'

'I was looking for the toilet,' Kate said. 'Then I heard someone cry out. What's going on up there, for goodness' sake?' She knew the answer to that but her only defence was to appear naive.

'That's nothing to do with you,' Broughton-Clarke said. It was obvious he did not believe her, and she felt icy cold.

'And if you know what's good for you, you'll keep quiet about it,' Chris Swift said quietly. 'We don't want any more nasty accidents, do we?'

Kate swallowed hard as various random pieces of information came together in her head and Broughton-Clarke pricked her neck lightly with the point of his knife she had not noticed he was holding. It was not a big knife, she told herself, but it was obviously razor sharp and quite long enough to cut a throat with. She fought a rising panic. She knew how very easy it was to cut a throat.

'What people do upstairs is their business,' Broughton-Clarke said, pressing slightly harder so that Kate felt a trickle of blood run down her neck. 'Nothing to worry about, you nosy little cow.'

'Nothing to talk about,' Swift added. 'Not so much as a single word, if you know what's good for you.'

What would have happened next she never knew because they all heard someone approaching heavily down the narrow corridor behind them.

'There you are, Roddy,' Ray Robertson said heartily. 'I was looking for you, mate. There's obviously a lull in proceedings. Can we have a private word?'

Kate slipped out of Broughton-Clarke's reach with breathless relief as the two men froze. For a moment she almost panicked again as Robertson grabbed her arm but he pulled her firmly out of the alcove and shoved her back towards the subdued crowds in the hall, some of them already milling about and demanding their coats from the harassed butler.

'Time for Miss O'Donnell to go home, I think,' he said to the other two men. 'No harm done, is there Katie? Just a little misunderstanding.'

Kate wasted no time in taking Ray Robertson's advice. She retrieved her coat and, heart thumping uncomfortably, followed a couple in evening dress out of the main doors. They headed for their car while she began the long walk down the drive towards the road hoping that when she got there she could beg a lift back into Amersham. But when she arrived at the gates she found to her astonishment that several of the departing cars had been stopped by police who had blocked the exit with their own vehicles, blue lights flashing. She stood uncertainly by for a moment wondering if she would be allowed to make her way out when she saw a familiar figure getting out of a familiar red Ford Capri parked behind the official vehicles and coming towards her.

'I was about to come and look for you,' DS Harry Barnard said putting an arm round her. 'Come and sit in my car. This is all about to get very interesting.' It was only when he got her into the car that he noticed the trickle of blood running down her neck.

'Who the hell did that to you?' he asked.

'Roddy had a knife,' she said. She felt suddenly sick as she realized how close she had come to a man who would have had no hesitation in using his weapon had Ray Robertson not intervened. 'I went upstairs and saw – or heard – too much,' she whispered. 'Roddy and Chris Swift grabbed me. Your friend Ray found me just in time.'

'I'll bloody have those two bastards,' Barnard said. 'I followed Swift here. He was delivering girls, bold as brass. Those two won't see the light of day for a very, very long time.'

It was almost a week before Kate and Harry Barnard met again away from the police station where she had made her statement, handed over the photographs she had taken at Broughton Hall and accepted that she would be an important witness when Roddy Broughton-Clarke and Chris Swift eventually came to trial on a charge of murdering Jenny Maitland and Ricky Smart. They met again at the Greek restaurant where he had introduced Kate to the delights of kebabs and ouzo.

'You won't be alone giving evidence,' Barnard said when they were settled at a table and had ordered *mezze*. 'When we rounded up all the girls who were at the hall that night, including the ones Swift had delivered personally, they fell over themselves to make complaints against Swift and

Broughton-Clarke, and Ricky Smart. Ricky was the one who procured the girls but Swift was the one who found the clients and made sure the girls provided exactly what was required. If they objected to any of their clients' demands all the men would make sure they did as they were told, mainly by threatening them, telling them they would scar them for life.'

'I can believe it,' she said quietly, recalling only too vividly the moments she had spent with a knife at her throat. 'So who killed Ricky? And why?'

'Believe it or not, Ricky seems to have drawn the line at murder, and kicked up a bit of a fuss. Jenny Maitland's death caused the three to fall out completely. We think Jenny was beaten at the Hall by one of the clients at the last party. She might even have been killed there. Roddy Broughton-Clarke wanted the body off the premises as fast as possible so he drove her into London and dumped her, probably stabbing her just to make sure she was dead. She knew far too much to be left alive.'

'It was a very sharp knife,' Kate said feelingly.

'Chris Swift is very keen to deny he had anything to do with either killing. He's blaming Roddy, though I doubt he'll get away with that in court. They've both been charged with the murders.'

'So that's why Andrei was so scared he would be next. He found out what was going on at the Hall and began making sense of it all.'

'Andrei Lubin knew enough to be very frightened,' Barnard said. 'That's why he closed up the studio and made himself scarce. He turned himself in the morning after he read in the papers what had happened at Broughton Hall overnight. He told us that Ricky had told him he was meeting Roddy to talk business. He'll be another witness at the trial.'

'Ricky probably wanted Andrei to know that he was doing well for himself, while Andrei's projects were running into trouble. He was always full of himself,' Kate said.

'He can't have realized how dangerous Broughton-Clarke and Chris Swift were,' Barnard agreed.

'And Tatiana? What's going to happen to her?'

'She's been charged with living off immoral earnings and

running a brothel,' Barnard said. 'It doesn't look as if they'll ever manage to mend the roof at Broughton Hall.'

'Poor Tatiana, she'll be mortified,' Kate said. 'She'll never be a top designer either,' Kate said. 'And what happens to the men who were so happy to pay them for the girls they used – or abused.'

'Tricky,' Barnard said. 'The girls didn't know the men's names, of course.'

'There were some well-known faces there,' Kate said. 'The girls could identify them from my photographs. Or do they get away with it? Wasn't there a guest list?'

Barnard glanced away for a moment. 'They were not even arrested,' he said. 'The raid was organized by the local police. They made their own decisions, for their own reasons.'

'Right,' Kate said, looking bleak. 'Although one of them may have beaten Jenny Maitland, possibly killed her.'

'They said they didn't have evidence to hold them. Using a prostitute isn't a crime.'

'And Muddy Abraham?' Kate asked.

'He'll be a witness too, but after that he'll go back to the States. The extradition request has already been approved.'

'There's not much justice there, is there?' Kate said, her eyes full of tears.

Barnard shrugged and put a tentative hand over hers. 'You have to learn to live with it,' he said.